The
KING'S JUSTICE

The
KING'S JUSTICE

Two Novellas

STEPHEN R. DONALDSON

G. P. Putnam's Sons / New York

PUTNAM

G. P. PUTNAM'S SONS
Publishers Since 1838
An imprint of Penguin Random House LLC
375 Hudson Street
New York, New York 10014

Copyright © 2015 by Stephen R. Donaldson
Penguin supports copyright. Copyright fuels creativity, encourages diverse voices, promotes free speech, and creates a vibrant culture. Thank you for buying an authorized edition of this book and for complying with copyright laws by not reproducing, scanning, or distributing any part of it in any form without permission. You are supporting writers and allowing Penguin to continue to publish books for every reader.

Library of Congress Cataloging-in-Publication Data

Donaldson, Stephen R.
  [Short stories. Selections]
  The king's justice: two novellas / Stephen R. Donaldson.
      p.   cm.
  ISBN 978-0-399-17697-5
  I. Title.
  PS3554.O469A6   2015   2015015843
  813'.54—dc23

Printed in the United States of America
10   9   8   7   6   5   4   3   2   1

Book design by Meighan Cavanaugh

This is a work of fiction. Names, characters, places, and incidents either are the product of the author's imagination or are used fictitiously, and any resemblance to actual persons, living or dead, businesses, companies, events, or locales is entirely coincidental.

For Jennifer Dunstan

who made it all possible.

Acknowledgments

My particular thanks to Susan Allison, who has helped me with some rather challenging books, and has been consistently supportive along the way.

Contents

The
KING'S JUSTICE

he man rides his horse along the old road through the forest in a rain as heavy as a damask curtain—a rain that makes dusk of midafternoon. The downpour, windless, strikes him from the long slash of open sky that the road cuts through the trees. It makes a sound like a waterfall among the leaves and branches, a damp roar that deafens him to the slap of his mount's hooves. Ahead it blinds him to the road's future. But he is not concerned. He knows where he is going. The broad brim of his leather hat and the oiled canvas of his cloak spare him from the worst of the wet, and in any case he has ridden in more frightening weather, less natural elements. His purpose is clear.

Shrouded by the deluge and covered by his dark gear, he looks as black as the coming night—a look that suits him, though he does not think about such things. Having come so far on this journey, and on many others, he hardly thinks at all as he rides. Brigands are no threat to him, even cutthroats desperate enough to hunt in this rain. Only his destination matters, but even that does not require thought. It will not until he reaches it.

Still his look does suit him. *Black* is the only name to which he answers. Many years ago, in a distant region of the kingdom, he had a name. His few comrades from that time—all dead now—knew him as Coriolus Blackened. But he has left that name behind, along with other pieces of who he once was. Now he is simply Black. Even his title rarely intrudes on who he has become, though it defines him.

He and his drenched horse are on this road because it leads to a town—so he has been told—called Settle's Crossways. But he would have taken the same road for the same purpose without knowing the name of the place. If Settle's Crossways had been a village, or a hamlet, or even a solitary inn rather than a town, he would still have ridden toward it, though it lies deep in the forests that form the northern border of the kingdom. He can smell what he seeks from any distance. Also the town is a place where roads and intentions come together. Such things are enough to set and keep him on his mount despite the pounding rain and the gloom under the trees.

He is Black. Long ago, he made himself, or was shaped, into a man who belongs in darkness. Now no night scares him, and no nightmare. Only his purpose has that power. He pursues it so that one day it will lose its sting.

A vain hope, as he knows well. But that, too, does not occupy his thoughts. That, too, he will not think about until he reaches his destination. And when he does think about it, he will ignore himself. His purpose does not care that he wants it to end.

The road has been long to his horse, though not to Black, who does not protract it with worry or grief. He is patient. He knows that the road will end, as all roads must. Destinations have that effect. They rule journeys in much the same way that they rule him. He will arrive when he arrives. That is enough.

Eventually the rain begins to dwindle, withdrawing its curtains. Now he can see that the forest on both sides has also begun to pull back. Here trees have been cut for their wood, and also to clear land for fields. This does not surprise him, though he does not expect a town named Settle's Crossways to be a farming community. People want open spaces, and prosperous people want wider vistas than the kingdom's poor do.

The prosperous, Black has observed, also attend more to religion. Though they know their gods do not answer prayer, they give honor because they hope that worship will foster their prosperity. In contrast, the poor have neither time nor energy to spare for gods that pay no heed. The poor are not inclined to worship. They are consumed by their privations.

This Black does think about. He distrusts religions and worship. Unanswered prayers breed dissatisfaction, even among those who have no obvious cause to resent their lives. In turn, their dissatisfactions encourage men and women who yearn to be shaped in the image of their preferred god. Such folk confuse and complicate Black's purpose.

So he watches more closely as his horse trudges between fields toward the outbuildings of the town. The rain has become a light drizzle, allowing him to see farther. Though dusk is falling instead of rain, he is able to make out the ponderous cone of a solitary mountain, nameless to him, that stands above the horizon of trees in the east. From the mountain's throat arises a distinct fume that holds its shape in the still air until it is obscured by the darkening sky. Without wind, he cannot smell the fume, but he has no reason to think that its odor pertains to the scent which guides him here. His purpose draws him to people, not to details of terrain. People take actions, some of which he opposes. Like rivers and forests, mountains do not.

Still he regards the peak until the town draws his attention by beginning to light its lamps—candles and lanterns in the windows of dwellings, larger lanterns welcoming folk to the entrances of shops, stables, taverns, inns. Also there are oil-fed lamps at intervals along his road where it becomes a street. This tells Black that Settle's Crossways is indeed prosperous. Its stables, chandlers, milliners, feed lots, and general stores continue to invite custom as dusk deepens. Its life is not overburdened by destitution.

Prosperous, Black observes, and recently wary. The town is neither walled nor gated, as it would be if it were accustomed to defend itself. But among the outbuildings stands a guardhouse, and he sees three men on duty, one walking back and forth across the street, one watching at the open door of the guardhouse, one visible through a window. Their presence tells

Black that Settle's Crossways is now anxious despite its habit of welcome.

Seeing him, the two guards outside summon the third, then position themselves to block the road. When the three are ready, they show their weapons, a short sword gleaming with newness in the lamplight, a crossbow obtained in trade from a kingdom far to the west, and a sturdy pitchfork with honed tines. The guards watch Black suspiciously as he approaches, but their suspicion is only in part because he is a stranger who comes at dusk. They are also suspicious of themselves because they are unfamiliar with the use of weapons. Two are tradesmen, one a farmer, and their task sits uncomfortably on their shoulders.

As he nears them, Black slows his horse's plod. Before he is challenged, he dismounts. Sure of his beast, he drops the reins and walks toward the guards, a relaxed amble that threatens no one. He is thinking now, but his thoughts are hidden by the still-dripping brim of his hat and the darkness of his eyes.

"Hold a moment, stranger," says the tradesman with the sword. He speaks without committing himself to friendliness or animosity. "We are cautious with men we do not know."

He has it in mind to suggest that the stranger find refuge in the forest for the night. He wants the man who looks like a shadow of himself to leave the town alone until he can be seen by clear daylight. But Black speaks first.

"At a crossroads?" he inquires. His voice is rusty with disuse, but it does not imply iron. It suggests silk. "A prosperous crossroads, where caravans and wagons from distant places must be common? Surely strangers pass this way often. Why have you become cautious?"

As he speaks, Black rubs casually at his left forearm with two fingers.

For reasons that the tradesman cannot name, he lowers his sword. He finds himself looking at his companions for guidance. But they are awkward in their unaccustomed role. They shift their feet and do not prompt their spokesman.

Black sees this. He waits.

After a moment, the sworded guard rallies. "We have a need for the King's Justice," he explains, troubled by the sensation that this is not what he had intended to say, "but it is slow in coming. Until it comes, we must be wary."

Then the farmer says, "The King's Justice is always slow." He is angry at the necessity of his post. "What is the use of it, when it comes too late?"

More smoothly now, Black admits, "I know what you mean. I have often felt the same myself." Glancing at each of the guards in turn, he asks, "What do you require to grant passage? I crave a flagon of ale, a hot meal, and a comfortable bed. I will offer whatever reassurance you seek."

The farmer's anger carries him. Thinking himself cunning, he demands, "Where are you from, stranger?"

"From?" muses Black. "Many places, all distant." The truth will not serve his purpose. "But most recently?" He names the last village through which he passed.

The farmer pursues his challenge, squinting to disguise his cleverness. "Will they vouch for you there?"

Black smiles, which does not comfort the guards. "I am not forgotten easily."

Still the farmer asks, "And how many days have you ridden to reach us?" He knows the distance.

Black does not. He counts destinations, not days in the saddle. Yet he says without hesitation, "Seven."

The farmer feels that he is pouncing. "You are slow, stranger. It is a journey of five days at most. Less in friendly weather."

Rubbing at his forearm again, Black indicates his mount with a nod. The animal slumps where it stands, legs splayed with weariness. "You see my horse. I do not spur it. It is too old for speed."

The farmer frowns. The stranger's answer perplexes him, though he does not know why. Last year, he made the same journey in five days easily himself, and he does not own a horse. Yet he feels a desire to accept what he hears.

For the first time, the tradesman with the crossbow speaks. "That is clear enough," he tells his comrades. "He was not here. We watch for a bloody ruffian, a vile cutthroat, not a well-spoken man on an old horse."

The other guards scowl. They do not know why their companion speaks as he does. He does not know himself. But they find no fault with his words.

When the sworded man's thoughts clear, he declares, "Then tell us your name, stranger, and be welcome."

"I am called Black," Black replies with the ease of long experience. "It is the only name I have."

Still confused, the guards ponder a moment longer. Then the farmer and the man with the crossbow stand aside. Reclaiming the reins of his horse, Black swings himself into the saddle. As he rides past the guards, he touches the brim of his hat in a salute to the man with the sword.

By his standards, he enters Settle's Crossways without difficulty.

In his nose is the scent of an obscene murder.

He finds the town much as he expects it. The street is dirt that has been scattered with gravel to provide purchase for the wheels of wagons, and also to give some protection from mud for the townspeople. But the day's heavy rain has overwhelmed the gravel. The street resembles a quagmire, and the alleys between the buildings are worse. Fortunately for the pedestrians, every place of business on both sides has a wide, raised wooden porch sheltered by a slanting roof. The folk of Settle's Crossways can move between taverns and general stores, milliners and inns, with little exposure to the downpour's aftermath.

Or they can pass between places of business and houses of worship. Some distance ahead, Black sees the crossroads that brings trade and travel from every point of the compass to and through the town. That intersection is a large open square. And opposite each other on its corners, northeast and southwest, are temples. Both are made of framed timbers, both have porched entrances with high doors, both thrust bell towers heavenward. There the similarity ends. The intended white dazzle of the Temple of Bright Eternal has been much raddled by the rain, while the black walls of the Temple of Dark Enduring glisten even at dusk as though they have gained an obscure victory.

Bright Eternal and Dark Enduring are the gods of the kingdom, worshipped as such, bombarded with pleas and praises. Yet their hymns sound much the same, and their liturgies vary little. In truth, they have too recently acquired their stature as gods for their modes of worship to become distinct. Also Black knows that they are not gods. He is more familiar with them than any inhabitant of Settle's Crossways, priest or parishioner. They are elemental energies, nothing more—and nothing less.

He is a veteran of what he calls the Balance Wars, the conflict of shapers hungry for power. That contest cost the lives of all his former comrades. More often than Black chooses to remember, it came close to killing him. Indeed, it would have reduced the known world to rubble if the King, a shaper himself, had not forsaken warfare to become a focus of balance, the human mediator between the unknowing, unthinking, and uncaring forces of bright and dark.

For good reason, Black distrusts temples. He fears that a preference for one god or the other will encourage the ambitions of shapers. In themselves, bright and dark are not fearsome. They are merely necessary. They are, after all, the elemental energies that enable the world—life and death, growth and decay—when they are balanced against each other. The danger is that taking strength from one makes the other comparatively stronger. Then the balance tilts. And it is imbalance that generates true power, the power of shapers to remake themselves and their allies and their desires.

Without the King—

Black does not think about such things. He knows too well what they entail. He does not wish to recall old horrors. The reek of a present atrocity is more than enough to resurrect wrath and fear from their graves deep in his soul.

The folk of Settle's Crossways want the King's Justice. No doubt they have tried to summon it. No doubt their congregations pray for it daily. But they do not know what it means. They have no idea what the King's Justice is.

When Black has secured a stable for his mount, he makes his way along the porches to the nearest tavern. It stands conveniently near the crossroads and the temples. The townspeople he passes stare at him, or make studious efforts not to stare. He has that effect, but he does not ignore it, despite its familiarity. He touches the brim of his hat to everyone, a greeting to assure men, women, and children that he is harmless.

Between him and the tavern, a mother and her young daughter approach. They have come from a milliner and are walking homeward. To them, also, Black touches his hat. But when he has passed them, the girl says, "Ma, that man has holes."

She is too young to understand caution.

Black halts as though a hand has been placed on his shoulder. While the mother tells her daughter, "Hush, child. Be polite. He is a stranger," Black turns to look more closely at the girl.

"But Ma," she insists. "He has holes in his *soul*."

The woman takes her daughter's hand, intending to urge the girl away. But she pauses when Black lowers himself to one knee in front of the child. Surprised, the mother stands still.

Black studies the girl, a child of no more than five or six years. She is clean and well-dressed, from a comfortable family, but he ignores such details. He ignores her blond ringlets and her open face and her unbruised knees. Instead he concentrates on the fact that she is not afraid. He concentrates on the kindness in her eyes. It suggests concern for him.

"Holes?" he asks gently. "In my soul?"

He knows too well that the girl is right. He has spent pieces of himself in more battles than he cares to remember.

The mother is anxious now. "Forgive her, sir," she says. "She will learn courtesy when she is older."

At the same time, the girl says, "I see them." She points at his chest. "They are there and there"—she points repeatedly—"and there and there."

Still gently, Black says, "You surprise me, child. There are few who see me. Even fewer see me clearly."

His manner encourages boldness. "Ma can't see what I see," she proclaims. "She thinks I make it up. But it is all true.

"Your holes hurt you. If they get bigger, you will die."

13

Black frowns, considering her words. After a moment, he admits, "That is certainly true."

The girl extends her hand. She means to touch him. "I can make them go away." Then she becomes less sure of herself. "They are too big. I can make one of them go away. When I am older, I can do more."

Before her hand reaches him, Black rises to his feet. Now he faces the mother, who is beginning to pull on her daughter's arm. "You are wise, madam," he tells her with less of gentleness, more of warning. "You have a gifted child. A precious child. You do well to protect her. She will have time enough for her gifts when she is a woman."

He knows now that this child *can* heal him. But he also knows that doing so will blight her childhood. She is a seer, one who sees. True seers are more rare than shapers. They do not cause imbalance. Rather they draw strength from within themselves. The girl is indeed precious. But she is too young to suffer the cost of what she can see and do.

The mother feels sudden tears in her eyes. She has been troubled for her daughter, disturbed by a child who pretends to see things which do not exist. But the stranger believes that such sight is not a pretense. This both comforts and frightens the woman. She casts one more glance at the man to confirm that he is serious. Then she hurries her daughter away.

Black *is* serious. However, he does not consider the child's presence dangerous, except to herself. Certainly he craves her healing. He aches for it when she is gone. Yet her gift has no bearing on his purpose. Her scent is as clean as her person. He does not regret sparing her.

Touching his hat to all who pass by, he continues toward the tavern.

Like the town itself, the tavern is much as he expects it to be. It has a wooden floor strewn with sawdust, a long bar with ale-taps along its inner edge and shelves of bottles and flasks behind it, a number of round tables with chairs for four or six, and an increasing count of patrons, some of whom have settled themselves for a night of drink. All this is indistinguishable from other taverns around the kingdom. The only differences here are the general affluence of the patrons, the consequent comeliness of the barmaids, and the room's air of unresolved distress. These men and their few women take comfort in drink rather than in each other. Comradeship, jests, roistering, and songs do not numb their fears.

Many of them look at Black as he enters, and of those many stare. But he touches his hat to them and leaves them alone. He already knows that the cause of the town's alarm is not present. If it were, he would smell it.

Its absence, also, he does not regret. He is patient. And he has been taught by blood and pain that no good comes of confronting his foes before he has prepared himself.

To begin his preparations, he seats himself at the bar one stool away from a man who is already dedicated to drowning his concerns in ale. Black does not remove his cloak, though his arms are covered by the heavy sleeves of his calfskin shirt. His hat he wears to cover the scars on his scalp. From the barkeep, a large man too well fed and lubricated by his own wares to contain his sweat, Black requests ale. He asks a bowl of stew, and bread with it. And when his desires are met, he concentrates on eating and drinking like a man who has no other purpose, though in truth he does not relish the stew, and the pungent ale does not ease his mind.

The barkeep's name is Bailey. His nature is friendly, but the town's alarm makes him wary. Also he is both interested in and suspicious of the stranger. He hovers nearby while Black eats and drinks.

After a time, Black asks with an air of indifference, "You are not troubled by brigands?" He knows this by the lack of walls and gates, and by the inexperience of the guards. "I am surprised. The forest can hide any number of evil men, and your crossroads surely offers many opportunities for plunder." He appears to address the barkeep, but in truth he is speaking to the drinker near him. "How does it happen that you are spared?"

"Trouble we had, sir," Bailey answers in his most pleasant tone. "In my Da's time, that was. Lives and goods were lost, fearsome quantities. My Da kept an axe here, under the bar, to defend himself. But the old wars have been good for us. Caravans now come with squadrons of men-at-arms, and even lone wagons are guarded by archers and pikes. No brigands trouble us now. They attack only in the deep forest, where they can be sure of escape."

Black is doubtful, but he puts the matter aside for a later time.

———

"You are fortunate, then," he observes. "Other regions of the kingdom are not so blessed."

"We are, sir," Bailey replies. "We are." He means to say, We *were*, but caution stops him. He knows, as all the town now knows, that strangers must be distrusted. Striving for still greater pleasantness, he asks, "You know the kingdom, then, sir? You are much traveled?"

Black has not met the barkeep's gaze. He does not now. "Much traveled," he assents, "yes." Then he deflects Bailey's prying. "Enough to observe that in favorable times the Temple of Bright Eternal attracts many good folk. It is Dark Enduring that responds to woe and hardship. Is his Temple well attended?"

He believes it is. The Temple of Dark Enduring is as large and well-maintained as its neighbor.

Bailey thinks to offer some dismissive response, but politely, pleasantly. Before he can choose his words, however, the man seated one stool away mutters with his mouth in his flagon, "Lately."

Anxious now, Bailey tries to say, Not so lately, sir. Dark Enduring has always been much respected in Settle's Crossways. But Black rubs at his left forearm, and words flounder in Bailey's mind. He does not intervene as Black asks without turning to regard the speaker, "Lately?" Black's manner suggests no particular interest.

The speaker is lean as a stick. His bare arms have the rope-like muscles and deep brown of a farmhand. He carries no weight on his frame, and his features droop like a hound's as he drinks. To Black he smells of sweat and grievance. His name is Trait, and if he is asked, he will say that he is bitter because the town's prosperity has passed him by. But that is not Black's question. Trait takes a long pull at his flagon, then says, "Since the murder."

Now Bailey intends to intervene in earnest. Several of his patrons have heard Trait, and a stillness comes over the room. Soon everyone will be listening. But Black continues to rub his forearm, and Bailey scowls because he cannot remember what he wants to say.

Black does not ask about the murder. He will learn what he needs to know soon enough. Instead he asks, "And that encourages attendance at the Temple of Dark Enduring? How so?"

Bailey contrives to blurt, "You are a religious man, sir?" But Black and Trait ignore him.

"That priest," Trait says. He frowns. "What is his name?" Then he remembers. "Father Tenderson. He says what we want to hear."

Black lifts his hand to Bailey, points at Trait's flagon. Bailey understands. He refills the flagon at an ale-tap and replaces it in front of Trait.

Still revealing no great interest, Black asks, "What do you want to hear?"

Trait gulps at his drink for a moment. Then he says with satisfaction, "Revenge. Retribution.

"That other priest. Father Whorry. He promises glory. He preaches that poor Jon Marker's boy is with Bright Eternal, all light and happiness. He says if we have faith what we lose will not grieve us. Who takes comfort in slop like that? Father Tenderson speaks truth."

From somewhere behind Black, a man calls out, "Enough, Trait. He is a stranger. He has his own concerns. Jon Marker's loss means nothing to him."

Trait grins sourly. He enjoys the reprimand. It makes him more substantial in his own eyes. "Father Tenderson," he tells Black more distinctly, "demands punishment. He prays every day for the King's Justice. He wants the man who butchered that boy burned alive." He knocks his flagon on the bar. "We all do. We pray for the same thing." Again he claps the bar with his flagon. "Revenge will comfort us."

Then he snorts more quietly, "Glory will not."

Black does not say, The King's Justice is not what that priest thinks it is. Instead he remarks, "Father Whorry sounds judicious. He values peace." Then he asks, "Can a stranger meet with him? I, too, value peace." His tone is noncommittal. "Does he frequent a tavern of an evening?"

The man behind Black responds loudly, "The good Father will be at his prayers. Settle's Crossways is his concern. Wait for the morrow, stranger. Your desire to accost him at such a time is unseemly."

Black does not apologize. While he considers his reply, Trait mutters into his flagon, "At his prayers, aye—if they belong in a common house. If not, he labors for peace by other means."

"*Enough*, Trait," commands the man behind Black again. He

approaches the bar. "Is this a fit occasion for your spite?" He slaps a heavy hand on Trait's shoulder. "Show respect, man, for Jon Marker if you have none for the priest."

Trait smirks into his flagon, but does not retort.

The man rounds on Black. "Do you mean to mock us, sir?" he demands. He is large, granite-browed, and muscular. His apparel suggests wealth by its fineness, and indeed he owns a well-stocked general store. Others consider him a bully, but he believes himself a man often justly offended—and able to act against insult. "Our concerns are none of yours."

Knowing the man, Bailey hastens to placate him. "Be easy, Ing Hardiston," he says in his most soothing voice. "This is a trying time at its best. A stranger might well give offense without the intent to do so."

Black ignores the barkeep. He faces Hardiston's anger. Still disinterested in his manner, he says, "Father Tenderson, then. Is *he* a drinking man?"

Trait stifles a guffaw with ale.

Ing Hardiston bristles. He has blows in mind. Like many another man, he fears for his sons, and his fear incenses him. He desires to deny that he is afraid. But Black's lightless gaze weakens him. Though he clenches his fist, he does not swing.

Casting a glare at Bailey, the storekeeper then returns to Black. "Ask him yourself, sir," he says with knotted jaws, "when you see him on the morrow. You will not trouble the folk of this town at night."

Black does not acquiesce. Nor does he refuse. He has taken

Ing Hardiston's measure and is not threatened. Rather than prolong the man's ire, he turns to Trait.

"Will you guide me to an inn, friend? I am unquestionably a stranger. Without aid, I may find myself in a flea-ridden bed when I prefer comfort."

For a moment, Trait hesitates. He enjoys his ability to vex Hardiston and is inclined to do as Black asks. Like the storekeeper, however—and Bailey as well—he finds the stranger's aspect discomfiting. Conflicting impulses keep him silent until he recalls that the stranger has bought him ale.

In a long draught, Trait empties his flagon. Then he nods to Black. "I will." Shouldering Hardiston discourteously aside, he stands from his stool.

Rasping an oath, Ing Hardiston returns to his table and his companions.

When Black also stands, Bailey rallies himself to request payment. He goes so far as to meet Black's gaze. However, what he sees there closes his mouth. Flapping one hand, he dismisses the question of coin. At the last, he manages only to wish Black a pleasant night.

Black nods gravely. "Perhaps it will be pleasant," he replies. Then he accompanies Trait from the tavern.

But he has no interest in a bed. His purpose requires him to trace the smell of evil to its source, and he has come no nearer since entering the town. His interactions in the tavern have not awakened his glyphs and sigils, his scarifications. A few steps along the porch, he halts his companion.

Full night has come to Settle's Crossways. The town's many lamps dim the stars, but those lights are too earthbound to obscure the now-cloudless sweep of the heavens. Briefly Black studies the dulled jewels of darkness past the eaves of the roof, though he has no need of their counsel. To Trait, he says, "Take me to Jon Marker's house."

Trait stares. He finds Black difficult to discern in the shadows. He will say, You asked for an inn. He will refuse Black's command. He will pretend obedience to the storekeeper's wishes. Though he has neither wife nor son himself, he has still some kindness in him, and he is disturbed by Jon Marker's loss. He will not comply with Black.

He does comply. He wants more ale. His mouth hangs open as he points to an alley across the street.

Together, Black and his guide cross the street. The alley takes them to a lesser street, a crooked way aimless to those who do not know the town. Here the odor Black seeks teases his nose, but it remains indistinct, not to be trusted. He does not release Trait.

Another alley admits them to a still-smaller street. Away from the main roads, there is no gravel to give purchase. Black's boots squish and slip in the mud. Trait moves unsteadily, wishing himself back at the tavern, but the inconvenience of poor footing does not compel Black's attention. He follows his nose and his companion to a house that stands pressed close to its neighbors.

The place is little more than a hut large enough for perhaps three rooms. Its size and humility suggest that its occupants are poor. Yet there are no sprung boards in its walls, no gaps around its windows. Its porch and roofs are solid. All have been painted in a recent season. The chairs on the porch, where a husband and wife might sit of a quiet evening, are comfortable. To Black, it has the air of a dwelling cared for because its people consider it a home.

But its neighbors have lanterns on their porches and lights in their windows. The house to which Black has come is dark. It looks empty. In another season or two, it will look abandoned.

"Here," Trait says. Then he finds the kindness to add, "Let poor Jon be. He is a good man. Good men are few."

Black dismisses his guide. He forgets Trait. He is on the trail. The smell is stronger here. It is not strong enough to be the source he seeks. Still it confirms that he is on the right path.

The scent is not that of human violence, of ordinary passion or greed too extreme to be controlled. For such a crime, Settle's Crossways would not need the King's Justice. The smell is that of shapers and wicked rituals.

Silent as shadows, Black ascends the porch to the door.

For a moment, he considers his purpose. Then he knocks. He is sure that the house is not empty.

After a second knock, he hears boots on bare boards. They shuffle closer. At another time, perhaps, he will feel sorrow for the man inside. At present, his purpose rules him.

When the door opens, he sees a small man much blurred by what has befallen him. His eyes are reddened in the gloom, and his gaze is vague, like that of a man deep in his cups, though he does not smell of ale or hard spirits. His sturdy, workman's frame has collapsed in on itself, making him appear smaller than he is.

He blinks at Black, uncertain of his ability to distinguish the stranger in the gloom. When he speaks, his voice is raw with expended sobs. He says only, "What?"

Black stands motionless. "Are you a temple-going man, Jon Marker?" he asks. "Do you find ease in sermons and worship?"

Perhaps that is why or how his son was chosen.

Jon Marker repeats, "What?" He does not understand the question. Then he does. "Go. Leave me alone. I do not deal with hypocrites. Let others pretend to worship gods who do not answer prayers. I am not such a fool."

Perhaps *that* is why his son was chosen.

Jon Marker tries to close the door. Even in grief, he is too polite to slam it. But Black stops him. Gently Black says, "Then I must look elsewhere." He smells no atrocity on the man, or in the house. The odor he seeks is here by inference, indirectly. It lingers with its victims when its source has moved on. "I need your guidance. Tell me of your son."

Now the door is shut, though Jon Marker does not close it. He and Black stand in the common room of the house, on uncovered floorboards, in darkness. Jon Marker blinks more rapidly, but his sight does not clear.

The stranger wants him to speak of his son. The command angers him. It was not a request, despite its gentleness. "I will not," he answers. His pain is too raw.

"You will," Black replies, still gently. "I require your aid."

Jon Marker gathers himself to shout. He gathers himself to lay hands on the stranger. But under his cloak, Black rubs a glyph near the small of his back with one hand. With the other, he reaches out to cup his inlaid palm to Jon Marker's cheek.

Jon Marker tries to flinch away, yet he does not.

Black's touch enters the father's ruin. It does not give comfort. It is deeper than consolation. It brings a wail from the depths of Jon Marker's heart.

"My son!"

Soft as the night's air, Black says, "Tell me."

For a moment, the father cannot. His wail holds him, though he does not repeat it. It echoes in the empty frame that his home and his family have become. But then he answers in broken chunks like pieces of his flesh torn from him.

"When my wife, my sweet wife. My Annwin. When she died. When the plague claimed her. She took it all. All of me. I thought she took it all. The plague—" His voice catches. "I could not endure my life.

"But I could. She left my boy. Our son, our Tamlin. As sweet to me as she was. As kind. As pleasant. As willing. And lost." His voice fills the dark room with ghosts. "As lost as I was. We were lost together. Without her, lost. Until he found himself for me. Or I found myself for him. Or we found each other. Together, we found—

"It was *cruel*. Cruel to me. Cruel to him. That we had to go on without her smiles. But his kindness. His sweetness. His willingness. He was a reason to go on. And he needed a reason, as lost as I was. And I loved him. With whatever I had left, I loved him. I tried to be his reason."

Quiet as the vanished sound of Jon Marker's wail, Black says, "Your love was enough. You saved him. His love saved you. Tell me."

With Black's palm on his cheek, Jon Marker becomes stronger. "I earned our way serving in Ing Hardiston's store. With Annwin to tend our home, and Tamlin laughing in his chores at her side, I did not chafe at Hardiston's harsh ways. But after the plague—" The man remembers anger. "Ing Hardiston has no patience for grief. I was dismissed, and lost, and could not earn our way. Also folk avoided us, thinking the plague clung to us still. Thinking us cursed."

A faint whisper, Black says again, "Tell me."

"But Father Whorry—" Jon Marker swallows a lump of woe and gratitude. "He is a priest and a hypocrite. He is known for whoring. But he has kindness in him. He persuaded Haul Varder the wheelwright to employ me. Lying, he told Varder I had been sanctified when I had not, and was therefore certainly free of plague. Free of curse.

"And Haul Varder also is kind, in his rough way. He did not fault me for keeping Tamlin at my side while I worked, though my boy was too small to do more than sweep the floor. Without knowing what he did, Varder helped us find each other, Tamlin and me."

Black is not impatient, but his purpose has its own demands. Still touching Jon Marker's cheek, he goes further.

"Tell me of the murder."

Jon Marker cannot refuse. "A terrible day came," he says while his whole body cringes. "A day like any other. The work was hard, but hard work is good, and my boy was goodness itself. As much goodness as my Annwin left in the world. When the day was ending, I told Tamlin to hurry home to fire the stove for supper. We had promised each other some hours of play when we had eaten." Again he swallows, but now the lump in his throat is anger at himself. It is weeping for his boy. "*I* sent him home. I sent him *alone*. The fault is mine.

"I did not find him again until he had been slaughtered. He was not in the house. The stove was cold. I searched for him, crying his name. I roused my neighbors. Some searched with me. We did not find him until we looked near the refuse-pit behind the houses. He had been discarded—" A third time, his pain chokes him until he swallows it. "What remained of him had been thrown in the pit."

There Black lowers his hand. He feels pity, but he does not take pity. He has heard enough. Soon he will learn more of what he needs to know.

When he releases Jon Marker, the man collapses. But Black catches him, holds him upright. "Be easy," Black tells him. "We are almost finished. Show me where your son is buried. Then you will be done with me. For my life, I will ask nothing more."

Jon Marker thinks that he has fainted. Still he hears Black clearly. Fearing even now for those he has lost, he summons the strength to turn his head. In a voice that has been scraped until it bleeds, he asks, "Will you dig up my sweet boy? Will you be so cruel? After all that he has suffered?"

"I must see the place," Black answers. He means that he must touch and smell it. "But I will only disturb his body if you do not tell me what was done to him."

He will not coerce Jon Marker again, though he has many forms of influence ready for his use, and some Tamlin's father will not feel. This restraint is how he expresses pity.

Jon Marker is angry now, as angry as he was when he buried his son. "Bastard," he pants, this man whose wife loved him for his mildness, his gentleness, his natural courtesy. "Whoreson."

"Even so," Black replies. He feels no insult. There is no vexation in his heart. "I do what I do because I must."

Jon Marker stands away from Black. He knots his fists. "He was *beaten*!" he shouts. No words can express the force inside him. The house is too small to hold it. "Beaten *terribly*, damn you! Worse than any dog. Worse than any slave among the caravans. But he was still alive—the healer thinks he was still *alive*—when he was cut from gullet to groin. If I believed in gods and prayer, I would pray that he died before his lungs and *liver* were taken."

Lungs, Black thinks, and liver. Lungs for air. Liver for heat. Air and heat are elemental energies, as natural and necessary as bright and dark. But they do not cause imbalance, they played no part in the Balance Wars, because no shaper in the known world can draw upon them. They are everywhere and nowhere, too diffuse to offer power. Therefore they have neither temples nor priests.

He does not understand why the boy was butchered in this fashion. There are no rituals for air and heat. But he can guess now why Tamlin Marker was chosen. The boy's father has told him enough for that.

The how of the choosing remains uncertain. Black can speculate, but he does not commit himself.

"I have caused you pain," he tells Jon Marker. "Accept my thanks. Show me your son's grave. I will not disturb it. Nor will I disturb you again."

Jon Marker's anger drains from him as swiftly as it swelled. He thinks that he has come to the end of himself. He is as empty as the house. He does not speak. Instead he shuffles to the door, opens it, and waits for the stranger to precede him.

When Black walks out into the night, Jon Marker is with him.

The man stays on the neighboring porches until they end. Then he moves into the street, taking Black toward the outskirts of Settle's Crossways. Briefly Black considers that Jon Marker will lead him to a cemetery, but soon he recognizes his error. The town has suffered a plague. There will be a bare field like a midden where the victims are buried. Tamlin may be among them. Some of the townsfolk believed that the disease clung to him. And likely many of the bodies were burned, a precaution against the spread of infection. No doubt the evil Black smells wished the same for Tamlin, to conceal the crime. Still Black is certain that Tamlin was not burned. He is certain that the boy's father would not permit it.

He and Jon Marker trudge through mire to the edge of the town. They leave the fading street to cross a long stretch of sodden grasses. Beyond it, they come to the field Black expects, an acre or more of churned mud where ashes and bones and bodies were covered in haste.

At the field's verge, Jon Marker pauses, but he does not stop. Awkward on the torn slop of the earth, he slogs to the far side. Then he goes farther to enter among the first trees of the forest. There he guides Black to a small glade with a mound of soaked dirt at its center. Between the trees, he has provided his son with the dignity of a separate grave, a private burial. When he nears the mound, wavering on his feet, he says only, "Here." Then he drops to his knees and bows his head.

Again Black says, "Accept my thanks." He, too, kneels. But he does so in the sloping mud of the grave. He places his hands on the mound and works his fingers into the dirt as deep as his wrists. After a moment, he closes his eyes. With all of his senses, he concentrates on the scent he seeks.

The rain has washed much away. In addition, the forest is rich with its own smells. And Tamlin's burial is at least a fortnight old. Black knows this because so many days have passed since he first began to track the smell of wickedness. But he has sigils for keenness and glyphs for penetration. The odor that compels him is distinct. He needs only moments to be certain that he has not misled himself with Tamlin Marker's death. He feels the truth of what Jon Marker has told him.

He recognizes the ritual, and does not recognize it. His thoughts become urgent, goaded by the discrepancy between what he expects and what surprises him.

Why was the boy beaten? Because he fought. Because his killer enjoyed hurting him. But that explanation does not account for the murder itself.

Still kneeling, he lifts his hands from the dirt. "It is not enough," he says, unaware that he speaks aloud. "One child, yes. An innocent boy. A beautifully innocent boy. But it is not enough for power. It does not enable sorcery. He is the start of a ritual, or he is its end. There must be others. Several others. Perhaps many others."

Jon Marker says, "There are no others," but Black does not heed him. Black is already certain that none of the townsfolk have been butchered as Tamlin was. The people he has met would react differently if they knew themselves threatened. The guards on the road would be more stringent in their duty, more numerous. Also the source of this evil needs secrecy until the ritual is ripe.

"They will be brutal men," he thinks, still aloud. "Men who relish harming innocence. Or cruel women who relish it."

He is sure of this, just as he is sure that the lungs and livers of the other corpses have been taken. Yet he does not understand it. Shapers do not pursue the impossible. They cannot draw their sorcery from air and heat.

Tamlin's father makes a sound of distress, but Black does not attend to it. He is immersed in his confusion. If his words have wounded Jon Marker, he does not regard the cost.

Still he is a veteran. He has fought many battles, he bears many scars, and he has been shaped for his task. His instincts are sure. Despite his concentration, he feels the men coming. As lightly as mist and shadows, he rises to meet them.

There is no moon to light the glade. Only the stars define the shapes of the trees. Yet Black sees clearly. Some of his sigils are awake. Some of his scarifications burn. He recognizes Ing Hardiston as the storekeeper approaches. The two other men he does not know. But one of them holds a longknife to Jon Marker's throat. The other advances a dozen paces to Hardiston's left. This man holds his cutlass ready. The storekeeper is armed with a heavy saber.

Black sighs. He knows that these men have no bearing on his purpose. He does not want to kill them. Under his cloak, he rubs his left forearm.

The man gripping Jon Marker lowers his longknife. The man with the cutlass hesitates. But Ing Hardiston strides forward. Though his fear is strong, his loathing of it—or of himself—is stronger. His anger shrugs aside Black's attempt to confuse him.

"You were warned, stranger," the storekeeper snarls. "You meddle where you are not wanted. It is time for you to die." His saber cuts the air. "If Marker is the cause of your coming, he has lived too long."

Hardiston's example restores his men. The longknife is again ready at Jon Marker's throat. The cutlass rises for its first stroke.

"Now you also are warned," Black replies. He is more vexed than irate. This interruption is worse than foolish. It is petty. "Jon Marker has suffered much, and I have refreshed his pain. I will permit no further harm to him."

When he touches his hip with his left hand, his longsword appears in his right. Its slim blade swarms with sigils for sharpness and glyphs for strength. Its tip traces invocations in the night.

Again the man with the cutlass hesitates. This time, he is shaken by surprise rather than slowed by confusion.

Ing Hardiston also hesitates. He yelps a curse. But his need to deny his fear is greater than his surprise. His curse becomes a howl as he charges.

Black is one with the darkness. His movements are difficult to discern as he tangles Hardiston's saber with his cloak. A flick of his longsword severs the tendons of Hardiston's wrist. In the same motion, his elbow crumples Hardiston's chest. As the storekeeper hunches and falls, too stunned to understand his own pain, Black spins behind him.

A flash in the night, Black's longsword leaves his hand. It impales the thigh of the man holding a blade to open Jon Marker's throat. The impact and piercing cause a shriek as the man topples away from Tamlin's father.

Black has no wish to kill any of these men. Unarmed, he

confronts the man with the cutlass. In a voice of silk, he asks, "Do you require a second warning?"

For a moment, the man stares. Then he drops his weapon and runs, leaving his fellows bloody on the grass.

When Black sees Jon Marker prone beside his writhing attacker, the veteran is truly vexed. He is on the trail and means to follow it. Yet he cannot forsake the man who has aided him. Moving swiftly, he retrieves his longsword and causes it to disappear. Then he stoops to examine Jon Marker.

He sighs again as he finds the man unhurt. Jon Marker is only prostrate with exhaustion. All his wounds are within him, where Black cannot tend them. Still Black gives what care he can. Lifting the unconscious man in his arms, Black carries him back to his empty house. There he settles Jon Marker in the nearest bed.

Though Black's purpose urges him away, he watches over the man who has helped him until dawn.

With the night's first waning, Black leaves Jon Marker asleep and returns to the stables where he bedded his horse.

The mount that awaits him there is altered since the previous evening. The ostler remarks on this as he hands the reins to Black. "Much changed he is, sir," the man says, "much changed. A different horse, I judged, that I did. A substitute for your sorry nag. Some fool plays a trick on me. But look, sir. The markings are the same. The scars here and here." The man points. "The white fetlocks. The notched ears. Notched like sword-cuts they are, sir. And the tack. I am not mistaken, sir, I swear it. There is no accounting for it. Rest and water and good grain are not such healers."

Black's only response is a nod. He has no reason for surprise. His mount has been shaped to meet his needs, as he has. For his long journey, and to enter the town, he required an aged and weary steed that would attract no notice, suggest no wealth. Now he means to travel with speed. The distance may be considerable. Also he may encounter opposition, though he does not expect it. Thus his mount must be a stallion trained for fleetness in battle, and so it has become.

When he has saddled his horse, tightened the girth, and swayed the ostler to refuse payment, he mounts and rides.

While he passes through Settle's Crossways, retracing the street that brought him here, he goes at a light canter, though the dawn is still grey, and he encounters few folk early to their tasks. Once he leaves the sleep-stunned guards behind, however, he gallops hard. He hopes to return before the morning is gone.

A league into the forest, he halts. For a time, he studies the air on both sides of the road with his sharpened senses. Then he turns his horse to enter among the trees and deep brush, heading east.

Though he has no cause to remember it, he has not forgotten

the lonely mountain that fumes over Settle's Crossways in this direction.

Through the close-grown trees and the tangled obstructions of brush, creepers, and fallen deadwood, he makes what haste he can. For the moment, he seeks only a path, one seldom trodden. A deer-track will suffice. When he finds one, he goes more swiftly.

The trail wanders, as such things do, yet he does not doubt his choice. Within half a league, the vague whiff that he detected from the roadside becomes more intelligible. It is still faint, obscured by wet loam and dripping leaves and passing animals. The rain masked it while he rode toward Settle's Crossways the previous day. Also it is diluted by time and other odors. Nevertheless it is the scent of his quarry's rituals. Sure of his discernment, he follows it.

His mount canters dangerously among the trees. It leaps in stride over fallen boles, intruding boulders, slick streams. Sunrise slanting through the forest catches Black's eyes in quick glints and sudden shafts, but he lowers the brim of his hat and rides on.

The smell of wild beasts grows stronger, and also a growing reek of rot. Abruptly he enters a clearing. It is well hidden, and he sees that a number of men have lived there. Perhaps they had women with them. Several sturdy shelters more elaborate than lean-tos stand at the edges of the open space. Discarded garments and bundles litter the ground. Among them he sees a short sword, several truncheons, an empty quiver. He does not need to look in order to know that the shelters once held stores of food, of meat and bread. These have been much ravaged by animals, but the decay of the remains informs him of their former presence.

In the center of the clearing is a wide fire-pit, its ashes sodden and cold. It has been abandoned for many days, more than a fortnight. And the corpse sprawled among the ashes has also been abandoned. Most of its flesh has been torn from the bones, the bones themselves have been cracked and gnawed, and the scraps of its motley garments lie scattered around the pit. The mangling of the body prevents Black from knowing whether the lungs and liver were taken intact. Still the scent that he seeks is strong here, despite the putrid sweetness of rot. He does not doubt that he is looking at another ritual murder.

The crime is old, but its age does not prevent him from imagining the scene. A band of brigands made this clearing their home. After their attacks on caravans and wagons, they returned here, hid here. But one night a man or men killed one of their sentries among the trees. When the lungs and liver were taken, and the man—no, the men—were ready, they burst into the clearing. They discarded their victim on the fire. By force of arms, or perhaps by mere surprise, they scattered the brigands.

And then—?

Black adjusts his senses to ignore the miasma of decay and feeding. He walks his horse once around the clearing, twice. Then he picks a faint track similar to the one that brought him here and follows it.

———

Within a hundred paces, he finds a second corpse. Hidden in the brush to his left, he discovers a third. Both are old and badly ravaged. He cannot determine how or why they were killed. Still the smell of evil clings to them. Studying them with a veteran's eye in the rising daylight, he concludes that both died the same night their sentry was cast into the fire.

He suspected the truth earlier. Now he is sure. The butchering of innocence is the end of the ritual, not the start. Therefore he is also sure that the culmination of the crimes, the completion of their purpose, will be soon.

Because he does not understand that purpose, he cannot guess why it was not acted upon immediately after Tamlin Marker's death. Still he believes that he has little time. He is reassured only by the knowledge that three men and a boy are not enough.

But half a league deeper in the forest, he finds a fourth corpse—and after another half-league, the shredded remains of three women tossed into the pit left by the falling of a dead tree. The count now stands at seven. If it reaches ten, it will be enough, if the ritual is of a kind that Black knows. If it climbs still higher, he will be in serious danger.

It does not stop at ten. Eventually he locates seven more bodies, men and women, all brigands by their apparel and weapons. Their odor tells him that their deaths are more recent than the first seven. In two instances, the condition of the corpses allows him to see that the lungs and livers have been harvested.

To himself, Black acknowledges that the perpetrator of this ritual is clever. Brigands who raid from coverts are ideal victims. Their absence will be noticed with gratitude. The reason for their absence will interest no one.

Alarmed now, he suspects that if he wanders the woods around Settle's Crossway for days, he will find a number of similar deaths. Some will be older than those he has already found. Perhaps some will be more recent. The source of this evil is growing stronger. Its intent must be extreme, if it requires such bloodshed. Why else has its culmination been delayed?

He judges, however, that he cannot afford to search farther. Unseen events are accumulating. Incomprehensible purposes gather against Settle's Crossways, or against the kingdom itself. He must try to forestall them.

With as much haste as his horse can manage, he returns to the road. Then he gallops back toward the town like a man with hounds and desperation on his heels.

But he does not reenter Settle's Crossways on the road. He is unwilling to be delayed by the guards, and he has no wish to silence them with sterner persuasions than he used the previous evening. Leaving the road, he returns to the glade where Tamlin Marker is buried, then re-crosses the plague-midden to reach Jon Marker's house by its neglected street.

There he does not pause to trouble the wounded father again. He loops his horse's reins around one of the roof-posts of the porch, knowing that his mount will remain until he needs it. Unaffected by the mud underfoot, he strides by streets and alleys toward the town's center.

At the crossroads where the temples of Bright Eternal and

Dark Enduring face each other, comfortable in their proximity, Black finds good fortune. A modest caravan is dragging its clogged wheels toward the town square from the west, and already the streets teem with merchants and townsfolk, hawkers and mountebanks, some surely hoping to buy what they lack, others intending to both buy and sell, still others striving to gull the unwary. Also the caravan will have its own needs for resupply. Therefore Black is sure that the wagons, their owners, their drivers, and their guards will remain in the square for some time. Since noon is near, they will likely remain until the morrow. He will have opportunities to speak with the caravanmaster later.

Rubbing his left forearm, he sways a distracted matron to direct him to Father Whorry's dwelling. She is a milliner, avid to purchase fine fabrics and threads from one wagon or another before her competitors acquire them, but she forgets her hurry briefly in order to answer Black. Then she rejoins the surge of the crowd.

Black separates himself from the townsfolk, touching his hat to everyone who gazes at him directly. Then he follows the matron's instructions.

The priest's residence is a mansion compared to Jon Marker's house, yet it is humble enough to suit the servant of a god. Like every other dwelling that Black has seen here, it has a wide porch linked to its neighbors' to provide passage safe from the sludge and traffic of the streets. The door has only an emblazoned yellow symbol, a stylized sun, to indicate that this is the home of a

Bright priest. Black knocks politely, though he senses that the house is empty.

But Father Whorry is already hastening homeward after a night in his preferred common house. He is a small man, rotund, with an anxious smile on his round face and a few long wisps of hair on his pate. He wears the brown cassock and yellow chasuble of his office, and might therefore be expected to walk with dignity. However, he clings to the notion that all Settle's Crossways does not know of his pleasure with women, and so his movements have an air of furtiveness as he attempts to pass unnoticed.

When he gains the privacy of his residence, he closes the door quickly, then sighs and slumps before turning to discover a stranger waiting for him in the gloom of the unlighted lamps.

Father Whorry aspires to a priest's imperturbable calm, but he cannot stifle a startled gasp as he regards the stranger. For a moment, his legs threaten to fail him.

"Father Whorry?" Black's tone is pitched to reassure this servant of Bright Eternal. "I must speak with you."

At once, the priest begins to babble, an incoherent spate of words to fill the silence while he struggles to recapture his wits. However, the stranger rubs his left forearm, and Father Whorry's alarm fades. When the stranger says, "You do not lock your door, Father. I took that for an invitation. Was I mistaken?" the priest has a reply ready, though he speaks too quickly for dignity.

"No, of course not, of course not, my son. All are welcome.

You are welcome. I am considered a servant of Bright Eternal, but in fact I serve all who hold our god in their hearts." He intends to ask the stranger's name, but the question escapes him. Instead he asks, "You wish to speak with me?"

Black pretends to smile under the brim of his hat. "I do." His voice is soothing silk. Beneath the scents of women, wine, and sweat, Father Whorry smells as innocent as a bathed babe. "But since I must put the same questions to Father Tenderson as well, we will spare ourselves effort and time if I speak to him and you together. Will you accompany me?"

Staring, Father Whorry manages to say, "Father Tenderson? He is an apostate. A former son of Bright Eternal. There is no truth in him." But the way the stranger rubs his forearm is un-accountably calming, and the priest has no difficulty adding, "But of course, of course. We are friends, that old blackguard and I. Bright Eternal forgives even those who do not wish it." He is pleased by the quality of his own smile. "Shall we go?"

Black touches Father Whorry's arm as though he, too, is the priest's friend. He guides Father Whorry from the house in a way that allows the small man to lead him.

Explaining that the crowds in the square will make passage there impossible, Father Whorry takes Black by side-streets and alleys to a residence that closely resembles his own. Of its exter-nal details, the only significant difference is that the symbol emblazoned on the door is a stylized stroke of lightning entirely black. Here, however, the windows are warm with lamplight, and a flicker at one of the panes suggests a fire in the hearth.

The Bright priest ascends the porch without hesitation. He is often a guest here, more often than he entertains his apostate friend. Father Tenderson's home is more comfortably furnished, and the Dark priest serves better wine. Father Whorry knocks on the emblem of Dark Enduring and waits at ease for an answer, sure of his welcome.

Black hears slippered feet on a rug before Father Tenderson opens the door, spilling light and good cheer over the arrivals.

The Dark priest is a tall man, and too lean to disguise the old sorrow in his soul. Yet his sadness does not mar him. His long face crinkles with ready smiles, the pleasure in his eyes promises easy laughter, and his open arms are full of greeting. Unlike his Bright friend, he would have hair aplenty on his head, though much grizzled, if he did not wear it cropped short.

In appearance, he is an odd man to urge vengeance and the King's Justice. But his preaching arises from bitter disappointment as well as deep grieving, from too much experience of pettiness and spite, and from more personal losses. For that reason, he believes, his words touch the hearts of many townsfolk. He gives them the only comfort he knows. And when he has preached with the eloquence of his own pain, he resumes the cheerfulness that is his nature.

"Father Whorry!" he exclaims. "And a stranger. Enter!" He stands aside with a sweep of his arm. "Enter and be welcome. I cannot feed you. It is early for my noonday meal. Nothing is prepared. But wine I have, and my fire is too good for one man alone."

Father Whorry ducks his head to enter, then raises it as he embraces his friend. He feels stronger in Father Tenderson's presence, as he often does, and now considers himself better able to face the stranger.

Father Tenderson pats his nominal opponent's head affectionately, then turns his gaze on the hatted and cloaked stranger. "And you are, sir? I believe I have heard mention of your arrival yesterday, but I do not know your name."

It is Black's immediate intention to sound ominous, to suggest threats. "My name is of no use to you." He has brought the priests together because he hopes to provoke revelations. "It cannot command me." As he speaks, however, he smells only cleanliness on the Dark priest. Like his friend, Father Tenderson has no malice in him. By that sign, Black knows that he must alter his approach. Resuming his silken tone, he adds, "But for convenience, I am known as Black."

"Black you are," observes the Dark priest with merriment in his eyes, "and are not. Yet you are welcome by any name. Please." He gestures toward the hearth, where three well-cushioned armchairs and a settee are positioned to enjoy the fire. "Be seated. Will you accept wine?"

Father Whorry nods vigorously. Black shakes his head. While Father Tenderson moves to a cabinet at the side of the room, selects a fired clay flask, and fills three goblets of the same material, the Bright priest scurries to the farthest armchair, hoping to put as much distance as he can between himself and Black.

Ignoring both men, Black seats himself upon the settee. It is too close to the fire for comfort, but he does not regard the warmth.

Carrying three goblets on a tray, the Dark priest offers one to Father Whorry. Black again declines in silence. "Should you change your mind," Father Tenderson suggests as he places the tray on the rug near the settee. Taking a goblet for himself, he settles his long limbs into the nearest armchair.

Black has much to consider. If he does not procure revelations by menace, he must use other means. And he suspects that the simple suasion he has used on Father Whorry will not prompt the honesty he requires. Also he believes that he will gain nothing by the form of coercion he imposed on Jon Marker. Answers he will get, but they will only be as useful as his questions, and he does not know enough to ask the right questions.

He remains silent until Father Tenderson says, "Now, Black. Father. You are here together for some purpose. Let us speak of it before my housekeeper's bustle interrupts us."

This opening surprises Father Whorry. He is easily flustered, but he is also familiar with the Dark priest's usual manner. He expects his friend to commence with casual inquiries to set the stranger at ease. Where are you from? What brings you to Settle's Crossways? And so forth. Father Tenderson's forthrightness makes the Bright priest's eyebrows dance surprise on his brow.

"Very well," begins Black. "You are aware, I hope, that you are both charlatans."

The priests stare, Father Whorry anxiously, Father Tenderson with wry sadness.

Black does not speak as he does to insult his listeners. Rather he attempts to shift the ground under their feet. If he succeeds, he may elicit replies that would escape him otherwise.

"You worship gods," he explains. "You encourage others in the same worship. Yet you are old enough to have some memory of a time when there were no temples. If you are not, your fathers were. In those days, no one imagined bright and dark as gods. They were known for what they are, elemental energies, nothing more. They exist, and they are mighty. But they are mindless. They do not think, or care, or answer. They are no more worthy of worship, and no less, than wind and sunlight."

Frowning now, Father Tenderson leans forward, his elbows on his knees, to give this visitor his full attention. Black's gaze stops a protest in Father Whorry's mouth. The Bright priest gulps wine to appease his indignation.

"There are four elemental energies," Black continues, "all potent. Together they make life possible in the world. But of the four, only bright and dark are accessible to shapers." When he sees that the word perplexes the priests, he says, "You may know such people as sorcerers. They have the knowledge and the means to draw power from one or the other, bright or dark. And when they draw power from one, they make the other commensurately stronger. They create an imbalance.

"It is true to say that the elemental energies make life possible, but it is also incomplete. The full truth is more fragile. It is both the energies themselves and the balance among them that enable life. Individually they are each too mighty to be survived. Any imbalance among them is fatal. It threatens every aspect of the living world.

"So much you know. Your fathers did if you do not."

"Then why do you tell us?" asks Father Tenderson. But he speaks softly. He is not impatient for Black's answer.

"The balance must be preserved," Black replies. "This task the King has taken upon himself. When one shaper seeks advantage, or several do, by calling upon bright, the King counters by making use of dark. Or the reverse. Thus he mediates between them.

"Certainly you are old enough to remember the old wars, or to have heard tales." Black sighs. He remembers too much. "They were terrible in bloodshed. Many good lands were laid waste. And the forces that the shapers called upon grew in ferocity until the King contrived to become the mediator of balance. Until he imposed his peace on the kingdom.

"He cannot end the evil that lurks in the hearts of our kind, but he can prevent a recurrence of the old wars. He can and does."

Under his cloak, Black touches two sigils. He rests one hand in a place among his scarifications. He has not slept, and has eaten little. These invocations refresh his strength.

Again Father Tenderson asks, "Why do you tell us this?" Unlike Father Whorry, he is neither alarmed nor indignant. He has not tasted his wine. His curiosity is growing.

Black answers by completing his explanation.

"The King's mediation is an arduous task. It requires a more than human vigilance. And his reserves are not limitless. Also those who serve his will are few. Many were lost in the wars. For that reason, he named bright and dark gods, and he commanded temples for their worship. By so doing, he hoped to gain several forms of aid.

"First, he sought to make the communities of the kingdom stronger by uniting them in shared beliefs. Second, he desired the priests of his temples to teach respect for forces too great to be controlled. From respect, humility might grow, humility to counter the arrogance that encourages men and women to tamper with their gods. Last, he believed that worship itself might steady bright and dark. It might make them less susceptible to abuse."

Black gazes deeply into Father Tenderson. Drinking, Father Whorry avoids Black's scrutiny.

"I have named you charlatans," Black concludes, "and so you are. You encourage the folk of Settle's Crossways in false beliefs. But you are also the King's best servants here. Indeed, your service as it appears to me is flawless. You, Father Whorry, preach forgiveness, while you, Father Tenderson, demand the King's Justice. You balance each other. And you are friends. Together you lessen the peril of Bright Eternal and Dark Enduring."

Black shows the priests his open hands. Then he knots them together. "Still there is evil among you. Jon Marker's son was murdered by a shaper."

This is too much for Father Whorry. He cannot contain his anger longer. He cries, "Do you upbraid *us*, stranger?" Emptying his goblet, he slaps it upended to the rug so that his hands are free. "Are we accused?" His hands make fists that tremble as he raises them. "There are no shapers among us, none. We do not condone evil.

"When you say that they—these sorcerers—that they draw upon Bright Eternal or Dark Enduring for power, do you mean that they pray to their chosen god, and their prayers are answered? I do not preach that any god answers prayer. Father Tenderson does not. We mislead no one. I tell my flock only that their god accepts and pardons them, as he does all living things. Why must we doubt ourselves now? What have we to do with shapers and foul murder?"

Black means to pursue his needs, but Father Tenderson intervenes. Turning to the Bright priest, he urges gently, "Calm yourself, Father. Put your mind at rest. Black does not accuse us. Unless I am much mistaken, he has not named his reasons for bringing us together yet."

Then he faces Black once more. "Let us be clear, sir." There is no good cheer in him now. Though he considers himself cowardly, he has his own anger in addition to his sorrow, and they speak for him. "I do not boast when I say that neither of us would hesitate to stand between any child of Settle's Crossways and murder."

Black watches him in silence, waiting. He does not doubt what he hears, but it is not enough. Unfortunately he cannot teach the Fathers to recognize the smell he seeks. He cannot ask them about their parishioners.

After a moment, the Dark priest recalls that he has not been blamed, though he is quick to blame himself. Ruling his emotions sternly, he settles his sorrow back to its depths and his limbs in his chair.

"Our good Father Whorry's theology is simplicity itself," he begins. As he speaks, he recovers his composure. "His heart is pure. Therefore his service is pure. I take a more oblique view. Perhaps I spend too much time alone." He attempts a smile, then exchanges it for a rueful frown. "But leave that aside. I admire the King's efforts to provide peace. I am grateful to him. But I am not troubled by his reasons for creating our temples, and I am not diminished by my role as his charlatan.

"To my mind—Father Whorry will forgive me for repeating myself, we have argued the matter often enough—the faith is more necessary than the god. Worshipping together is more necessary than the god. And speaking what is in our hearts—as a form of worship, you understand—is more necessary than all else. Dark Enduring"—he raises a placating hand to his friend—"please, Father, I know your objections—is merely an excuse for wounded souls to come together so that they can say or hear what is in their hearts.

"The King, if I have understood you, sir, would not disapprove of either of us."

"He would not," Black confesses. He has his own faith. The Balance Wars must not be permitted to resume. He has faith in his purpose. "Still there is evil to consider. There is Tamlin Marker's murder to explain."

Father Whorry remains angry. "And you expect that of us? An explanation?"

Black shrugs. "You have knowledge of the townsfolk that I do not. Perhaps that will suffice.

"You know what was done to Jon Marker's boy?"

Father Tenderson nods with sadness in his eyes, but the Bright priest speaks first. "All Settle's Crossways knows."

"Do you also know how it chanced that Tamlin Marker was alone? That his killer was able to take him and remained unwitnessed?"

Now it is Father Tenderson who replies. "We have heard poor Jon's account. Directly or by rumor, we have heard it. He sent the boy home to fire the stove."

Black sits motionless as a stone. He reveals nothing. "And you do not call it *unlikely* that Tamlin's killer was ready to take him at the moment when mere chance provided his opportunity?"

Both men are struck by the question. They have not considered the matter in that light. Father Whorry's brows squirm. He rubs his hands together like a man attempting to wash away some stain. Father Tenderson stares with his eyes wide. He is too full of chagrin to contain it. When he speaks, his voice is hoarse.

"I call it unlikely *now*. Fool that I am, I did not think—" For a moment, he cannot continue. Then he asks, "How is such readiness possible? Do these shapers—?"

Black cuts him off. "No. Shapers are not seers. They do not

foresee. If they did, some among them would see cause for restraint. The explanation I seek does not rely on sorcery."

"Then how?" demands Father Whorry. "It is impossible. How was it done?"

Black cannot answer. The priests must help him. He changes his approach.

"Jon Marker," he states, "lost his living in Ing Hardiston's store after his wife's passing." He does not tell the priests how he knows this. "You, Father Whorry, went to his aid. You found employment for him with a wheelwright named Haul Varder.

"But Jon Marker is not a temple-goer. He does not belong to your flock. Indeed, he scorns both temples and priests. How does it chance that you alone in Settle's Crossways sought to aid him?"

The Bright priest wants to shout a retort. He believes that now he is surely being accused. Yet he is out of his depth, and much of his anger is directed at himself. For that reason, he twists and cringes. How had he failed to grasp the unlikelihood of Tamlin Marker's taking? He has spent too much time besotted with wine and women. Though Black does not compel or confuse him, Father Whorry cannot refuse to answer.

"The man needed help." He is shamed by the smallness of his voice, or by his own smallness. "What else could I do? Bright Eternal does not discriminate. You say my god does not care. If that is true, it is also true that he does not judge. I offered Jon consolation, but he would not take it. Yet his need was severe. I did what I could."

To Black, Father Tenderson murmurs softly, "His service is pure. There is only kindness in his heart."

"And kindness in Haul Varder's," the Bright priest asserts more stoutly.

The taller man turns to his friend. Still softly, he urges, "Be honest, Father. Haul Varder is not known for kindness."

The Dark priest makes Father Whorry squirm. He feels driven to bluster. "His childhood was one of misery. All Settle's Crossways knows this. He did not learn kindness from his mother. Now his manner is dour and ungiving. What of it? He is known for self-interest, yes. He is much in demand, especially by caravans and wagoneers. But he could have readily found another to bend his iron and lathe his spokes. Settle's Crossways does not lack young men who want work. It was kindness that chose Jon Marker."

With the mildness of affection, Father Tenderson says, "More honest, Father."

The small man surprises himself by blurting an oath. Then he recants. "Bright Eternal forgive me." He speaks to his friend rather than to Black. "*More* honest? Well, if I must. For Tamlin Marker's sake.

"Haul Varder is also known for absences. He is commonly absent. If he did not have a good man to tend his forge and his iron, his business would founder.

"But"—Father Whorry sees a gleam of hope that he can win free of his friend's insistence—"he was present on the last day of Tamlin's life. The boy worked with his father, sweeping floors and such. Jon Marker would not have sent his son home without Haul Varder's leave. He is too courteous and diligent to be presumptuous with the man who pays his labor."

An instant later, the Bright priest claps his hand to his mouth as though he has just heard himself utter an obscenity. In his heart, he is crying, Bright Eternal! God forgive me! Have I *accused* Haul Varder?

Father Tenderson spreads his hands. To Black, he says, grieving, "You see how matters stand. I do not regard the wheelwright as charitably as my friend does. He bargains meanly for his services. He treats men who cannot pay with disdain. He has neither wife nor child, and does not regret his lack—or does not acknowledge that he regrets it. His absences are many. Some are prolonged. All are unexplained.

"Yet I also must be honest. I know no ill of the man. Like Jon Marker, he is no temple-goer, but that is not a fault in him."

There the Dark priest turns away. He gazes into the fire, searching the flames as he searches himself. "Father Whorry's kindness serves as courage. *I* did not aid Jon Marker. I had not the heart to approach that harmed man. His losses filled my veins with weakness.

"I talk and talk. My good friend occasionally bridles at my profusion of talk. But when I open myself to my god and my flock, I obscure more than I reveal. The truth is that I am weak. My friend is the better man. He is the better priest."

Black remains motionless. He considers what he has heard. He does not doubt either priest. They have given as much guidance as they possess, and it is more than they expect. Still he is baffled. He is both thoroughly shaped and well taught. His experience of sorcery, ambition, and greed is long by any measure. It has cost him pieces of his soul. Yet he knows of no ritual, even among those most vile, that requires lungs and livers. The King himself cannot draw upon air and heat.

Abruptly, Black stands. While his hosts scramble, surprised, to their feet, he says, "I have troubled you enough. A simpler question remains. Then I will disturb you no longer."

Father Whorry only gapes. He is much distressed, though less by what he has said than by what he has been caused to think. Against his will, he wonders whether he is culpable for Jon Marker's loss. He asks himself why he trusted Haul Varder's apparent kindness. Father Tenderson would not have committed that cruel error.

For his part, however, the Dark priest recovers from painful concerns more swiftly. He is practiced at submerging his anger and woe, his many regrets. Black has given him cause for consternation, but it does not stifle his native curiosity.

"Answer one query, sir, and I will answer yours," he replies with a semblance of his customary cheer. "You spoke of four elemental energies. Bright and Dark are two. What are the others?"

Black frowns. He finds that he does not wish to speak of such things. Naming them dismays him. It gives them a substance that he desires to deny.

Yet he is indebted to these men. Some debts he avoids when

he can, as Bailey, the barkeep, will attest. Others he repays in full. And on its face, Father Tenderson's inquiry is a small matter.

"They are air and heat," he replies, "as necessary as bright and dark. But they cause no concern. No shaper calls upon them. They are too diffuse. The knowledge to concentrate them does not exist."

He hopes that he speaks truth.

"Accept my thanks, sir," returns the Dark priest warmly. "I am edified. And your question?"

Black feels a need for haste that he cannot explain. "The caravan," he says. It has come from the west. Perhaps it comes from lands unknown to him. "I must speak with its master, but I do not know the town. Where do such men spend the night?"

Father Tenderson laughs. "Or women, in this case," he answers without hesitation. "Her name is Kelvera, though her men call her Blossom for obscure reasons. As for where she spends the night—" With a glance, he refers the question to his friend.

Lost in acid thoughts, Father Whorry names an inn without realizing that he is addressed or knowing that he answers.

Father Tenderson sees Black's desire to depart. In a few words, he directs Black to the inn. Then he says with wry mirth, "You will not think me rude, sir, if I do not escort you to the door. I am concerned for my friend. He needs the solace of more wine. I recognize the signs."

Black bows by inclining his head. Then he goes. Within himself he is running, though his stride is unhurried. He is sure of his ability to locate Haul Varder, but there are questions to which he desires answers before he approaches the wheelwright.

Among them is this. What use can a shaper make of lungs and livers? However, he does not expect to find an explanation in Settle's Crossways, or from any caravaner. Instead he hopes to understand a more practical matter.

How had one shaper attracted enough followers to kill so many brigands and suffer no losses without some rumor of those followers finding its way to the priests, or attaching itself to Haul Varder?

If the wheelwright is innocent, the shaper and his followers must have come to this region from a considerable distance— and must have contrived to remain entirely secret for an unlikely number of days.

Black means to go directly to the inn Father Whorry named. As he skirts the edges of the crowded square, however, he encounters the mother and daughter who addressed him when he first entered Settle's Crossways.

The mother's name is Rose, and she was widowed by the same plague that claimed Annwin Marker. For that reason, her anxiety for her fey daughter, Arbor, is greater than it was. And it has grown still greater since her meeting with the stranger. Her good husband had the gift of calming her. He saw no harm in little Arbor's real or imagined sight, and his unconcern eased Rose's heart. Without him, she has been troubled daily by the fear that her daughter's wits have strayed. But now she has a new fear. The stranger's belief that Arbor's sight is real is beyond her comprehension.

In Settle's Crossways, a town remote from the larger world, and ignorant apart from the gossip of wagoneers and caravaners, the gift of unnatural sight is not preferable to an unbalanced mind.

But Arbor is not afraid. During the past day, she has spoken often of the stranger with the holes in his soul, and of her desire to help him. She has insisted that she can heal his holes, one or more of them. Seeing him again excites her. While Rose flinches in alarm, Arbor succeeds in pulling free of her mother's hand. She runs toward the stranger as though she means to leap into his arms.

Black sees her. He sees her desire to touch him. But he also sees her mother's fear. And he has his own reasons for caution. He knows what may become of the girl if she aids him while she is too young to understand what she does. He holds up one hand while the other secretly invokes a sigil of command.

Surprised by herself, the girl stops.

Rose hastens closer. "Arbor!" she cries in a voice that trembles too much to sound stern. "He is a stranger. Leave him alone."

"But, Ma—" Arbor protests.

Still asserting his command, Black asks, "Your name is Arbor?" His tone is quiet reassurance.

The girl nods. She does not resist as her mother reclaims her hand.

Black meets the mother's wide stare. "And your name, madam?"

His command reaches her. Unwillingly, she replies, "Rose." But then she musters her resolve. "What have you to do with us, sir?" She aches for her husband's presence at her side. He would speak more confidently. "You called my daughter precious. I do not understand you. She is precious only to me."

Black nods. Soothing as water, he says, "Then hear me, Rose. Arbor has a gift for which I have no name. It is clear in her, though I cannot account for it. I am certain only that it is not ripe. When she is older, it will manifest more strongly, and more safely. For the present, it must not be spent on a stranger"—he gazes at Arbor ruefully—"even a stranger with holes in his soul." Then he faces Rose again. "But you are precious also. You have your own gift. You call it fear or grief, but it has other names.

"There is a man who needs your gifts, both yours and Arbor's. He is Jon Marker." Seeing Rose's bafflement, he adds, "You know of him. You know what he has lost. But perhaps you do not know that he is utterly alone.

"It would be a great kindness to befriend him."

If Arbor feels an impulse to touch Jon Marker's pain, she will do herself no harm.

Rose is confounded. Her stare becomes a frown. It becomes dismay. "You wish me to befriend a man I do not know? A man I have never met?"

Black still holds up his hand, though it no longer commands. "Father Tenderson will introduce you," he says because he wants to hurry away. "Or Father Whorry."

Then he touches his hat and withdraws into the crowd.

Rose follows the stranger with her eyes until she loses sight of him. She hardly feels Arbor tug at her hand. She hardly hears her daughter ask, "Can we, Ma? Can we meet him? The man who needs us?" The stranger has turned the mother's world on its head, and she is no longer sure of her balance. She is nodding, but she does not know what she will do.

She does not know that Black has already put her from his mind. His thoughts run ahead of him rather than behind, traveling a road to a destination he cannot see, as he sifts through the throng until he clears the square. When he is able to gaze down the street, he scans it for the sign of the inn he seeks.

Soon he locates it. It is where the Dark priest told him it would be. At once, he ascends to the series of porches on that side and strides toward his goal. In his haste, he neglects to touch his hat to the townsfolk. They stare at him harder as he passes.

As he expects in a town of this size, the inn is also a tavern. Its swinging doors admit him to a room both larger and more elaborate than Bailey's establishment. It has chandeliers for light and padded chairs at round tables for its patrons. Long mirrors behind the bar reflect the bustle of serving-maids and boys carrying a greater variety of viands than Bailey can offer. And in its own fashion, the place is as crowded as the square. Father Whorry has advised Black well. A profusion of wines, ales, and spirits flows as wagoneers, caravaners, and their guards demand refreshment after their long deprivation. Half or more of the men and women who have come with the caravan will resume their journey on the morrow with aching heads and complaining stomachs.

Amid the confusion, however, the shouts for service or companionship, the noise of camaraderie, and the clatter of eating, Black identifies the caravan-master without difficulty. She has the arms of a muleteer, the hands of a gravedigger, the hair of a wind-storm, and the bulk of a steer, but it is not by those signs that he knows her. He is sure of her because she sits at the only table that does not strain to accommodate too many patrons. Also her back is to the wall and her face to the door, she drinks sparingly, and the two men she permits to share her table defer to her as they eat.

As Black enters, the caravaners pay no heed, but every gaze that resides in Settle's Crossways snaps to him as though he has come flinging daggers.

Like the inn itself, and its patrons, this does not surprise Black. He expects it, not because he is a stranger, but rather by reason of his actions against Ing Hardiston and the storekeeper's comrades. He judges that Hardiston would not talk about his own defeat willingly, or permit his deeds to reflect discreditably on him. But the storekeeper needed a healer, as did one of his men. An explanation would be required. Therefore he will have told his version of events—a courageous, honorable version—to everyone he encounters. By now, half the town has heard Ing Hardiston's tale.

This does not trouble Black. He has no use for the town's good will. And he sees no indication that Hardiston's tale has reached the caravan-master. She notices his arrival as she notices everything, but she betrays no reaction that will prevent him from speaking to her, or discourage her from answering.

Ignoring the townsfolk, he makes his way among the tables until he stands in front of Kelvera.

When she meets his gaze, he says her name with his accustomed silk. Without asking her permission, without removing his hat and cloak, he seats himself opposite her. She rests her forearms on the table. He does not. Her companions stare at him, openly astonished, but he does not regard them.

"Kelvera," he says again. "Forgive my discourtesy. I must speak with you. The matter is urgent."

He surprises her, though she gives no sign of her reaction. She is experienced and wily. In her many years of long journeys, guiding caravans through lands unknown to all but her and her captains, she has seen much, heard much, learned much. She knows a shaped man when she meets with one. They are rare in this kingdom, and have become more so since the ending of the old wars. Still she is certain that if this man exposes his arms, he will reveal an astonishing variety of glyphs, sigils, scarifications, and inlaid metals.

Holding the stranger's gaze, she tells her companions, "Another table."

They rise from their chairs at once, though they do not mask their reluctance. One is her captain of guards. He commands the defense of her train. He does not pretend equanimity as he draws a poniard from his belt, shows it to the stranger, then stabs it into the table where it is ready for Kelvera's use. The other man is her captain of wagons, responsible for managing the diverse owners, burdens, teamsters, and beasts of her train. More readily than the guard captain, he goes to request a seat at a nearby table.

Black does not acknowledge the captains. Waiting, he ignores the poniard.

The caravan-master leans back in her chair. She does not judge the shaped man or determine her response in advance. Nor does she invite him to share her meal. When she has appraised him for a moment, searching her memories of other travels through this land, she says, "Call me Blossom." Endless days of shouting have made her voice gruff as a grindstone. "You are?"

"Black," he replies without hesitation. He is already sure of her. She will answer him or she will not. If she does, she will do so honestly. If she does not, she will betray no hint of what she withholds.

"Black, hmm?" muses Kelvera. "Interesting." Her tone suggests disinterest. "Not a name I know."

Black shrugs. He does not respond.

The caravan-master studies his silence. With an air of distraction, as though she is unaware of what she does, she reaches out and taps the hilt of her guard captain's poniard. "An urgent matter, you said? Then speak. I cannot guess your mind."

Black nods. "Blossom," he says. Despite his haste, he hopes to distract her from her natural suspicions. "Why are you called Blossom?"

She raises her eyebrows. "*That* is what you wish to know? And you call it urgent? I am Blossom because it pleases me."

Black almost smiles. "And I am Black because I have forgotten my other names. My travels have been as long as yours. I forget what I can. The rest is urgent. If it were not, I would forget it as well."

Kelvera feels a tension in her shoulders easing. Rare as they are, shaped men are dangerous, and this one more so than others. Now, however, she understands that he is not dangerous to her. Frowning, she draws the poniard from the table and pushes it away from her.

"Then speak," she repeats. "Those who trust me to lead them have their secrets. I will keep them. But anything else—" She spreads her hands to indicate the world she knows.

"Have you incurred losses?" he asks abruptly.

She squints at him. "What, *ever*?"

"In this kingdom," he explains. "On this journey."

"No," she answers. Then she admits, "Attacks are inevitable. The wealth of my caravans is legend. But my captain of guards knows his duties. His men are well trained and armed. One guard took a spear in his thigh. An arrow killed the personal servant of a dealer in fine spices. We left seven brigands dead. I do not call the outcome losses."

Black nods again. "And no desertions?"

Kelvera slaps her hand on the table. She pretends indignation. "I treat my people well, men and women. They do not desert." After a moment, she laughs humorlessly. "Not in this kingdom. The old wars began here. They ended here. This land is considered perilous. Shapers and wild powers are said to remain, perhaps hidden in this very forest. Even cowards do not desert here."

Black's manner remains abrupt. "When did you last pass this way?" He means from west to east, from the strange deserts in the far west to the richly mined mountains a hundred leagues eastward.

The question catches Kelvera off guard. She counts backward in her mind. "Two seasons ago? No, more. But less than three."

"Did you incur any losses *then*? Any desertions?" Black needs an explanation for Tamlin Marker's killer's ability to claim so many brigands without the aid of followers known in the town. "Did any wagons leave your train?"

The caravan-master collects her thoughts. "Any wagons?" She dismisses losses and desertions. "In this kingdom? Before the destinations they hired me to reach?"

Any matter that a shaped man considers urgent is important to her as well, though her reasons are not his. If Black is not dangerous to her, his presence and his questions imply danger nonetheless. His interest is a warning she means to heed.

For the third time, Black nods.

"Yes," she replies slowly. She makes certain of her memories. "But not in Settle's Crossways. A league to the east. In virgin forest. Near that misplaced mountain, the old fumer. For no discernible reason."

Soft as feathers on clean skin, Black urges, "Tell me."

"We had not left the desert," she answers, still slowly, "when a wagon purchased a place among us." She trusts him to know of the desert she mentions. "Its owner was an old man. More than old. He appeared ancient, with a face cut by the erosion of years, skin worn thin until it seemed transparent, and a frame much emaciated. He wore a long robe that may once have been red, but was now faded to rust. His beard, white and well-kempt, reached to his waist. Altogether he resembled a hierophant who had given his life to the worship of a desert god."

Black prepares another question, but Kelvera does not pause. Having chosen to answer, she answers fully.

"Still his movements were not decrepit," she continues. "Indeed, his steps were sprightly when he elected to walk, which was seldom. Also his voice was not ancient, though it quavered. At times, laboring caravans raise a mighty din, yet he was able to make himself heard.

"We required a name. He allowed us to call him Sought.

"With him, he brought four guards, and also a teamster for his oxen, but no personal servant. We called his lack of an attendant strange, yet his wagon was stranger. It was all of wood, more a house on wheels than a wagon, and painted the same worn hue as his robe. Also it was made without windows—without as much as chinks between the boards—to ease the heat within. Its only opening was a door at the rear, a door too sturdy to be forced, which remained locked at all times."

The caravan-master shrugs. She has no cause to doubt her choices. "I accepted his company. I did not begrudge him his strangeness, and the price he offered was generous. But I would have accepted him without payment for the sake of his guards.

"My men are good. His surpassed them. I have rarely seen arms and armor of such quality. Their training was diligent, their skill prodigious, and their vigilance in their master's name exceeded all bounds. If they ever ate or slept"—she remembers them with as much awe as her nature allows—"I say this seriously, Black—they did so only when he admitted one or at most two of them to his house. With four such men in my employ, I could dispense with ten others and call myself well defended."

For a moment, Kelvera drifts among her memories. To prompt her, Black asks, "He named his destination, this Sought?"

Her full attention returns to the shaped man. "He did not," she replies more sharply. "He said that he would go with me as far as I went. Then he would find another caravan to continue his journey."

"Yet he turned aside?"

She folds her arms. "As I have said. He did not emerge from his wagon while we rested here. But when we had passed a league beyond Settle's Crossways, his teamster pulled his oxen from the road. There the old man informed my captain of wagons that he was content. He needed rest, he said. He would bide where he was for a time. His guards would suffice to fend for him."

"Fend for him?" Black interjects. The phrase troubles him. It matches his hasty speculations too closely.

Again Kelvera shrugs. "So he said. As he asked no return of coin, I had no cause to refuse him."

Black is silent for a moment. Within himself, he wonders whether his purpose will require him to confront a foe he cannot comprehend. A foe against whom his own powers will have no meaning. Despite his ability to forget, and his singular resolve, he is forced to acknowledge—not for the first time— that he is afraid.

Yet he masks his uncertainty. His manner is unchanged as he asks, "The place where he joined your train. Is it known for its winds?"

"Known?" snorts Kelvera. "Say infamous. It is an unholy hell of winds. Their dust can strip the flesh from bones. Every outcropping of rock has been sculpted until it resembles a fiend yearning for release. Those winds—" She shakes her head to dispel thoughts of over-turned wagons, mangled deaths, spilled goods, maimed beasts. "There is a price in pain to be paid for crossing that stretch of desert."

By these words, Kelvera tells Black that the land of her birth holds to an alien theology, one which would not be recognized in the kingdom he serves. The temples created by the King have not yet excreted such arcana as hells and fiends. Perhaps sorceries are possible in the west that are inconceivable here.

He knows now that he has entered deep waters. For him, they may be bottomless. Nevertheless his purpose is at its most compulsory when he fears it.

As he gathers himself to thank the caravan-master, however, his doubts prompt one more question.

"A dire desert, then," he remarks. "What gods are worshipped there?"

If the old man is in truth a hierophant—

Kelvera rolls her eyes. "What else?" She has her own reasons to scorn religions. "Wind and sun. In that region, there are no other powers that can be asked for mercy." Then she shrugs once more. "Those prayers are not answered."

Thinking, Lungs and livers, air and heat, Black can delay no longer. He must obey his purpose.

But when he rises from his chair, the caravan-master stops him with a gesture. He has warned her. She has a warning of her own to deliver.

Leaning close, she says, "Heed me, Black," a whisper no one will overhear. "You are a shaped man. That Sought was not. Be wary of him."

Black raises an eyebrow at her recognition. She does not need to say the words he hears. If the old man is not shaped, he may yet be a shaper. Also his guards are fearsome.

More formally than is his custom, Black replies, "Accept my gratitude, Blossom. I am in your debt."

This debt he hopes to repay.

Kelvera returns a smile as disturbing as his. The more she

thinks on him, the more she desires to understand the danger. It may spill onto her caravan. "Perhaps," she suggests, "we will meet again."

She means to add, When we do, we can discuss who is in debt. But Black forestalls her. He is in haste. "We will not," he says like a man who is already gone. Giving her no time to respond, he strides for the doors.

Still he wants guidance. It will shorten his search. At the doors, he pauses to grip the arm of the most recent arrival, a burly chandler still wearing his leather apron mottled with dried wax. Black invokes his sigil of command as he demands the location of Haul Varder's workshop.

The chandler glowers, torn between umbrage, distorted rumors, and an inability to refuse. He tries to sound angry as he directs Black. To some extent, he succeeds.

At once, Black releases the man. Through the swinging doors, he leaves the inn and enters the glare of the midafternoon sun.

He is at his most certain when he is afraid.

Two streets and three alleys from the inn, he finds the wheelwright's smithy and woodshop. The structure resembles an open-sided barn, providing abundant space for Haul Varder's forge at one end and his lathes at the other. Near the forge stands an anvil. Between and above the ends, he has storage for his iron and hammers, for his supplies of wood, and for racks to hold his chisels, saws, and other tools.

The place is near the edge of the town. But this stretch of Settle's Crossways is not extensive. Black judges that he is two hundred paces from Jon Marker's house, perhaps three hundred from the caravan's road. Above the workshop's roof to the east, he can see the tops of the nearest trees.

He hopes to find his quarry there, but he is not surprised when he does not. If the ritual that required Tamlin Marker's murder is near its culmination—and if the wheelwright is involved, as Black now believes—the final preparations are being made. And they are certainly not being made in the town. They are not being made anywhere that risks witnesses. Their perpetrators will seek seclusion against even the most obscure mischance.

The ashes in the forge are cold. They have been cold for some time. The sawdust around the lathes has not been swept. The lathes themselves wear a fine fur of dust, as do their tools. If Black had spent more time questioning townsfolk, he would no doubt have learned how long the shop has been unattended. But he does not need that knowledge. The scent of evil is strong here, as acrid as acid, as bitter as kale, and fraught with intimations of bloodshed. To his shaped senses, it is as distinct as murder, overriding even the stink of cold ashes and the warm odor of drying resins. He will be able to follow it.

A brief stroking of his thigh summons his horse. While he

waits, he searches for some sign of Haul Varder's intent, some indication left by carelessness or haste. But the search does not have his full attention. Kelvera has answered his more practical questions. It is his need for understanding that troubles him. He cannot gauge the peril ahead of him. He is forced to consider that an impossible ritual may be the only possible explanation for the smell that haunts his nose.

His mount greets him with a soft whicker as it trots forward. Despite the hard use he made of it earlier, it is strong and ready, as refreshed as a horse that has enjoyed days of rest and rich pasturage. The ways that it has been shaped are subtle, difficult to discern, but they are potent. The beast will not fail him until he fails himself.

He checks his horse's girth and tack, an old habit. Then he mounts. Though he is no longer patient and believes that he knows his way, he circles the workshop twice, testing the air in every direction. When he is done, he trots toward the eastern outskirts of the town.

There near the fringe of the forest, Settle's Crossways is a haphazard collection of buildings. The shifting sunlight shows him several large warehouses belonging, no doubt, to prosperous merchants. It shows him hovels where the town's poor scrabble for shelter, hoping that their proximity to the warehouses will ease their efforts to find work. And among the hovels and warehouses, he discovers a scattering of more sturdy homes. These lack such amenities as roofed porches. Their owners are not reluctant to enter with mud, dirt, and the droppings of horses and cattle on their boots. Still they are solid houses, made to last. They belong to men or families who do not care for appearances, but who mean to be secure in their homes.

Black does not expect to see lights in the windows at this time of day. They face the westering sun. Their occupants do not yet need lamps. But the windows of one house glow. Covered as they are with oiled cloths, they give him no glimpse of what waits inside. With the sun on them, they should not glow as they do. Yet they are unmistakable in the dwindling afternoon.

The scent of evil leads Black to the lit house.

He dismounts. Silent as nightfall, he approaches the door. When he places his palm there, he knows at once that his quarry is absent. This is Haul Varder's house. The odor of his doings permeates the door, the walls, the glowing windows. Black is sure. But the wheelwright is not here.

Someone else occupies the house. Someone else lights lamps against the coming darkness. That someone, alone, has lit a profusion of lamps.

Black considers departing as he came, in silence. He can follow the obscenity of Tamlin Marker's murder unaided. He does not fear the men who killed the brigands. But an impulse overtakes him, and he knocks.

The quaver of an old voice calls, "What?" An old woman's voice. "Go away. He is not here. Leave me to my prayers."

Black does not ask permission to enter. Lifting the latch, he steps into a room lit by a noonday sun of lamps, lanterns, and candles.

———

The old woman sits in a comfortless wooden chair surrounded by many lights. Her hearth is cold, but she does not need its warmth. The flames give abundant heat. A dew of sweat glistens on her brow and gathers in the seams of her face, giving her the look of a woman who has labored too long in the last years of her life. Nevertheless she wears a heavy shawl over her shoulders, and she clutches it to her breast as though she imagines that it will protect her.

She turns her head unerringly toward Black, and he sees at once that she is blind. The milky hue that covers her eyes is too thick to permit sight. Still she has heard him. She knows where he stands, just as she knows every lamp, lantern, and taper around her. She keeps them lit at every hour of the day and night. When one or several go out, she refills or replaces them with no fear that she will set herself or the house aflame. It is not Haul Varder who desires them, though the woman does not need them. They are her prayers.

"You dare?" she croaks at Black. She sounds both querulous and frightened. "Be gone. Leave me. When he catches you, he will teach you to respect his mother."

"I do not fear him," Black replies like the coming night. "You have no cause to fear me. Only tell me what he does, and I will go. Only tell me where he is, and I will go."

"*Tell?*" the old woman retorts. The puckering of her mouth betrays her toothless gums. "*I?* Tell *you*? I will tell you nothing. You are a blackguard who preys on weakness. I am a gods-fearing woman, gods-fearing. I do not go to the temples. I cannot walk so far. But that does not make me evil. I worship *here*, do you understand? I worship *here*. There is no temple-goer more devout.

"If you do not go—if he does not catch you—I will call down Bright Eternal's light to consume you. I will cast you into Dark Enduring's agony."

To an extent, Black believes her. He does not doubt that she will hurl her lamps and lanterns at him, as many as she can reach. He does not doubt that her aim will be good. But he also knows that he will not burn. His cloak and his shaping will ward him. Still he seeks to calm her. If she acts against him, her house will become conflagration. He will be forced to rescue her. He may be forced to find aid for her before he can resume his purpose.

In his mildest tone, his softest silk, he asks, "Who speaks of evil? I did not."

"Blackguard," she snaps. As her fright fades, her bitterness grows. "Do you think to confuse me? I know you. You are the canker that rots the heart of this town. You do not speak of evil *now*. You are too cunning for that. But you did *then*. You were not so bold to say it to my face, but you said it. You said it behind it my back, a gods-fearing woman's back. You said it and did not admit your wrong. You did not ask my forgiveness."

Sweat gathers on her brow. It trickles into her eyes. But she does not blink it away. It is not sorrow or regret. It is an old woman's trembling fury.

"If you had said it to my face, I would have told you that I see as clearly as you, indeed I do. And I have a clearer sight of my duty. There *was* evil in him then. He was a wicked boy, cursed son of a cursed father. Did you think me blind to it? But there is no evil *now*. With my own love and my own strength, I ripped it from his heart after his father forsook us. With punishment and prayer, I drove it out. *Out*, do you hear me? I scarred him with my love until he had no room in him for evil.

"He is a good man *now*." She smacks her lips in satisfaction, but does not ease her clutch on her shawl. "A good neighbor with a good living. A kind man who aids the less fortunate. A hard-working man who provides for his gods-fearing mother, his lonely mother, his blind mother. He cares for her with the diligence of a priest.

"When he catches you, he will drive you from the house. He will drive you to your ruin. When he is done with you, you will beg me on your *knees* for forgiveness"—quavering, she summons the fullness of her anger—"*and I will not give it.*"

Black has heard enough. Such men as Haul Varder do not spring from the earth. They are shaped much as Black himself has been shaped, though by different means. If his purpose and his circumstances permit it, Black will take pity on Haul Varder, for surely the wheelwright's mother did not.

Tracing a pattern across his chest with one hand, Black grips the edge of his cloak with the other. "He will not catch me," he assures the old woman. "I will catch *him*."

Then he swings his cloak in a sweeping gesture that extinguishes every light in the house. When the woman begins to wail, he turns his back on her, strides outside, and leaps for his horse. At a gallop, he rides in pursuit of his quarry.

He cannot gallop when he enters the forest. The trees are thick, and the day's light becomes dusk quickly among them. If he turns aside until he comes to the road, he will make better haste. Nonetheless he stays within the woods, following the scent of Haul Varder's crimes. He is on a track the wheelwright has taken many times. It will lead him to his destination. Trusting his horse to give him as much speed as it can, he sharpens his senses so that errant breezes or undiscovered corpses will not urge him astray.

He expects an ambush. He knows nothing of the old man who calls himself Sought. He knows only what Kelvera has told him of the man's bodyguards. It is possible that they are ignorant of him. They have come from a land far to the west, where the King's mediation does not hold sway. Their ignorance may be complete. Yet Black thinks otherwise. He will be surprised if Haul Varder has not been in Settle's Crossways during the past night and day. He considers it unlikely that the wheelwright has not heard gossip of the stranger who spoke with Trait in the tavern, the stranger who injured Ing Hardiston and another man at Tamlin Marker's grave. He believes that Sought's men will be ready for him.

The sun's setting behind him casts spots like fragments of Varder's mother's prayers through the boughs and leaves, spots that dance and waver in the low wind, obscuring more than they reveal. Each instance of brightness darkens what lies behind it. But Black does not regard them. He has other senses, forms of perception that are not misled by the sun's last fireflies. He trusts what he is able to discern. All other concerns he puts from his mind. That he does not, can not, understand the purpose that drives his quarry dismays him, but it does not affect his resolve, or his haste, or his confidence in his mount. It does not make him less the servant of his own purpose.

Lungs and livers, air and heat. And a hierophant from a land infamous for its winds, a land where wind and sun are worshipped as gods. If it is true that air and heat are elemental spirits, as necessary to life as bright and dark, it may also be true that a shaper born to a parched and baking world knows how to call upon gods that have played no part in Black's homeland's wars.

The ability to make use of such knowledge here is incomprehensible to Black, but his lack of understanding does not make it impossible.

His mount stretches to leap a fallen tree. It skitters aside from a thicket of longthorn briar, avoids a sinkhole in a wandering stream, picks a careful path between large boulders. Its care makes him a target for his attackers.

He is aware of them while they still only hear his approach. He counts four men armed with sabers and other weapons. He recognizes their stealth. He knows that the wheelwright is not among them.

He detects a crossbow aimed at his hip from the brush on one side, a spear poised to throw from the shelter of an old oak on the other. A man with a dagger ready crouches to spring from atop the nearest boulder. Directly ahead of Black, ten or more paces distant, stands a fourth assailant, waiting with his quarter-staff in case Black is able to evade three simultaneous assaults.

Black's movements are mapped in his mind, as precise as though he has foreseen them. Snatching up the edge of his cloak, he catches the bolt of the crossbow in the tough canvas as he vaults from the far side of his horse. The spear plucks at his shoulder, but does not harm him. The man leaping from the boulder lands in the mount's empty saddle.

An instant of surprise slows Black's attackers, an instant of harsh cursing. During that heartbeat's pause, Black slaps his horse's rump, causing the beast to buck the man from its back. Prompt to its training, its shaping, the horse begins to trample the fallen man.

Two or three paces of ground are now clear in front of Black. As one assailant bursts from the brush and another charges past his oak, both drawing their sabers, Black invokes his longsword. Kelvera has warned him against the skill of Sought's men. As he engages them, he sees that she did not exaggerate. His own skill suffices against one such opponent. Only the many ways in which he has been shaped enable him to counter two.

Parrying with his utmost speed, he shifts his ground until he has a boulder at his back. With both men in front of him, he fights for his life.

Thrust and parry, slash and counter, his blade and theirs weave a skein of imminent bloodshed through the gloom. The last glints of the sun strike sparks like stars on the swift iron, gleams briefer than blinks. Black's horse has fled among the trees. The beast has left one of Sought's bodyguards broken or dead. There is much to be said for killing both of his immediate attackers, and also the last, who still waits. He imagines that Sought relies on them. Their deaths may prevent the culmination of the ritual that claimed Tamlin Marker. But he cannot be certain of this. Perhaps Haul Varder is all the aid Sought needs. Also he is not confident that he *can* kill his opponents. They are indeed exceptional. And they do not tire, though he resists them with all the strength of his body, all the gifts of his shaping, all the experience of his many battles. If he grants one of his foes an opening, he may be able to cut down the other. But then he will be wounded himself. Killing them both is not a likely outcome.

Without hesitation, almost without thought, he changes his tactics. He fights now, not to harm or drive back his attackers, but rather to make himself a different target. He means to cause them to adjust their footing. And when he sees a subtle alteration in how they balance themselves, he takes his chance.

Headlong, he dives between them, hoping that their blades will not find his back as he passes.

They are wrongly balanced to turn and strike while he is exposed. For the merest instant, they interfere with each other. Neither man can swing without hazard to his comrade.

Black's dive becomes a roll. He surges to his feet facing the foes he has passed. In the same motion, he springs to assail them.

He understands what will happen now. He recognizes it as it occurs. The last bodyguard is charging. Black feels the blow of the quarterstaff coming. He knows how to evade it, but he does not do so. Instead he accepts it. When it strikes the back of his head, he accepts the shock, the blinding pain, the fall into unconsciousness.

The blow will not kill him. He is too hardy. But it will take him where he needs and fears to go.

When he returns to himself, he is bound spread-eagled by his wrists and ankles. At first, he knows only that he cannot move. Then the pain finds him. The agony in his head is like that of a spear driven through his skull. The back of his head is a sodden mess. Blood drips down his neck to his shoulders. Waves of nausea and the bright echoes of the blow that took him make his guts squirm. They prevent him from opening his eyes. Of his circumstances, he knows only that he is helpless.

His wound is not mortal. It is worse than mortal. It has made him a victim.

The heat is tremendous. It seems to scald his skin. It has probably burned away his eyebrows and lashes. The hair on his head may be gone. When he tries to blink, his lids scrape his eyes.

Nevertheless the ways in which he has been shaped go deep. His bleeding slows. With every breath, his nausea eases. Gradually tears moisten his eyes. In stabbing surges, the pain of his head spreads through him. It restores sensation to his limbs. He finds that he is able to close his fingers. He can move his toes.

Now he feels the pressure of rope on his wrists and ankles. It is woven of sisal or some other harsh fiber. It will not break. And it allows no more than a slight flexing of his elbows and knees. He can bend his joints to achieve subtle shifts of his posture. He cannot gain leverage.

He is not ready to see where he is. But the rough touch of the surface at his back tells him that he is pinned against native rock. It is crude, studded with protrusions and gaps, written with ridges. He can imagine that he is bound to a boulder, but he believes that he is not. He believes that he is fixed to a wall. The fierce heat and its brimstone reek convince him that he is in a cavern.

Though his eyes are closed, he knows that the space is filled with ruddy light.

From some distant source comes a low sound like the slow boiling of a cauldron.

Then the life returning to his nerves makes him aware that his plight is worse than helplessness. The heat on his skin tells him that he is naked. More than his cloak and hat have been taken from him. All of his garments have been stripped away. Even his boots are gone. Even the bindings of his loins—

He is exposed for what he is. Every detail of his shaping is visible, every detail except those on his back. From neck to foot, the elaborate sweeps and whorls of his scarification are revealed. They speak a language known to every shaper in the kingdom. The deeply tattooed sigils name and define him. The burned glyphs invoke the powers imminent in his scars. The thin bars of purest silver inlaid under his skin summon the energies of bright and dark to enhance his senses, his strength, his resolve. Together, the inlays, his glyphs and sigils, and his scarifications bind him to his purpose.

If he hoped now, which he does not, he would hope that Haul Varder's ignorance of shaping, and Sought's presumed ignorance of how bright and dark are called upon, will protect him from a complete betrayal of the King. If Sought's learning suffices to interpret what he sees—to interpret all he sees—Black's body will tell him how the King's mediation can be foiled.

Black has found that he is able to close his fingers. Now he clenches his fists firmly. He means to conceal what little he can.

When he begins to distinguish voices from the sound of distant boiling, he opens his eyes and blinks them clear.

He is bound to the wall of a cavern the size of the square where roads intersect in Settle's Crossways. The ropes at his wrists and ankles are tied to iron stakes pounded into the rough stone. Much of the floor in front of him is level until it is cut off by a rift or crevice that extends the width of the cavern. This fissure is the source of the reddish light and the terrible heat. It is also the source of the boiling. Clearly it goes far down into the heart of the rock.

From the rift arises a thick, acrid fume, but it does not fill the cavern. Around the walls are a number of natural tunnels, and the cavern's ceiling has the shape of a funnel. Drawing air from the tunnels, the hot fume streams upward and away until it emerges from the throat of the mountain, the old fumer in the east.

The air from the tunnels is all that prevents the heat from destroying Black and his captors.

Off to one side stands a wagon that resembles a house on wheels. Its only door is open, but Black cannot see inside.

With him in the cavern are four men. Three he recognizes by their arms and armor, by the way they move. They are the guards he fought in the forest. The fourth is surely Haul Varder. He has neither weapons nor protection. He is naked to the waist in the heat, and his chest weeps sweat. He has a black beard like a glower, the muscles of a blacksmith, the solid frame of a laborer. His hands are so heavily callused that he cannot close them completely. Of the four, only he watches the wagon. Only he is impatient. In his eyes, the ruddy light burns like excitement or fear.

The three guards keep watch on Black, but they betray no particular interest in him, no animosity for the death of their comrade. Black's helplessness contents them. They will react to him only if he struggles, and then only if his struggles threaten to free him.

Sweltering, Haul Varder paces the stone. He has been promised much, and has done much to fulfill his role in Sought's ritual. He has in him a wellspring of cold rage that has enabled him to commit deeds he would not have imagined without the old man's promises. At Father Whorry's urging, and because Sought wished it, he accepted Jon Marker as his shop servant. Grinding his teeth, he endured Jon Marker's insufferable courtesy and meekness and labor, though he knew the man's demeanor was false. He knows too well that all courtesy and meekness are false, feigned by men who seek to conceal their contempt, men who know him and his mother and hold only scorn. Still he did as he was bid. Because he had dealings with men who had dealings with robbers and cutthroats, he could guide the old man's guards to the camps of brigands. With his own hands, he took insufferable Jon Marker's insufferable son. With the old man's guidance, he harvested the boy's lungs and liver while the boy still lived. In every way, he has served Sought's commands and whims, and has endured the old man's disdain. He desires what he has been promised more than he craves respect. For him, all respect is false. He will never trust in it.

No, Haul Varder does not wish for respect. He covets fear. It is his dream, and the old man's promise, that he will be feared. That he will be feared so extremely that strong men will loose their bowels and women will grovel in the dirt.

———

He is impatient to see the old man's promise honored.

Vexed and suffering in the heat, the wheelwright waits as long as he can. Then he shouts at the wheeled house, "Enough! It is *enough*! I have endured too much of your preparations and researches. Is there no end to your dithering? When will you let me kill him?"

He believes that Black's death will transform him. It will make him fearsome.

"*Kill* him?" the old man answers. In normal tones, his voice is a quaver that masks its strength. Now it is a shriek. "Imbecile! We *do not* kill him!"

In a fury of haste, Sought leaves his dwelling. He springs to the stone with the lithe confidence of a much younger man, a newer priest. His beard spills aside in the breezes from the various tunnels. He wears a long robe colored or dulled to the same hue as the light from the fissure. It is voluminous and flutters about him, giving the impression that inside it he has spent decades in near-starvation. Its secret is that it conceals many pockets containing various powders and implements, some or all of which may be needed at any moment.

The stiff mass of his eyebrows gives him a look of perpetual astonishment, yet he is not surprised by Haul Varder's presumption. He is only surprised at himself. Immersed in his last preparations, in the near fruition of his life's work, he forgets too easily that lesser men are sheep-headed fools. It is only the near-mindless fidelity of his guards that allows him to stand so close to the achievement of pure glory.

Exalted by the heat, Sought sweeps forward. Clutching the wheelwright's sweat-slick arm, he drags the man closer to Black. An arm's length away, he halts. "We do *not* kill him," he repeats, openly exasperated. "Are you blind? Look!"

He points to the sigil on Black's right shoulder. "There." He indicates a glyph decorated with scars on Black's ribs. "There." He directs Haul Varder's gaze to an extravagant whorl in the flesh of Black's lower abdomen. "*There.*

"The signs are plain. This man is the King's Justice. We are indeed fortunate that he has come against us. I will make good use of his enhancements. Yet for that very reason, he must live. If he is slain, the King will know it. Even at this distance, he will attempt to intervene.

"You do not understand the danger. I have spent an age of my life in study, and lakes of blood as well. Still I cannot measure the reach of the King's powers. I know only that they are great. To end the wars as he did, they must be great indeed. We will not risk his awareness of what we do."

Then Sought shrugs. He releases Haul Varder. Swallowing his ire, he says, "When we are done, we will not care who knows. The King can feel as much fear as any man. Until then, his Justice will serve us. We will take his inlays"—he muses for a moment—"perhaps two or three of his glyphs"—then he continues more strongly—"and as much blood as he can spare. But we will not allow him to breathe his last until our task is complete."

None of this surprises Black. He knows there is sorcery in his blood, a necessary effect of his shaping. He knows Sought can take power from his veins as well as from his silver, and from other details also. And he finds that he now understands more than he imagined. The conundrum that has baffled him since he heard Jon Marker and studied Tamlin Marker's grave is the impossibility of concentrating the elemental energies of heat and air so that they will serve as a source of power. But here that riddle is answered. The slow boil of stone in the crevice will supply Sought with all the concentration he can require.

Then there will arise a form of sorcery for which the King is unprepared. No amount of resolve and strength will suffice to preserve the balance to which the King has given his life.

His fists Black keeps closed. Perhaps Sought has not studied them. Perhaps the hierophant does not know that there is thin silver under the surface of Black's palms.

Haul Varder does not understand Sought's caution. He does not care to understand it. Explanations and warnings only aggravate his impatience. He is entirely aware of the old man's scorn. He does not trust Sought to fulfill any promise. Yet if there is doubt in the wheelwright's eyes, if there is fear, he does not know it. His rage overcomes every qualm, every scruple, every hesitation.

"Then do it," he demands. "Cut him. Take what you need. Keep your word. I am done with your endless preparations. They are *timid*, old man. They show that you are unsure of yourself.

"He is helpless now. He will not be more helpless in an hour's time."

Sought replies with a smile like a wolf's. The wheelwright's insults stoke his own hot hungers, but he does not speak of them. Instead he offers his mildest quaver.

"Very well. I am ready. At your request, we will begin."

Holding Haul Varder's gaze, the hierophant nods to his guards.

They have been well instructed. They know their master's will. It rules them. One remains with Sought and Haul Varder. His comrades cross the cavern to enter the wagon.

When they emerge, they are carrying two square-cut timbers, one twice the length of the other. They have rope. Near Black, they lean the longer timber against the wall. With rope, they lash the shorter timber across the longer. When they are done, they have fashioned a rude cross.

Haul Varder snorts at the sight. "What purpose does *that* serve?" The wellspring of his rage provides an abundance of bitterness. "Is this some trick? He cannot be made more helpless than he is. I can do whatever I wish to him as he stands."

Black has a better understanding of the old man's intent. Any ritual of shaping must begin with natural flesh. He is not surprised when the guard at Sought's side strikes the wheelwright's head, a clout that drops him to the stone. While Haul Varder writhes in pain and shock, stunned by the blow, Sought's servants drag him to the cross. With practiced ease, they bind his arms to the shorter timber. His ankles they secure near the floor. When they are done, Tamlin Marker's killer is as helpless as Black.

The guards do not remove Haul Varder's trousers. Sought has seen Black's legs. He has studied them. He knows that their shaping contributes much to Black's purpose, but will not serve his own.

As the wheelwright recovers, he shakes his head frantically. "This is not—" His voice fails him until the effects of the blow diminish. Then he is able to shout. "This is not your promise! Bastard! Whoreson! I did not consent to *this*! You assured me I did my part when I killed the boy. When I harvested him." His eyes glare in his head like a madman's. "*This is not your promise!*"

Sought now stands in front of Black. He is planning his cuts, his maimings. He does not disguise his eagerness as he answers Haul Varder.

"You did your part. Indeed, you did. I acknowledge it freely. And I will fulfill my promise. You will see how I fulfill it. But the boy's death required your willingness. For my ritual, innocence must be voluntarily taken. If one of my men did the deed for me, the effect of the outcome would be lessened.

"Now I do not need your willingness. It has no further use. For the fulfillment of my promise, you are merely an implement. By choice or not, you suffice."

Haul Varder screams his rage and fear, but Sought no longer heeds him. The gaze with which the priest regards Black suggests that the old man is amazed to come so near his goal, but Sought knows only his own eagerness. After so many years of toil, so many victims, so much extreme deprivation, so much arcane study, he now stands in the perfect place for his purpose, and has been given the perfect tools to achieve his ends. No hierophant has ever accomplished what he attempts here. He finds that he must take a moment to calm himself so that his hands will not tremble.

From hidden pockets, he draws out a delicate knife of aching keenness and a small vessel shaped like a trough slightly curved. Pressing the vessel to Black's flesh, he sets his blade to an inlay below Black's collarbone. With extreme care, he cuts to remove the silver. Black's blood he collects in his vessel.

This is a pain with which Black has long and extensive experience. He accepted it during his shaping. He does not accept it now. Howling hoarsely, he twists as much as he can from side to side, playing the part of a man who squirms in a wasted effort to escape excruciation. Yet his demonstrated agony is a charade. He uses it to disguise the way he invokes the inlays of his palms, the way he strains to free his right arm from its bonds. He knows that he will not break the rope. He has never had such strength. Yet with time and effort, a bolt hammered into stone may be worked loose.

If Sought and the guards do not recognize what he strives to do—

From the place where the bolt enters the wall comes a small sifting of grit, nothing more.

With one thin bar of silver removed, the old man sets his vessel aside. He confronts Haul Varder. Vexed by the wheelwright's screams and curses, Sought gestures to his guards. One man steps forward to gag Haul Varder's mouth. The gag is driven so deep that Varder retches. He can scarcely breathe. He cannot scream, though his gaze is white terror.

Satisfied, Sought finds a place among Haul Varder's ribs, a place unlike the inlay's location in Black's chest. He opens a substantial flap of Varder's skin, inserts the silver, then settles the flap over it. Responding to Sought's nod, another guard uses a leather-hook and twine to sew shut the wound so that the inlay will not shift.

As his servant treats the wheelwright, Sought returns to Black.

Briefly the hierophant considers his task. When he has made his choice, he slashes with his knife again and again at Black's sigil of command, taking care only to catch Black's blood in his vessel. He does not stop until the sigil is marred beyond use or name. Then he proceeds to remove another inlay from Black's chest.

During these cuts, Black continues his raw-throated howls, his twisting, his show of anguish. The slight flexing of his elbow allowed by his bonds does not enable him to exert much force, but he does what he can. And he does not only pull. He jerks upward, downward.

The drift of grit from the place where the bolt enters the stone is not enough.

When the second of Black's inlays has been imposed on Haul Varder, this time deep in the man's belly, and the wound has been sewn shut, Sought begins to draw cuts on the wheelwright's flesh. Some are symbols and whorls that Black recognizes. Others form patterns unfamiliar to him. Soon Haul Varder's torso is a sheen of sweat and blood, his beard is a mute cry for help, and his eyes flutter on the edge of unconsciousness.

For the moment, the old man is content with his work. A sign to his guards brings one of them to remove the gag from Haul Varder's mouth. While the wheelwright whoops for air, Sought retrieves his supply of Black's blood. Obeying a silent command, the guard grips Haul Varder's head and tilts it back. The guard's fingers gouge Varder's nerves until Varder's mouth is forced open.

The old man pours Black's blood down his ally's throat until it has all been swallowed.

Black feels that he is suffocating in the heat. Sweat runs from his body. His new wounds pump trickles of blood. But he ignores those sensations. While Sought's attention, and that of his guards, is occupied with the wheelwright, Black works against the bolt that secures his right hand.

He cannot work long. The hierophant soon returns to him. Sought has much to do to complete his designs. Black endures as best he can, feigning torment, while another of his sigils is destroyed and two more inlays are cut out. As best he can, he fights the bolt. Yet despite his straits, his growing weakness, his imminent betrayal of the King, he finds comfort in Sought's actions. The old man has not touched the signs he indicated to Haul Varder, the signs that demand the King's attention. He avoids attracting the King's notice. Also Sought has not harmed the place on Black's hip that summons his longsword. The priest believes that Black cannot move his arms. Therefore Black cannot invoke his powers. Sought has not examined Black's palms.

The hierophant's knowledge is not as complete as Black feared.

Haul Varder is unconscious now, or he has fallen into the compliance taught by his mother's harsh love. He does not struggle as he is wounded with Black's inlays and the wounds are sewn. He does not protest as Sought's cuts proliferate on his chest and belly, his arms and shoulders. He does not resist drinking Black's blood.

While the wheelwright is shaped, Black risks more obvious efforts to loosen the bolt. He knows that he has little time. Sought's ritual approaches its culmination.

Still the grit falling from the bolt is not enough.

For the first time, Black hears Sought speak to his men. "I must pause," he says. With studious care, he mops blood and sweat from Haul Varder's torso. "One more inlay will be enough. More than enough. But the last cuts are crucial. I must see clearly what I do, and I am old.

"Ready the organs while I rest. Scatter the powders I have prepared on them. Say the words I have taught you. Then bring our harvest out. There must be no delay at the end."

Two guards enter the wagon. They do not return quickly. When they do return, they carry between them a large wooden tub crusted with old blood.

The organs, Black thinks, straining his right arm until the muscles and sinews threaten to tear. The lungs and livers. To invoke heat and air. To rule them. Not the fierce heat from the crevice. Not the comparative cool of breezes from the tunnels. Rather the elemental energies themselves, the gods of heat and air. Concentrated here as they are nowhere else in the kingdom, or in the known lands.

Still Black does not believe that Sought can draw force from air. The hierophant needs lungs only to stoke the fire in the rift, to fan the flames like a bellows. His ritual will evoke the sorcery of heat.

When the old man stands before him again, Black summons his last desperation.

Another inlay Sought cuts out of Black, this one from Black's lower abdomen near his groin. Playing his charade, Black stretches against his bonds like a man on the rack. But he does not exert his full strength. He allows his growing weakness, the effect of his losses, to affect him. When this silver is gone, and his blood has been collected, he slumps in the posture of a man defeated.

He waits until Sought has returned to Haul Varder, until the wheelwright is being cut, until the old man's eagerness and the attention of the guards regard only the ruined man. Then Black puts all that remains of him into his right arm and *pulls*. He pulls until his heart threatens to burst.

Grit trickles from the hole made by the bolt. The bolt wobbles. For an instant, its resistance is greater than Black can endure. Then a cruel effort draws the iron from the stone.

His arm is free.

He is close to fainting, but he does not hesitate. One guard notices his success. Sought himself notices. They will act. One two three, Black slaps the places on his marred body that demand the King's awareness. And with his summons, he sends a piece of his soul. He cannot do otherwise. It is his soul that the King will hear, his soul that the King will understand.

By so doing, Black commits himself to death. Even a shaped man cannot live long when so much of his soul is gone.

Still he regrets nothing. He is near the end of all fear.

And he does not falter in his purpose. A guard rushes toward him. Sought turns in surprise and outrage. Black responds as swiftly as his failing strength allows. He claps his hand to the glyph on his hip that manifests his longsword. With the hilt in his grasp, he swings outward. The tip of his blade catches the guard's throat, but Black does not pause to observe the effect of his slash. His return stroke hacks at the rope binding his left hand to its bolt.

The rope is tough. Though it is damaged, it does not part.

The old man is shaken to the core of his ambitions, his hungers. He knows what Black has done. He knows his peril. But he also does not hesitate. He has come too far for too long to draw back. He snarls an instant's incantation. With one trembling hand, he sketches an arcane symbol across the air.

Black's longsword becomes smoke in his hand. It dissipates quickly, tugged away by the breezes from the tunnels.

The guard is on the floor. He clutches at his neck. Blood

gasps from the severing of his windpipe. Already he is too weak to seek help from his master. In moments, he is dead.

Two servants remain to the old man. They await his bidding.

"Curse you!" Sought yells at Black. He is incandescent with rage. "Curse you to all the hells that were, or are, or will be! Curse you eternally!"

Black replies with a smile that does not encourage confidence. He has taken the hierophant's measure now. He knows that Sought's knowledge is incomplete. He knows the ways in which that knowledge is incomplete. And he knows that the old man's hungers will overcome both his outrage and his danger.

Also Black knows that his own task is not done. His purpose demands more of him.

Writhing in his robe, Sought masters himself. He has only one hope left, and his craving for it is endless. He turns away from Black. To his remaining men, he shouts, "The organs first! *Quickly!* We must complete the ritual before the King can intervene!"

The guards do not delay. They have no personal fears. Despite their great skill with weapons, they are Sought's puppets. As one, they turn to the tub of lungs and livers. Carrying it to the crevice, they heave it and its contents into the depths.

A roaring from the fissure answers them. Black hears louder boiling. He sees flames at the lip of the rift.

"*Now the wheelwright!*" shrieks the old man. "Let him see how I keep my word!"

The guards obey. Returning to the wall, they lift the cross between them. Haul Varder attempts some weak protest, but he is not heeded. Carrying him bound to his crucifixion, Sought's servants approach the fissure. Without ceremony, they drop their victim into the seething heat, the flagrant light.

The roar in the rift resembles the priest's eagerness. It resembles his hunger. A gyre of flame rises into the cavern, circling itself until it is sucked into the funnel of the ceiling.

"Now!" Sought exults to Black. "Gaze on what I have wrought! Gaze and know despair!"

His men stand as though they have forgotten themselves. One or both of them can kill Black now, but they do not move. They have come to the end of their instructions. They wait for their master's commands.

Black does not know what preparations the hierophant has performed in secret. Like the guards, he waits.

The roar has a voice. Black almost understands it, but its meaning is confused in the fissure, in the deep boiling, in the tremendous increase of heat.

A hand of fiery stone grips the rim of the crevice. A shape of flame climbs into view. Black sees a head that may once have been lava. He sees shoulders as heavy as boulders, yet as liquid as molten wax. A second hand grasps the rim. It melts purchase for its fingers in the rock.

Loud in ecstasy or agony, the outcome of Sought's promise to Haul Varder heaves upward. A knee that mars what it touches braces itself on the floor. The voice howls, *"At last!"* Another heave brings the old man's creation to its feet at the edge of the rift. *"Now I am made FEARSOME! I am fear INCARNATE.*

"She will not hurt me again!"

Haul Varder has become lava, or the lava has become him. He retains the shape of a man, though he is twice Black's size. His eyes are the blaze in the heart of a forge. His voice is living heat, and his hands are formed to incinerate lives. His proximity alone turns flesh to tinder. Standing where they have been left to wait, Sought's last servants burn like fagots.

He is Sought's triumph, and his own. No human force can stand against him. He will make infernos of towns and forests. He will burn entire lands to ash. He is ready to rampage wherever he chooses.

For a moment, the old man regards what he has achieved, exulting in his own greatness, and in his creation's. He has proven himself. He has done what no man before has or can. At another time, he would be content. Now, however, seeing the fruition of his life, he wants more. He wants to prove himself against the King.

Then Haul Varder's heat drives Sought back. And when he turns away, he perceives that the crisis of his ambitions has found him. Black and Haul Varder and the smoldering corpses of the guards are not alone.

From the tunnels on one side of the cavern, darkness pours inward. It flows like water over the stone. It is colder than the oldest ice, deeper than the gulfs between the stars. Though it only flows, and does not seek or act, its presence spares Black the worst of the wheelwright's fire. When it reaches Haul Varder's feet, it begins spilling into the crevice, where it or the lava cease to exist.

At the same time, the tunnels on the far side grow brighter. The brightness emerges in globes of purest radiance. Some are smaller than others, but all resemble instances of the sun's best light. They float in the air without apparent aim, riding the breezes. Some are carried upward and swept away, funneled into the night above the mountain. Others bob here and there, avoiding only the flow of darkness on the floor. Those that collide with Haul Varder's fire do not harm him. They are not harmed themselves.

Driven by fear and eagerness, the hierophant retreats to the wall of the cavern. There he watches to see what his creation will do. He has no need or desire to control Varder. He has written his own protection into the man's chest. Now he feels a student of power's desire to learn where his efforts will lead.

The wheelwright peers at the eerie manifestations. He stamps a foot into liquid dark. He swats at floating bright. Then he laughs like thunder. The sound of his mirth and scorn stuns Black's hearing. It shakes the organs in Black's chest.

"Is this how your King responds?" Haul Varder asks. His voice is sure triumph. "He is a fool! These forces are mindless. They have no purpose. They cannot harm me. They cannot stop me.

"When I reach him, I will hold his terror in my hands!"

———

Sought tastes fulfillment. The King's powers do not hurt his creation. They cannot.

Nevertheless Black smiles once more, a smile that would chill the heart of any man able to recognize it. "You are mistaken," he replies to Tamlin Marker's killer. "They do not need minds. They have mine."

The sound of Varder's laughter scours the cavern, but Black does not heed him. With sigils, glyphs, and scarifications, the King's Justice reclaims his longsword. For this sorcery, evaporation and distance are not obstacles. The remaining fragments of his shaping suffice. They enable him to recall his blade from the ether of its dispersion.

Cooled by the frigid touch of dark, he has strength enough to cut the rope that holds his left wrist. Made brittle by flowing cold, the bonds that secure his ankles part more easily. Though much of his soul and his vitality are gone, he is able to stand.

Under his breath, he prays, "One last effort, my lord. With your help." Then he moves toward the wheelwright.

In a staggering run so that Sought's creation of fire and stone will not have time to slap him aside, he thrusts the length of his sword deep into Haul Varder's belly.

While the transformed man roars heat and fury, Black collapses to his knees. But he does not release his grip on his longsword.

Too late, Varder reaches for Black. He means to fling his foe into the fissure. He means to pluck the blade from his belly and shatter it. He is strong enough to crumple the finest steel, and his wound is no more than an annoyance. But before he can strike, dark flows up Black's body and arms, and a globe of bright bursts in the wheelwright's face. Dark secures Black's hands to the sword's hilt. The utter cold of dark follows Black's longsword into Haul Varder's vitals. And bright enters Varder's throat when he tries to roar. A light that lava cannot consume is agony in the wheelwright's gullet, the man's chest.

Stricken by more pain than his made flesh can endure, Varder topples backward. He falls into the fire and fury of his shaping, and does not rise again.

Black does not hear the old man's wail of frustration and terror as Sought flees from the cavern. Kneeling near the lip of the rift, Black smiles for the last time. But this smile threatens no one. It is glad and grateful, and it is all that he has left.

When he falls himself, slumping into the embrace of dark and bright beside the fissure, he is not afraid.

He does not know that time passes. He does not know how long he is unconscious. Yet by small increments he becomes aware that he is at peace. He has no fears and is not driven. For this he feels gratitude. He does not question it.

Eventually, however, his pain returns. Blunted at first, then more sharply, jagged distress reclaims the back of his skull. He has been maimed of several of his inlays, some of his scarifications have been damaged, and one or more of his glyphs and sigils have been ruined. His right arm tells him that it has been wrenched in its socket. Also he has many bruises. If his soul is at peace, his body is not. Each beat of his heart forces him to acknowledge that he is alive.

His hurts are a form of grief. He feels dampness on his cheeks and knows that he weeps.

Later he finds that he cannot imagine where he is. He lies on softness, is covered by softness. There are pressures around his head and body that suggest his wounds have been bound. But there was no softness in the cavern where Haul Varder suffered and died. There was no one alive to bandage Black's wounds.

Someone has cared for him.

The King? he wonders vaguely. In some way that Black cannot identify, he has been healed. Not made whole, precisely, but more whole than he was. The King is capable of such consideration. Yet Black knows of no sorcery that can transport him from the edge of death in the mountain to a place of comfort. He knows of no shaper who can apply bandages at any distance. And his pains assure him that his wounds have only been tended. They are not mended. If he has been healed, it is not a healing of his body.

When more time has passed, Black becomes aware that he is not alone. He hears the low murmur of voices. He hears a woman's muffled weeping, and a man's awkward attempts to soothe her. He feels a hovering presence.

Sighing because he has not been granted death, Black opens his eyes.

As his sight clears, he sees that he is lying in a bed in a small room. The bed and the room are those in which he parted from Jon Marker.

A man sits in a chair at the head of the bed. It is his presence that hovers. With an effort, Black recognizes Father Tenderson. The priest of Dark Enduring has finally summoned the courage to approach Jon Marker.

Against the wall where Black can see her when he turns his head, a woman sits with a child cradled in her lap. The woman is Rose, and she is weeping softly, restraining her sorrow as much as she can so that she will not disturb Black. The girl in her lap is her daughter, Arbor. Arbor is wrapped around herself, as rigid as death. A feverish sweat beads on her brow. Her eyes do not open. She does not appear to breathe. Her skin has the stricken hue of tallow. Her mother's caresses give her no solace.

Jon Marker stands beside Rose. His good face is twisted in distress, and he wrestles with himself to find words that will comfort Rose, though no one has comforted him. He knows her distress well.

Father Tenderson sees that Black's eyes are open. The tall priest leans closer. "Ah," he begins uncertainly. "Black. Sir. You are awake. Do not try to speak. Conserve your strength.

"You will wonder how you come to be here. There is much I do not know, but I will tell you what I can."

The sight of Arbor in Rose's arms tightens like a fist around Black's heart. He finds that some purposes do not end. They are like roads without destinations, or roads where every step is a destination. He twitches a hand to silence the priest. He does not need to hear Father Tenderson. Instead he coughs to clear his throat, though pain claws his chest as he does so. He fights a rawness that reaches from his mouth to his lowest belly until he is able to whisper, "No."

Father Tenderson leans still closer. "No? Sir? No?"

"The girl." Black coughs again, tearing scabbed wounds. "Arbor. Did she touch me?"

The priest is startled. His eyes grow wide. "She did. How do you know?"

Black shakes his head, dismissing questions and explanations. "Then help her."

He is too weak to do what must be done.

Abrupt tears come to the tall man's eyes. "Do you think I would not, if I could? She is beyond me. Touching you hurt her. I cannot account for it. She is beyond any healer."

Black aches for the strength to swear. "Stop," he croaks. "Forget yourself. Hear me.

"Your god does not answer prayer. The King does." Trembling, he thrusts away the blanket that covers him. "Touch me here." He shows Father Tenderson the three places on his body that compel the King's notice. "Hold your hands here. Speak in your heart of what the child has done. You will be heard."

The priest stares. Black's demand, and the sight of Black's shaping, shakes his courage to its poor foundations. There is a wildness in his stare. He considers himself a coward despite his self-justifications. If Rose had not asked him to introduce her to Jon Marker, and if she had not accompanied him to this bereft house, he would not have come. He would not sit at Black's side now.

But he is also ashamed of his weak spirit. He is ashamed of his hesitation. Arbor's plight is a blade twisting in his heart. Also he knows that in his place Father Whorry would act first and question the meaning of his deeds later.

Trembling himself, Father Tenderson rests his hands where Black has shown him. He does his best to forget that he is afraid. In silence, he describes what Arbor has done, and how she has been afflicted. As he does this, he feels a rush of weakness. He almost faints. He hears no answer.

Yet the room is suddenly crowded with light. An unspeakable cold fills the air.

An instant later, both light and cold are gone. Father Tenderson's weakness passes. He does not understand what has transpired. He has imagined—

But he sees Black relaxing. After a moment, he is sure that Black now breathes more easily. Black's faith is stronger than the priest's.

When Rose gasps, the suddenness of her outburst snatches Father Tenderson to his feet. Unnoticed, his chair clatters on the floor behind him. When he turns to Rose, he sees her arms wrapped around her daughter, and Arbor's arms clutching her mother's neck. Clinging to each other, both mother and daughter sob aloud. Now, however, their cries are relief and gladness. Arbor has returned from the horror of what she has done for Black.

Beside Rose and Arbor, Jon Marker kneels. He is unaware of himself as he closes his arms around them both. He shares their surprised joy. He needs it as much as they do.

After a few moments, the Dark priest retrieves his chair. He seats himself near Black again. He is still trembling, but now he trembles for different reasons.

He does not ask Black what has just happened. He has witnessed a mystery and will not question it. He has believed that men and women need to share what is in their hearts. Now he has seen his conviction confirmed. He calls it worship.

He cannot find words to express his appreciation. Also he suspects that Black has no use for it. "If you wish it," he says instead, "I will tell you now how you come to be here. I have no other gift to give."

When Black has considered his circumstances, and his desire for an end to his journeys, he manages a slight nod. Though his concern for Arbor is eased, he remains confounded. Why is he not dead? Why has he not been allowed to pass away? Whispering again, he admits his curiosity.

Father Tenderson replies with a smile that mixes rue and

wonder. "Much," he begins more briskly, "I cannot explain. I do not know what you have done. I do not know how you have survived it. Still a cloud has been lifted from my heart, and perhaps also from Settle's Crossways. Some questions I can answer.

"That you are here is Blossom's doing. To account for herself, she said only that she knew you were in danger. When her caravan left for the east, she halted in the place where she had last seen the hierophant Sought and his guards. With two of her men, she left the train and entered the forest to search for you. She did not know where you had gone, but she guessed that Sought's purpose, and yours, would take you to the mountain.

"Her guess was confirmed when she discovered Sought's corpse on the mountainside. She could not determine the cause of his death, though by appearance he died many days ago. Yet"—the priest takes a deep breath, holds it to steady himself, then releases it slowly—"he was neither decayed nor eaten. Rather he was clad in a thick hoarfrost despite the preceding night's warmth. Perhaps the cold preserved him. Certainly it preserved his last expression. He died with astonishment on his face."

As the servant of Dark Enduring speaks, Jon Marker rises to join him. Tamlin's father knows Kelvera's account. It was to him that she gave it. But he has embraced Rose and Arbor, and has found solace. Now he feels a need to gaze upon Black.

"Knowing then," continues Father Tenderson, "that she had guessed correctly, Blossom pursued her search. And after a time, she found you. You were being dragged among the trees by a horse. With what must have been your last strength, you had hooked your arm through one stirrup. By that means, the horse was able to pull you toward Settle's Crossways.

"Confident that the horse was yours, obedient to your bidding, she and her men lifted you onto their own mounts and followed the horse to this house. She could not explain the horse's choice, or yours. And she did not remain to hear what you would say when you awakened. If you awakened. When Jon Marker had helped you to his bed, she informed him that she was required by her caravan. Having told her tale, she and her men rode away."

Now Tamlin Marker's father speaks. He knows that he is in Black's debt, though he cannot explain the debt's terms. Certainly Black saved him from Ing Hardiston's ruffians, but his life is a small thing, and he places no great value on it. His sense of indebtedness is deeper. It is as the priest has said. A cloud has been lifted from his heart. He owes Black some acknowledgment.

"I was at my wit's end," he confesses. He speaks haltingly, unsure of what he must say. "I was able to bind your wounds. I settled you as comfortably as I could. But I did not know how to succor you. Did you need food or drink? I could not rouse you. Did you require a healer? I could not imagine a healer in Settle's Crossways who would know how to mend a man so cut and scarred and"—he falters until he finds a word—"and embellished from neck to foot. I floundered until Father Tenderson brought Rose and Arbor to aid me.

"And then—" His voice breaks. "Then I thought—"

The priest intervenes to spare Jon Marker. He has listened to the many woes and hurts and angers of Dark Enduring's worshippers. He has learned to keep his composure.

"By chance, however," he says, "or perhaps by some form of providence"—he smiles crookedly, knowing his role in his temple—"yesterday Rose asked me to introduce her and Arbor to Jon. In my timid fashion, I agreed to do so this morning. You know why I have not come before. We arrived to find this good man growing frantic.

"At once, however, other matters became more frightening than your straits. Seeing you, Arbor broke from her mother. 'He has holes in his soul!' she cried. 'He will die! I can heal them!'

"I was of no use. I did not understand. Nor did Jon. Before Rose could prevent her, Arbor ran to your side and placed her hands on your chest.

"At once, she screamed, a howl too fierce for so small a girl. Then she collapsed. She became the lost thing you saw in Rose's lap, a child overcome by who you are. By what you have done. By what was done to you. It was more than she could bear.

"We do not discount what you have endured. We will not. Still I say that her suffering was greater. You do not act in ignorance. You are able to estimate the cost of your deeds. She is not. She cannot prepare herself for the price of what she does.

"For that reason, I—" He glances around. "We?" When both Jon and Rose nod, he declares, "We will treasure what has been done for her above what has been done for us."

———

Black does not reply. He has no words. Indeed, he hardly attends to the priest. He approves Father Tenderson's sentiments. He wants no gratitude. To his way of thinking, he deserves none. He has merely served his purpose. But now a choice awaits him. He was not permitted to die. Therefore he is now free to determine how he will live. His wounds will heal. The remains of his shaping will suffice to mend him. And when he is well, what then?

He can attempt to make a home for himself in Settle's Cross-ways, or perhaps in some nearby town that is ignorant of him. He can join a caravan and accompany it wherever it goes. Or he can return to the King, where he will be shaped anew and dispatched to resume his purpose.

While Black searches himself, Father Tenderson and Rose agree to depart. The priest has his temple's duties, and Rose does not wish to tempt Arbor with Black's nearness. The mother promises Jon Marker that she will return later with food and better bandages. She smiles easily at his embarrassed thanks. Then she and Arbor are gone.

While Father Tenderson speaks briefly with Jon, Black rouses himself to forestall the priest's departure. The priest is as ignorant as Rose of Arbor's gifts. They will need a measure of guidance.

"Father," he says hoarsely. "Hear me a moment longer. I cannot explain Arbor's gifts. She will need her mother's protection, and yours." He has not strength enough to name Father Whorry also. "But when she is well again, she will be able to heal you. No harm will come to her."

———

Nor will she be harmed by giving her gift to Jon Marker, a man whom she will not be able to resist.

The priest is surprised. His head jerks up. His eyes grow wide. Is he in need of healing? Truly in need? He knows that he is, for the weakness in his soul when he touched Black, and for the weakness of his courage. But he does not know how he has become transparent to Black's discernment.

Another mystery. This one also he will not question. Instead he makes what he will later call a leap of faith. Bowing to Black, he says, "You have done enough. Settle's Crossways no longer needs the King's Justice."

He feels that he is fleeing as he leaves the room, the house. He wants time to think. More than that, he wants to consult with Father Whorry. He needs to hear his friend's simpler judgments of what he has seen and learned.

Alone, Jon Marker remains at Black's bedside. The wounded stranger's plight still perplexes his kindness, though he has been relieved by Black's awakening, and by Arbor's recovery, by Rose's generosity, and by the priest's easy spate of talk. He has not repaid his debt. He shifts from foot to foot. Stilted in his courtesy, he asks if Black needs water. He asks if Black can eat. He offers to make soup when he has fired the stove.

Black has no reply. His thoughts go elsewhere. As he regards his host, he considers his purpose in a new light. It is not an unending struggle against such men as Sought and Haul Varder. It is not measured by his opposition to bullies like Ing Hardiston. It stands at his bedside now. It belongs to men like the priests, to women like Rose, to children like Arbor and lost Tamlin.

When he is well, he will return to the King. He needs his purpose as much as it needs him.

The
AUGUR'S GAMBIT

eep in what I pleased to call my laborium, surrounded by walls of dark stone, by trestle tables black with old blood, by vessels for discarded bones, tissues, offal, and rank fluids, and also— a much-needed improvement—by foul drains that emptied into fouler sewers, I strove by the guttering light of candles to surmount the obstacles arrayed against me.

Of course, by *arrayed against me* I mean that they had nothing whatever to do with me personally. I was merely a servant. The obstacles were not mine, and their participants took no more than private notice of my existence. Rather they pertained to the doings—that is, the machinations, chicanery, and obfuscations in pursuit of obscure ends—the doings, I say, of my Queen, Inimica Phlegathon deVry, the fourth of that name, and the first monarch in seven generations of Queens to hold sway over a court largely embroiled in treachery.

On its face, such engagement in double-dealing and the general quest for advantage was strange in a realm as prosperous as Indemnie, blessed as it was with nature's abundance in every form. Streams that became rivers poured fresh and cleanly from the Fount Peaks which dominated the heart of the island. Rich forests draped down the slopes of the Peaks gave timber aplenty for every purpose. Mines among the Fount foothills yielded necessary ores and meretricious gold enough to sate most appetites for wealth. In every direction from those foothills to the coasts lay arable fields of such fertility that crops of every description appeared to spring forth unbidden by effort or indeed attendance. And the seas themselves teemed with edible life. Our horses grew fat, our cattle fatter, and many of our folk both high-born and low fattest of all.

True, the isle was not large—or so I deemed it, though it was larger than my knowledge of it. By the vast measure of the surrounding seas, Indemnie was little more than a scrap of flotsam alone in an immeasurable world. A determined man on a good horse could have ridden the land from south to north in four or five days, had he not been compelled to skirt the Fount Peaks. A more leisurely canter around our coasts would have occupied no more than two fortnights.

Still my Queen's realm was altogether comfortable. Gifted in every way by earth and weather, Indemnie's five barons and their sovereign had no obvious cause to strive against each other with such stubborn duplicity.

During the first years of my service to Her Majesty, I had

conceived that our populace must have come to the island from some savage people passionate for slaughter and cruelty—come, and then lost either the ability or the will to return to their home-lands. Spared by wealth from the impulse to kill each other, they sought advantage by less bloody means. Now, however, events and demands had taught me better wisdom.

The reign of Queen Inimica Phlegathon deVry III, like that of her mother, and of her mother before her—indeed, like those of Indemnie's seven generations of monarchs—had been admirably placid. The court's present thirst for conniving was too recent to be blamed upon our forebears.

In some other life, I might have grown as fat as Indemnie's folk, and cared as little. Alas, I was cursed by one small gift—and as a youth I had been foolish or foolhardy enough to make it known. Therefore I was now my Queen's Hieronomer, her seer into the unknown—indeed, into the unknowable. It was my task to advise her in all matters pertaining to Indemnie's future. Hence the obstacles arrayed against me. And in this opaque endeavor I had but one ally—one ally, and no resources apart from a devoted heart and a desire for comprehension to keep my head upon my shoulders.

Of my gift itself I seldom spoke. Oh, I was no charlatan. I gained insights of substance from blood and offal, intestines and malformations. In my own fashion, and on my own terms, I could scry more keenly than any practitioner of catoptro-mancy, certainly more than any mere caster of bones or in-terpreter of dreams. But the fashions of Inimica Phlegathon deVry IV were not my own—and her terms were decidedly not. It was chiefly by devotion rather than by augury that I served her, fearing for my head as I did so only somewhat less than I feared for Indemnie.

With the precision of entrails—the squirming of my own would have sufficed, but I read the same outcomes in chickens, lambs, piglets, and one still-born infant—I saw that the island and all its people were doomed.

High against one wall of my laborium hung two bells which could be jangled by ropes from several distant chambers in the opulent manor-house which served as the residence and seat of Indemnie's monarchs. One summoned me to attend upon my Queen privately, the other to observe her unseen. It was this second bell which scattered my thoughts now. Prompt to my duty, I doused my hands in a cistern to remove the more blatant traces of blood, adjusted my black robes—black not to produce an impression of mystery, but rather to conceal their stains—applied a brush to the worst tangles of my hair, and left my workrooms with a vague pretense of dignity, taking care to lock them behind me. Then I trudged up the many long and generally disused stairs within the walls of the house to search for my Queen.

The edifice had been styled simply the Domicile by its founder, Inimica Phlegathon deVry I, and there were no tales or indeed hints attached to her reign which suggested that she had ever required secret passages and hidden stairs. Yet she must have foreseen the changing exigencies of future monarchs— foreseen them herself, or been advised by some nameless personage with gifts resembling mine. The stairs and corridors I traveled were old, thick with dust, and unlit except when gleams or glows leaked inward from occasional chinks and embrasures in their walls. They had been unused for uncounted years.

The bell which had summoned me did not reveal where I might find Her Majesty, but my choices were few and familiar. Also she had informed me the previous day that Baron Glare Estobate was expected in the Domicile, and that he had requested or demanded—or had perhaps been hailed to—a private audience with his sovereign. She was unspecific about such details. I assumed therefore that she would receive him in her public boudoir, a chamber in which she could pretend to both ease and intimacy, but which in fact served no purpose other than to create the illusion of privacy. And when I had made my way thither, and had cracked open a door masked by one of the Domicile's many hanging tapestries, I found that I had arrived in time to hear the Baron announced.

Knowing my Queen's wishes in such circumstances, I slipped through the door and stood behind the tapestry, where I would be able to hear without difficulty, and to catch more than a glimpse of what transpired without betraying my presence.

Her Majesty's putative boudoir was large and ornate, as befitted the prosperous ruler of a prosperous land. Tapestries depicting farmlands, men at hunt, regal festivities, or squat ships warmed the walls, while the floor between them was piled with rugs more welcoming than my poor mattress. To one side of my covert, curtains nominally intended to conceal a bed which could have pleasured a party of twelve had been drawn aside to convey an impression of invitation, though to my certain knowledge they had never been closed. And everywhere was light. Forenoon sunshine slanted to the rugs from a number of high windows, and its effect was embellished by an abundance of lamps burning scented oils. Altogether the chamber proclaimed itself a place in which any secret which did not fear illumination could be unveiled freely.

The irony may have been impenetrable to many of the men with whom Inimica Phlegathon deVry conversed here. It did not mislead me. I had learned that my Queen spoke here when she particularly wished her lies to be believed—or when she wished those who spoke with her to believe that their own lies were indistinguishable from truth. Therefore she stood so that the sun's light dazzled other faces than hers.

As for the Baron himself, Glare Estobate, I was uncertain of his penetration. Foppish in attire and coarse in manner, with a thick snarl of beard that concealed his mouth entirely, thereby distracting attention from the hard glint of his eyes, he called to mind a wild boar playing the part of a sycophant. Unsure of him, I suspected that he courted others only as a means of courting himself.

Rumor said of him that his lusts were dark—and that they were painful to endure.

Making a leg, he presented himself. In a growl which may have been a failed simper, he proclaimed, "Your Majesty, I have come at your command. Three nights and six horses I have spent on the road, such was my haste to obey your summons." Without pausing for her reply, he continued, "Your herald's words were explicit. 'Your hopes await you.'" His growl became overt. "But I rode past the harbor. No ship of mine sits at anchor. No vessel of any baron sits at anchor. Only the boats and coracles of fishermen." With apparent effort, he remembered courtesy. "Your Majesty."

Resplendent as ever, Inimica Phlegathon deVry faced the Baron. As I had often observed—at some cost, I might add, in sweated sheets and twisted dreams—she was a magnificent woman. Ripe of breast and slim of waist, she dressed to accentuate some few of her many advantages, displaying an expanse of bosom and her regal carriage. Silks thin as gauze draped her form as though at any moment they might waft away. Held by a string of fine pearls, a ruby worthy of Indemnie's Queen rested in the delicate hollow of her throat. As for her features—well, her skin was flawless, her mouth and nose as delicate as works of art, her lips a moist pink, her brow apparently incapable of displeasure or doubt. The light of the sun crowned her auburn hair. And the brown luster of her eyes promised that they would warm to any desired word or touch. All in all, she was so finely wrought that even a careful study of her person might fail to discern that she was not in her best youth—or that she had been some fifteen years a mother.

"My lord Baron," she replied in a voice like liquid music, as self-harmonized as a madrigal, "my herald's words were indeed explicit. They were also honest. Yet I confess a woman's wish to provoke you. My summons did not refer to the vessels which you have kindly commissioned to search the seas surrounding our friendless isle. Rather it concerns your other ambitions."

A variety of emotions confused Glare Estobate's visage. References to his ships inspired one response. Comments concerning *a woman's wish* and *ambitions* surely evoked another. To which should he give prompt response? For a moment, he forgot himself enough to knot both fists in his beard and tug in opposing directions. On one side, the three ships which he had contributed to my Queen's questing had been a considerable drain on his treasury. On the other, anything that Inimica Phlegathon deVry said of his ambitions might be equally expensive. She was known, after all, for her whims—and for her happy willingness to inflict their price upon her barons.

I could have counseled him to put his ships from his mind. By my arts, I knew them utterly lost. As, indeed, did my Queen. Also history was against him. Full of pride, his vessels had sailed from Indemnie's harbor on varied eastward headings. From the direction of the sun's rising, no ship ever returned.

However, it was not my place to speak in such an audience. I remained hidden and watchful.

With an effort, the Baron mastered his hands. Squinting fiercely, he retorted, "Your Majesty, you confuse me. My ships *are* my ambitions. Only their success will appease—" He caught himself. "I mean gratify my liege."

My Queen granted him a smile that would have ravished an ox. "You place too little value upon yourself, my lord Baron," she observed lightly. "Both your deeds and your person are more worthy in my sight than you know.

"Are ships truly the sum and limit of your ambitions?"

Glare Estobate's face became a scowl, beard and brow and all. His eyes flicked a glance at the canopied bed, then returned to confront his monarch's gaze. Clearing his throat, he replied in a congested tone, "Speak plainly, Your Majesty. I have ridden hard and long to no visible purpose. Innuendos will not relieve my confusion."

Inimica Phlegathon deVry's smile became yet more ravishing. "Then I will be plain, my lord Baron." Musicians relished their melodies in her voice. "I wish to make of you my husband."

The Baron did not appear appropriately surprised. Nor did he evince quick eagerness. Rather his scowl threatened thunder. It threatened wild lightnings. "To what advantage?" he demanded without pause for consideration. "Do you conceive that my ambitions will be sated by a place in your bed? I am not such a fool. You see some advantage to yourself. You do not desire my person. And you have already secured the succession. Wedlock with you will not provide for my sons"—he muttered a curse under his breath—"or indeed for my daughters."

In contrast, none of his mistresses would complain of it if his attentions were directed elsewhere.

"Where does *your* advantage lie," he concluded, "Your Majesty?"

"Advantage, my lord Baron?" The Queen granted the word an inflection of amusement. "It is true that I have secured the succession, as did my mothers before me. That is as it must be. Still I am surprised to hear your ambitions so simply named. Do you not crave stature among your fellow barons? Do you not desire a voice among my counselors? Do you not yearn for *influence*, Glare Estobate?" She let the corner of her mouth twist humorously. "And are you truly incurious to taste the pleasures of my bed?"

Though I heeded closely, I did not hear her reveal where her advantage lay.

However, the Baron did not pursue that query. He barked a laugh. "My confusion grows, Your Majesty." His mien said otherwise. Now he looked avid as a pouncing cat. "Less than a fortnight has passed since my friend and ally, Baron Thrysus Indolent, informed me that you have proposed marriage to *him*. Proposed, he assured me—and was accepted."

His beard bristled with triumph. "Will you wed us *both*, Your Majesty? Will you dare such mockery? If you do, all Indemnie will cry out against you."

For my part, I heard him as though I had received a blow. That my Queen had proposed wedlock to Thrysus Indolent— and had been accepted—was known to me. I had been present on that occasion, as I was now. And I was not unduly struck by her offer to Glare Estobate, though I had no conception of her motive. I had been likewise present when she had engaged herself to three other barons before Thrysus Indolent. That the toll of the land's lesser rulers was now complete did not unsettle me unduly.

But that Baron Indolent had confided in Glare Estobate—! That was a blow indeed. To my mind, Thrysus Indolent was much the sharpest, and therefore the most dangerous, of my Queen's subjects. Of his predecessors in courtship—if her machinations may be so styled—I would more readily have expected indiscretion from Praylix Venery, who could not have kept a secret if it were locked in a vault. As for Quirk Panderman, his dedication to wine was so profound that his engagement to his sovereign might well have escaped his mind. And Jakob Plinth was too dour and self-contained to betray ambitions of any kind. When he had accepted his monarch's offer, he had done so with an ill grace, indeed with an air of duress, apparently fearing the fate of his present wife if he refused. Assuredly he would not have spoken of his coming nuptials until—or unless—events compelled him to confess them.

In contrast, if Thrysus Indolent had indeed spoken—and had confided in Glare Estobate, of all men the one most likely to take violent umbrage—he was playing a deeper game than I could then explain. One deeper than I could justify.

However, Inimica Phlegathon deVry's game was likewise deep, as it had been from the first. I had labored until my eyes watered and my brain ached to find and refine the auguries she sought. And when I was not cutting and prodding and interpreting, I had studied her seeking itself, hoping thereby to improve my ability to answer her. Yet I could not apprehend her lies and reversals, her demands and rejections, her constant play of openness and concealment. She remained as hidden from me as I from the Baron. Glare Estobate's challenge did not disconcert so much as a hair on her head.

As though she could dismiss Thrysus Indolent's revelation with a twist of her hand, she countered, "Must I conclude, then, my lord Baron, that I am refused?"

His beard positively bristled with triumph. "You must. Thrysus Indolent is my ally and my friend. Should I accept, I will be gravely disadvantaged by the loss of both friendship and alliance. It has perhaps escaped Your Majesty's notice that such bonds have become precious in Indemnie. I cannot suffer the consequences of your proposal."

"And you do not consider," she asked lightly, "that you will be disadvantaged by the loss of *my* friendship? *My* alliance?"

Glare Estobate snorted. "Your offer is surpassingly expensive, Your Majesty. My treasury cannot bear the price of a wedding— and certainly not the price of standing at your side while you turn all Indemnie against you."

To this charge, my Queen replied with a sigh which would have melted a pillar of salt. "My lord Baron," she returned, "I am not fickle. Nor am I deliberately unkind. I have indeed proposed matrimony to Thrysus Indolent. But his was merely the fourth of my offers. Now you alone are not pledged to me. By this test, I determine the disposition—I may say the loyalty—of men who name themselves my subjects." Her manner suggested that he now stood higher in her estimation, although her words implied otherwise. "The consequence of your refusal is that I must now try you further. I will amend my proposal.

"If you will grant a provisional acceptance, an acceptance dependent solely upon the outcome of my dealings, I will devise some means to sway you."

Again his fists grappled with his beard. Again his visage threatened storms. The extremity in his eyes suggested that words did not suffice for him. Doubtless he would have preferred to face Inimica Phlegathon deVry with a saber.

But while he wrenched his thoughts to and fro, his monarch defeated him. Where beauty did not serve her, words were entirely sufficient. Her response dismembered his turmoil like the flick of a blade.

"The succession, my lord Baron, is perhaps not as secure as you suppose."

That utterance unmade the Baron's resolve. His various indignations were transformed. His resistance fell from him like a snatched cloak. For a moment, he gaped, almost visibly attempting to voice the cry which was obvious to my mind. Not secure? Do you intend to disinherit your daughter? But his temerity did not extend to such a query—I may say, to such an affront. Rather he croaked unsteadily, "Provisional?"

Inimica Phlegathon deVry wore her assurance as though it

could not be sullied, either by doubt or by threat. "Provisional only, my lord Baron. Until I have demonstrated my sincerity."

Glare Estobate's beard shuddered. His mouth could not muster the strength to express his view of her sincerity. Instead he could only ask, "How?"

Draped in silks and sunlight, she appeared irrefusably regal. "How?" she echoed. I saw a teasing glint in her eyes. Perhaps she considered feigning incomprehension. If so, she discarded the notion. With more crispness, more authority, than she had heretofore allowed herself, she announced, "Spring is upon us. On the summer solstice, I will host a great ball in the Domicile. Every personage of note will attend.

"Upon that occasion, I will name my betrothed for all to hear."

Before Baron Estobate—or indeed I—could so much as begin to estimate the purposes and perils of her intentions, she concluded with drums beating in her tone like a march to the gallows, "At that moment, my lord Baron, your acceptance will cease to be provisional."

I did not scorn his consternation. Hidden, I shared it. She offered wedlock as a test of loyalty? And she proposed publicly to spurn four so that she might reward one? If it were not errant folly, it was plain madness. She hastened one of Indemnie's dooms. Indeed, she might bring it upon us in a single stroke.

And yet she was my Queen. In that respect, if in no other, my dismay was greater than the Baron's. He risked only his head in a game he lacked the penetration to play. I hazarded head, heart, and all in her service.

Glare Estobate had rediscovered wrath. He may have wished to roar. Certainly he appeared primed with outrage, poised to hurl vituperation at the walls. Yet the untroubled polish of Inimica Phlegathon deVry's demeanor closed his throat. He found no chink in her perfection. At the crisis of this encounter, his wits failed him—his wits or his courage. Rather than cry indignation, he could only writhe in frustration as he dropped his gaze.

"Provisionally, then, Your Majesty," he gasped as though he had suffered a beating. "I accept."

Graceless as a marionette, he made a leg and withdrew like a man routed.

Snared within myself, I remained where I was until my Queen asked softly, "You heard?" Then I had no choice other than to emerge from my concealment like a boy caught in a shameful act.

She lifted an eyebrow at my plain disconcertion. "What think you, Hieronomer?"

I swallowed several times. "I am scarce able to name my thoughts, Your Majesty." Questions crowded my throat. Have you taken leave of your wits? Did you not hear that Thrysus Indolent has already betrayed your machinations? What gain is there in setting the barons at each other's throats?—a tinder keg which may well take flame ere your demented ball turns every hand against you? How are you able to imagine that such false dealing will forestall the doom—indeed, the dooms—which crowd close upon us? Yet I had no words for such demands. The only query that I was man enough to utter was, "Did you speak truly? Is the succession threatened? Do you mean to disinherit your daughter?"

To shield her daughter's place from challenge, she had commanded the child's father murdered in his bed.

My Queen frowned at me, when she had only smiled for Baron Estobate. "Hieronomer," she replied, "we have spoken of this." In her tone, an as-yet distant vexation swelled. "Or if not of this explicitly, of other matters similar enough. Your knowledge of my dealings does not concern me. In truth, I require it. It will aid the accuracy of your auguries. But I fear your grasp of my intentions. It will make you dangerous."

Though I knew how she would answer, I could not stifle a protest. "How so, Your Majesty? I am your servant in all things."

"We have spoken of this," she repeated more sharply. "You confessed it to me when you entered my service. I merely heed your counsel.

"You must know of my doings. You must be cognizant of the deeds and forces which shape Indemnie's fate. But should you apprehend the policy which guides my dealings, you will either approve or disapprove. In either case, you will continue to serve me. And in either case, you will serve me falsely. The honesty of your auguries will be distorted, perhaps fatally, by the judgments of the mind that scries.

"I must rely on you, Mayhew Gordian. You have uttered that

to me which cannot be recalled. At your prompting, I have considered futures which cannot be turned aside. I must not now undermine your gifts. I will not."

Fearing that her ire might draw nearer, I bowed my contrition. "I am chastened, Your Majesty. You well recall my counsel, as I recall the terms of my service. I must trust that my surprise," indeed, my dismay, "will serve you, should it transpire that your daughter is set aside."

My Queen did not hesitate. "Then I return to my inquiry." To that extent, she trusted me still. "Glare Estobate has revealed much which may cause Thrysus Indolent to grind his teeth. What think you of these gambits?"

There I stood on surer ground. I met her gaze well enough to say, "Your deeds as they stand foment rebellion, Your Majesty. Now we have learned that Baron Indolent seeks to weaken your rule for his own purposes. He stirs the hot cauldron of Glare Estobate's heart. Whether he guessed that Baron Estobate would blurt his revelation is an intriguing detail, but of secondary import. The central point is that Baron Indolent plots some harm to you—or to the realm. So much has been made overt.

"Alas, I cannot determine the nature of that harm by words alone."

Indeed, I doubted that I would be able to determine the truth of Thrysus Indolent even in my laborium. The greatest frustration of hieromancy, and also the greatest peril, is that it answers specific questions with generalities. Only general questions receive specific responses.

Briefly Inimica Phlegathon deVry mulled my assertions. "Rebellion?" Then she shook her head, scattering auburn intimations through the light on her hair. "I think not. The barons of Indemnie are small men. Those clods and sheep-tuppers have not the manhood to act against me."

In response, I invoked what small dignity I possessed. "In this, Your Majesty, my arts assure me otherwise. The signs are unmistakable." I yearned to convey the scale of her peril. "Only the form that the rebellion will take remains obscure."

However, she appeared impervious to my alarms. With a glance toward the tapestry from which I had emerged, she indicated her readiness to dismiss me. "Return to your den, my fox of the unknown. Glean what you can concerning Thrysus Indolent's plots. And scry again regarding ships. I crave tidings from any quarter, but in particular from the east. We will speak again when you have some report." A small catch flawed the music of her voice. "I fear the east."

Having no other recourse, I bowed again and gathered myself to withdraw.

As I neared the tapestry, she commanded like a sting, "Sacrifice a child if you must."

With those words, she swept all thought of self-preservation from my head. I wheeled on her as though I were armed. "*I will not.*"

Through the clamor of my heart, I heard her as though from a distance. "You will if you must." She was a woman speaking in some other chamber. "Inquire of Slew. He will obtain"—she lifted her shoulders—"what you require."

I stood before her trembling, deprived of voice. From the windows, the sun cast a blur across my sight. Slew was known to me, a man whose visage of gnarled oak presided over the arms and thighs of an ox. He performed an array of unsavory tasks for his sovereign. I believed him the slayer of the man who had fathered Inimica Phlegathon deVry's child.

By increments, she appeared to return as though her mind had wandered far. As she assayed my silence, she frowned once more, but slightly, a sign that her displeasure was not yet grave.

"Mayhew Gordian," she informed me, "I do not fear your disapproval of my deeds. You are aware that I must know the unknown. My need is extreme."

Then the small tightness of her brows eased. Now she appeared to regard me with a sympathy which she customarily reserved for men whom she meant to mislead or betray.

"I am not unfeeling, Hieronomer. It has not escaped my notice that I make hard use of you. Perhaps you suffer the pangs of a need for which your straits preclude satisfaction. Food and wine you have in plenty. Lodgings, garments, warmth. The rooms and implements necessary to your arts. Any sacrifice that you desire. And I have offered both attendance and aid— even my own—but those comforts you have declined. Nevertheless some common need remains to plague you.

"If you will but name it, it will be assuaged."

The thought that she now offered the use of some hapless woman or man for my pleasure—or indeed of some girl or boy—exceeded endurance. I did not regard myself highly, but I had not yet sunk to such depths. Nor were the tattered remnants of my conscience so readily suborned. With an effort, I recovered my voice, though I spoke hoarsely.

"I have seen too many entrails, Your Majesty. I have no common needs." More clearly, I conceded, "Should no other augury suffice, I will consider a child," though I hoped that I would be man enough to cut my own throat first.

Then I turned away again. Thrusting aside the tapestry with hands that shook, I effected my departure from the boudoir.

I believed that I could have sacrificed Slew without quaver or qualm. Alas, every hieronomer knew that the entrails must be young. An excessive experience of life introduced too many conflicts, too many knots of passion, wrong, and failure. Only the viscera of the innocent spoke truly.

Still I preferred to contemplate disemboweling Slew as I descended to my laborium. His blood would not make me regret my existence.

When I gained my chambers, I found the door unlocked. This did not alarm me. I was too much distracted for ordinary fright. And I knew of one other key. For that reason,

I was not taken aback to discover a woman waiting in my laborium.

I knew her for a woman by no sign other than her possession of a key. Though she was seated upon a stool and must have expected my return, her face was entirely hidden by the hood of the dun wool cloak which also concealed every detail of her form. Under other circumstances, the young delicacy of her hands might have exposed her, but now they were covered by her sleeves.

Yet I was sure of her. When I had swallowed the taste of my exchanges with Inimica Phlegathon deVry, I said gently, "Your Highness," bowing though she could not see me past the rim of her hood. "You are ever welcome here." I did not add that I was especially grateful for her presence now. "How may I serve you?"

Straightening her back, she lifted her head without revealing it. In a tone too arid for her years, she replied, "You do not serve me, Hieronomer. I serve you." Then she added less drily, "How often must I insist that I wish to be addressed by my name? If you do not, I must continue to call you Hieronomer."

I smiled. She had that power over me despite my recent distresses. "Very well," I answered, "Your Highness. I make no future promise. For the present, however, I will deny you the dignity of your title. Excrucia, you are very welcome."

She was Excrucia Phlegathon deVry, my Queen's daughter—and presumed heir.

She sighed. "Ah, dignity. You and no other man considers

me worthy of any title. Still I am pleased, Mayhew. Your name suits you."

I smiled more broadly. "Then accept my thanks. Among my few pleasures, I regard your use of my name most highly." I did not cite the comfort of her friendship, or the value of her aid.

"Most highly," she echoed. Now she sounded like a land in drought. "You are not often thus fulsome. You must have returned from yet another opaque audience with my mother."

In my turn, I sighed. For a moment, I scrubbed my face with my hands, striving to efface my Queen's command from my features. *Sacrifice a child*— When that expedient failed, I slumped to a stool and seated myself near my visitor.

At once, she adjusted her posture so that still I could not gaze upon her visage.

I knew the cause of her modesty or shame—knew it, and was deeply vexed. At other times, I had respected her reluctance to be seen, doing so because I had no wish to discomfit her. Now, however, Her Majesty's instructions had provoked me out of my customary circumspection. Goaded by an unfamiliar ire, I elected to confront her daughter.

"Excrucia Phlegathon deVry, you are widely considered the plainest and dullest woman in the land. That is unfortunate." Who would not appear both plain and dull beside Indemnie's ruler? "But it is your further misfortune that I do not find you plain, and to my certain knowledge you are far from dull. Also I am desperate. Therefore I ask of you deeds and dangers which my service to your mother will not permit me to perform."

Indeed, I relied upon Excrucia's common repute to render her unworthy of notice, perhaps even of refusal. Such qualities might ward her where I could not.

To my relief, she laughed. "Now you mock me, Mayhew. I have incurred no perils in your name. Rather the tasks which you request provide only fascination."

That happy condition would not endure. Nonetheless I silenced my wish to speak of future hazards. She was not the cause of my anger—or of my alarm. Also her presence assured me that she had much to relate.

"Your Highness." I faltered. "I mean to say, Excrucia." Then I summoned my resolve. "Your perils are perhaps greater than you suppose. I have come from eavesdropping upon an audience between Her Majesty and Baron Glare Estobate." Reluctant to inspire condemnation of Inimica Phlegathon deVry in her daughter, I revealed only that which I deemed compulsory. "In the course of their converse, Her Majesty suggested to the Baron that the succession may not be entirely secure."

There I halted, awaiting some response.

My ally granted me a glimpse of one eye past her hood. "I suppose Mother is wise to caution the barons. Certainly they will be wise to fear her wrath." Her voice resembled bleached bone as she added, "There has been an attempt on my life."

In an instant, my world reeled. In a day of unpleasant blows, this jolt snatched me to my feet. Indemnie was not a realm in which attempts were made upon the lives of daughters—or indeed of sons. We were too prosperous, and had been too long at peace. Trembling again, and unable to speak, I stood over Excrucia. Another man would surely have demanded, *Who dares?* I was able only to knot my fists and stare.

She did not flinch. Doubtless for her own preservation—I mean her emotional preservation—she had learned a measure of her mother's self-possession. Also she did not fear me. In a tone devoid of emotion, she explained, "Five nights past, I awoke well before dawn. Some sound, or perhaps some current in the air, must have disturbed me, though I do not recall it. Opening my eyes, I found a dark form near my bed. It approached with its hands raised. I saw the polished sheen of long knives."

Within her cloak, she shrugged. "Fortuitously Vail's saber swept the assassin's head aside ere the knives plunged."

Gaping, I croaked like a toad, "You suffered no hurt?"

Her hood shook a negative. "Mother was irate that Vail did not preserve the assassin's life. She wished my intended slayer questioned. She wished him tortured. However, Vail outfaced her displeasure. After a time, she conceded that his quickness was apt.

"Doubtless she is wise to hint that the succession is endangered." Here Excrucia's voice suggested the breaking of brittle twigs. "And doubtless also she is wise to do no more than hint. Through Glare Estobate, she informs the barons that she is aware of betrayal while leaving them uncertain as to the extent of her knowledge, or even of her suspicions. They will do well to hear her hints as threats."

I found that I had not the strength to remain upright. Seating myself once more, I slumped like a broken thing. I had acted inconsiderately when I first sought her aid, but I was not yet so devoid of scruple that I could contemplate harm to her person without faintness.

Vail, I thought, shaken as aspen leaves high on the Fount Peaks. Damned, blessed Vail. He was Slew's comrade—almost Slew's brother in appearance—but his tasks were not Slew's. He served as Excrucia's bodyguard. In Indemnie! An isle where even household guards were no more than a formality. I had long distrusted him, but now I was weak with gratitude for his diligence in his duty—and also for his skill.

"Well," I breathed, endeavoring to calm myself. "Well. It is plain that events have proceeded further than I knew." Hieronomy suggested future movements and outcomes, but was notoriously imprecise concerning *when* those developments might occur. "Hazards I foresaw, but I had supposed them distant," certainly no nearer than Inimica Phlegathon deVry's coming ball. "Now I confess my folly."

Sinking inwardly, I said as well as I could, "Your Highness, I must cast you aside. I no longer require your service. That you are already endangered is insufferable. I will not allow your peril to be increased in my name."

"Nonsense," she retorted. Beneath the dryness of her tone ran an unexpected trickle of mirth. "You do not endanger me. My heart is not made to flutter by my efforts at your behest." She sounded remarkably untroubled for a girl who had come near to death. "And my name is Excrucia. Should you neglect it again, you will earn my regal displeasure."

When I looked up at her, she laughed openly, allowing me to see her face.

Well.

In the ordinary course of events within the Domicile, I had seen Excrucia's features often enough. My Queen did not permit her daughter to attend public occasions hooded or veiled. Still the sight of the girl's face did not fail to strike me.

She might justly be styled plain when she regarded her world and those who inhabited it without expression. Her skin did not glow. Her features were blunt and irregular, with somber eyes too near-set and mouth too wide—and all dominated by a prominent nose. Moreover, her appearance was not improved when she frowned, which she did often, in concentration or social discomfort. At such times, she might have been no more than a young fishwife.

Ah, but when she laughed—when humor or sarcasm or indeed kindness ruled her—when interest, curiosity, or eagerness struck their sparks—she was ignited to beauty. Then her mien was transformed. She concealed herself when she could because she knew too well that she was plain—and perhaps because her mother's example, or her mother's disappointment in her, caused her shame. But our colloquies in my laborium were often blessed by such reminders as she now presented—reminders that she was not as she customarily appeared.

Her face was one that a better man than I could have loved.

Her laughter and her smile enabled me to forget for a moment that I was angered by my Queen, dismayed by her deeds—and altogether baffled by Indemnie's plight.

Sadly the moment passed. Recalled to my straits, I spoke with a measure of asperity.

"Excrucia, then. Your service itself does not endanger you. That I grant. Rather my fear is of your mother's disapproval.

"Oh, she does not wish you ignorant. Mere study will not incur her ire. But that you pursue your studies at *my* bidding—" I swallowed anxiety. "Excrucia, your aid will infuriate her. That you will be barred from further contact is certain." With difficulty, I refrained from adding, That she will have my head is probable. More quietly, I explained, "She relies upon *my* ignorance. She requires it absolutely."

My words banished Excrucia's smile. Instead she frowned— a frown that I was unable to interpret. And she did not relieve my uncertainty. Her tone revealed only restraint as she offered, "Yet you seek to defy her."

Beyond question, I should have sent her from me. I should have refused all further converse. She was my Queen's daughter and heir. I had no claim upon her, no right to cause her the slightest discomfort. Nevertheless I deemed myself desperate. Moreover I was too much alone with my dreads and doubts. I could not hold back.

"I seek to *understand* her."

Excrucia started in surprise. "She does not wish to be understood? She does not wish her *Hieronomer* to understand her?"

I ground my teeth, striving to silence my unruly heart. Any utterance might prove fatal, were it reported to Indemnie's ruler. But I found that caution no longer ruled me. Inimica Phlegathon deVry had proposed marriage to all five of the island's barons. She urged the sacrifice of a child. An attempt had been made on her daughter's life. And that daughter was my only ally. Common fears were forgotten.

"She believes," I replied with some care, "that comprehension will falsify my auguries." Quick to clarify, I continued, "As I once did myself. But now, Excrucia—" Being unable to both grind my teeth and speak, I squeezed my hands between my knees. "I have come to the end of what viscera and pooling blood can tell me. I have sacrificed chickens, piglets, lambs, and calves without number. On one occasion, I gutted a stillborn infant." The memory set my bowels squirming. "I have gazed upon Indemnie's dooms until I yearn for blindness, yet I find no outcome that is not ruin. And still—"

I suppressed an oath. "Guided by my poor efforts, your mother wrestles with our fate, she confronts it daily in her chosen fashion, but I am able to glean no *reason* for her deeds. She is Indemnie's ruler. I cannot credit that she desires ruin. Yet her dealings hasten our end.

"I must serve her. She is my Queen. I am helpless if I do not understand."

These protestations my companion absorbed with no more than a deepening of her frown. In my present state, I would not have been surprised had she elected to revile me. She was her mother's daughter and heir. I considered it implausible that she did not aspire to her mother's assurance and hauteur. Certainly she must remain loyal to her mother—or if not to her mother, then to her place in the succession. Yet when she spoke, she conveyed no disapprobation. With an air of impersonal concentration—indeed, with an apparent irrelevance, as though she had not grasped the import of my concerns—she observed, "She dreams that our ships will return with hope."

By her manner, Excrucia startled me to sharpness. "Yet they do not. Those that quest northward encounter only ice. They return with rime still in their rigging. To the west, they wander until their stores are depleted to no purpose among barren atolls defended by jagged reefs. In the south, they are met with storms which challenge their best seamanship, and some are lost. And from the east no vessel finds its way homeward. No ship commanded to that heading has ever returned."

By such signs, as by my own scrying, I was certain that one of Indemnie's dooms would come upon us from the east.

The other, alas, gathered against us on our isle itself. And no amount of scrutiny, no quantity of entrails and blood and art, informed me which fate would be the first to befall. Indeed, I was unable to determine which was the more to be dreaded.

However, Excrucia was not ruffled by my tone. Nor did she appear discomfited by the plain thrust of my speech. Frowning still, and still with an impersonal air, she remarked, "For that reason, she provokes the barons. She toys with them to expose their conniving. What other course lies open to her? If she cannot hope for help beyond the seas, she must confront perils near at hand."

Then by increments her brow eased its clench. A nascent smile plucked at the corners of her mouth. Her eyes as she regarded me were rich with warmth.

"Now, Mayhew"—she appeared to tease—"I begin to understand the studies that you have asked of me. I undertook them willingly, having no better use for my time, but their purpose has eluded me. Why have you wished to know the earliest origins of our people upon this island? Why are you not content to imagine that we sprang full-grown from the earth? Why are you troubled by such matters as history and lineage, when Indemnie's future is open to your arts? Why have you inquired particularly concerning alchemy in every guise and use? And why, oh, why do you attend so closely to the successions and practices of Indemnie's rulers?

"But now at last I have you. You seek to comprehend any hidden force and factor which may bear upon our dilemmas. By doing so, you hope to understand my mother. You have confessed as much, but now I grasp the reach of your ambition.

"You do not merely wish to understand her. You are not content to serve her. You seek comprehension as a means to her salvation."

Have I not said that she was her mother's daughter? The dullness ascribed to her was a ruse. She wore a feigned lack of wit like a cloak to disguise her true acuity. Indeed, it was a form of deliberate plainness. It spared her the burden of the expectations which her birth and station might otherwise compel her to bear. Such concealments freed her to feel and think and act as she chose.

As for my expectations, she wore them lightly, seeming to take pleasure in them.

When I could find no reply other than to spread my hands, acknowledging their emptiness, she continued. Still with warmth in her gaze and a tease in her voice, she said, "You aim high, Mayhew. It is not conceivable that a man of your stature and gifts can effect the salvation of Indemnie's Queen—and certainly not when her own duplicity undermines her every step. Therefore you must aim higher still." By increments, Excrucia's tone grew grave. "If you would save her, your only path to that end is the salvation of Indemnie itself. And *that*, Mayhew, is a task too high for a man of *any* stature or gifts."

"As you say," I interposed so that she would not say more. Already she named my futility too baldly. "I aspire to a feat beyond the compass of any man. Who would know the truth of this, if I do not?

"Yet if we are greatly fortunate," and if my thin courage held, "perhaps it will not exceed one small Hieronomer aided by his Queen's daughter and heir."

Now I beheld a new light in Excrucia's eyes, one unfamiliar to me—a glimpse of daring that surpassed simple eagerness or curiosity. The smile with which she regarded me was a gift as broad as a grin. "Then, Mayhew," she said like a girl laughing, "we will make the attempt. And to begin, I must inform you that I have completed my studies.

"I have now perused every volume, scroll, and tattered parchment preserved in the Domicile. A strenuous endeavor, I do assure you." Briefly she caused her eyes to cross, perhaps hoping to win an answering smile. "If you are willing, and your duties permit, I will share my learning."

I sat before her mute, striving to mask the force of my relief. I had made shameless use of her, yet she rewarded my presumption with bounty. It was possible, or perhaps probable, that her studies had been as futile as my own. Nevertheless her willingness in my cause surpassed my prayers.

At my silence, she lifted an eyebrow, awaiting some response.

Swallowing weakness, I said unsteadily, "Your Highness. Excrucia Phlegathon deVry. Friend. I am yours entirely." Then I thought to add, "Do not mistake my silence. It signifies astonishment, nothing more. I am amazed that you condescend to aid me. Nothing less than my Queen's summons will coerce me to delay your tale."

To this offering, she granted another laugh. "Flattery? From the Queen's Hieronomer? I am raised up in my own estimation. There is no other man in all the realm who would trouble to flatter me."

I would have suspected her of mockery, either of me or of herself, but I heard no jeer in her laugh, no self-pity in her tone.

Defying my natural disbelief—indeed, my native caution—I deemed her pleasure genuine.

While I marveled at her, her humor receded, allowing a frown to reclaim her brow. Her gaze left my face and appeared to consider a more distant vista, as though she endeavored to refresh from afar her recall of scrolls and parchments.

"In truth," she began, "the scale of my learning is not large. What records our ancestors preserved are both random and fragmentary, rife with hints but miserly with knowledge. The tale which I have gleaned is as much supposition as fact. Yet I doubt not that it will hold your interest."

I murmured an assent that did not deflect her from her thoughts.

"In sum, then," she informed me, "it appears plain that the realm began as five separate colonies widely scattered around our shores. Their documents do not reveal any early knowledge of each other. Nor do they account for the establishment of these colonies, apart from one suggestive fragment which mentions 'abandonment.' Alas, that fragment expresses neither desire nor execration regarding this abandonment. It confirms merely that our first ancestors came to Indemnie from some other land. That they all came from the same homeland is implied only by the fact that their documents are written in our tongue.

"On one detail, however, the earliest surviving records of the five colonies are in agreement. At the time of their establishment, this isle was utterly barren."

Involuntarily I gaped at Excrucia, but she did not pause to acknowledge my surprise. In a tone desiccated by concentration, she said, "The soil was rock and sand. There were no native plants. And no planting could be attempted because there was no water. Some few small springs were discovered, but the streams issuing from them were worse than brackish. Whoever drank therefrom became gravely ill, and some perished. If the colonists were indeed abandoned, they were abandoned to die."

Ere I could expostulate, she continued more briskly, "Regarding their survival itself, I stand on firm ground. We are here. We prosper. The colonies grew to become baronies. The barons were united under the rule of the first queen. So much is certain.

"Regarding the means by which they procured their survival, however, I have gleaned little. On one parchment I read these words. 'By my command, and having no other hope of life, my gift-kin and adherents—and I myself—have turned all our efforts to the search for *chrism*, sacrificing our stores of food and water in the attempt. Only our livestock and game animals were spared.' The outcome of that search is not described, but it must have succeeded. Like the others, that colony endured. This detail is confirmed by the name of the document's author, a name which endures among us. He called himself, 'Lord Tromin Phlegathon.'"

I held up my hands to interrupt Excrucia. The name Phlegathon twisted in my vitals, as did the notion of "gift-kin," but for the moment a more pressing concern gripped me. "Are there other references to this *chrism*? Have you determined what it is?"

The word was entirely new to me. I could not guess its import.

Frowning more deeply, she replied, "I have not. Of references I encountered perhaps a score, but they offered no word of explanation. In one scroll, I read the words, 'Lord deVry having discovered *chrism*, we were at last able to secure water.' A parchment devoid of names states, 'With *chrism* sufficient to our needs, we began to flourish.' It must have been common knowledge among the colonies that *chrism* was vital to their survival. All knew what it was, and why it was necessary, else some scribe would have recorded the knowledge to preserve it. Yet I have found no such record."

What, none? Unable to arrange my thoughts, and unwilling to demand an account which Excrucia could not supply, I mused instead, "Livestock and game animals? If the straits of the colonists were dire, why were such beasts spared?"

She implied uncertainty with a shrug. "As I have confessed, my tale is largely supposition. However"—for a moment, her gaze returned from its distance to meet mine—"the word 'hieronomer' occurs with some frequency, even on the oldest parchments. I surmise, therefore, that the beasts were preserved for the use of the colonists' hieronomers. Indeed, I suspect that the colonists relied upon hieronomers in their quest for this *chrism*."

Well. So much I understood. Hence my first interest in lineage. Like the people of Indemnie, I with my small gifts could not have sprung full-grown from the earth. Names such as Phlegathon and deVry spoke of my Queen's earliest ancestors. I also had such ancestors, though they were nameless. So I had always

believed. To the best of my knowledge, I had inherited my apti-
tude for augury from my mother's mother, a village hieronomer
of no small repute in her day. I had therefore concluded that
those abilities which I possessed—and which my two sisters, my
brother, our parents, and our friends alike did not—were an
effect of lineage. My gifts, like their uses, were an expression of
blood.

However, I did not speak of such matters. My own lineage
surely played no part in Indemnie's dooms. Rather my concerns pertained to Excrucia's—by which I chiefly mean to her
mother's. It was Inimica Phlegathon deVry who would bear the
brunt of impending crises, not her lowly Hieronomer.

Nodding my acceptance of my companion's conclusion, I
inquired, "Have you been able to determine what followed from
the discovery of *chrism*?"

She nodded, her gaze once more fixed upon her studies or her
thoughts. "To some extent, I have. That which I have gleaned
resembles a preliminary sketch rather than a true portrait. The
rendering becomes more complete in more recent years, but the
older portions are mere outlines.

"For the colonies, foul springs were made clean rivers, how
I know not—though I surmise that the transformation was
achieved by some effect of *chrism*—or, more likely, by the use of
chrism in the hands of those colonists referred to as gift-kin. In
similar fashion, barren rock and lifeless sand became loam.
Grasses became crops. Shrubs became trees. Habitations were
built, first scanty, then more enduring. Here one document cites

the efforts of the adherents. Another praises them, though without explicit cause. By increments which would perhaps astound us, the colonists prospered. They began to multiply. And as they grew, these burgeoning populations began to encounter each other.

"That these encounters were greeted with recognition rather than animosity is a further supposition—one, however, which is supported by their shared tongue, by the absence of any hint of conflict in their few records—and also by a substantial increase in the number and clarity of their documents when contentions later arose between the colonies. These contentions plainly concerned access to lands, or to stands of timber. Perhaps they also concerned available sources of *chrism*, though the writings say as much only by inference. However, there is this in addition. These contentions did not end in bloodshed. Rather they were resolved by negotiation."

To myself, I thought, Hence Indemnie's long history of peace. Though the colonies were five, they were one people, all transplanted or abandoned for no cause that I could discern. They had no natural antipathy.

Still I sat silent, unwilling to interrupt Excrucia's tale.

Once again, her gaze returned to her surroundings, and to me. "It will interest you, I think, to hear that these negotiations were not conducted by names such as deVry and Phlegathon. The scrolls speak of Lords Plinth and Estobate. One parchment cites a Harmoty Indolent. And another states that all matters pertaining to leadership and rule were managed by families that were not 'gift-kin'—who were therefore presumably descended from the 'adherents.' The tasks of the gifted were deemed too vital to be vexed by the more mundane affairs of expanding populations."

This also I understood. If hieronomers were required to discover sources of *chrism*, their services were surely much in demand.

"Taken together," Excrucia continued, "the records thereafter prompt little imagining. Indemnie became increasingly bountiful. The colonies grew apace—as did their subjects of contention. Their negotiations became ever more complex, the resolutions ever more formal. Thus it ensued—naturally, to my mind—that clear boundaries were established, clear rights codified. The lands thereby demarked became baronies as their lords or leaders elected to style themselves barons—a reflection, I believe, of the form of governance practiced in their lost homeland.

"Still the sources of contention grew as the populations increased. One scroll asserts that the hieronomers of the baronies began to offer conflicting auguries. Another implies that the alchemists were disinclined to respect the governance of men who were not gifted. And the barons themselves chafed at the difficulties of achieving agreement when each held differing desires. Eventually they concluded that the only peaceful solution to their various dilemmas was to raise up a monarch whose word would bind them all.

"In addition, they concluded that only a gifted monarch

would be able to command the loyalty and service of the isle's hieronomers and alchemists. Therefore they arranged a union between the two oldest families believed to have the purest blood. And when the joining of Amelda deVry and Arrant Phlegathon produced a daughter, that child upon her coming of age was proclaimed Queen Amarra Phlegathon deVry, the first of her line."

Briefly my companion sighed. "So my tales ends. The sequence of the Queens you know." Then her manner quickened. "However, the records hold one other secret which will interest you. The Articles of Coronation signed by the barons of the time grant to the Queen authority in all matters pertaining to the well-being of the realm as a whole. So much appears both natural and necessary. But the Articles also stipulate the manner in which the succession is to be secured—and thereby they account for the choice of a Queen rather than a King."

I found that I was holding my breath. I had long pondered the curious detail that each of Indemnie's Queens had birthed a daughter ere offering her hand in wedlock—and that this child had been universally accepted as the legitimate heir. But I had been unable to grasp the purpose of the custom.

As she spoke, Excrucia watched me closely, gauging my reaction. "I will not quote the document itself. It is lengthy. But in sum, it recognizes that sexual congress may produce a bewildering variety of offspring, some or all with a claim upon the throne, yet the child of a woman's body is hers beyond question. Therefore the Articles require that the Queen must give birth to a daughter ere she chooses to wed. To that end, she must procure the guidance of a hieronomer, presumably to ensure that she does not produce a son in error.

"Further, the child's father must be and forever remain unknown. His identity must be concealed so that he—and any other offspring of his loins—can have no claim upon either his royal daughter or his royal paramour. Similarly, any man whom the Queen subsequently elects to wed will have no claim, either direct or through his children."

While I stared, momentarily struck witless, Excrucia recounted her conclusions.

"By such measures, the barons plainly sought to prevent any challenge to the rule and succession of Indemnie's Queen. Their history of negotiated resolution rather than violent conflict assures us that they wished to preserve the realm's future from civil war. But the rather extreme severity of the stipulation suggests that those barons had another purpose as well, one which is not named in the Articles.

"I cannot resist one final supposition, that the terms of succession were intended to guard the purity of their monarch's lineage. Queen Amarra Phlegathon deVry, first of her line, was the daughter of two families known to be gifted. I suspect that the barons desired every later Queen to be similarly gifted, with as little admixture or dilution of her ancestors' abilities as possible.

"This, I think, explains the insistence upon hieronomers. Their task was not merely to choose a father who would produce a daughter. It was also to choose a father descended from the founding gift-kin."

Under my companion's scrutiny, I floundered for a response. My Queen was of the isle's purest blood? She, too, was capable of hieronomy? Why, then, did she not perform her own auguries? Of what use was I? Was her fear of my comprehension an exact expression of her own straits? Knowing and judging her own purposes, did she thereby falsify her ability to scry?

But I could not burden Excrucia with such concerns. Compelled by her gaze, I summoned a more immediate question. "Gift-kin?" I echoed, striving to regain my wits. "It appears that the term must refer to men and women who share the abilities common to hieronomers and other augurs—and that these abilities are passed from mother and father to child." Or to grandchild, as in my own case. "You now grasp my interest in lineage." Then I shook myself, hoping thereby to master my unspoken confusion. "Do you believe that alchemists also are gift-kin?"

Of alchemy I knew little, but on the instant I felt certain that it required blood, as did my own gifts—blood and heritage.

My companion nodded without hesitation. "I am sure of it. I can think of no other reason for Indemnie's alchemists to refuse fealty to any monarch not gifted—or for the barons to support the wishes of their alchemists in such formal and stringent terms. Indeed, the well-being of the realm depends as much on the services of alchemists as on those of hieronomers."

As much, I thought, or more. To my poorly informed mind, the services of alchemists appeared both more practical and more reliable than my auguries. By common repute, those services had been essential to the construction of the Domicile. They were also much credited in the formation of Indemnie's harbors, and in many smaller achievements across the realm.

While Excrucia studied my visage, I considered my duty to my Queen. And when I had considered it, I replied in a voice made thick by uncertainties, "Then I must speak with an alchemist."

Excrucia's scrutiny of my features became still more acute. At the same time, her tone resumed the aridity of concentration— or perhaps of rigidly suppressed emotion.

"Nothing could be simpler. I will instruct Vail to summon such a man. Doubtless Vail will not abandon my protection himself. However, he will command others in my name. Some days may pass—alchemists are considered a self-absorbed lot, resistant to compliance—but your wishes will be satisfied."

After an unseemly delay, I rallied myself to thank her. She had already done much in my aid. I could hardly estimate the amount of gratitude that she had earned from me. Was she not effectively defying her mother for my sake? She was. Also her very life was in peril. Nevertheless my bewilderments and doubts precluded a profuse expression.

Her regard did not waver. Her tone did not soften. "Then you must answer a query of mine, as I have answered yours."

Earlier I had confessed my motive. Now I could not imagine what further concern might trouble her. Still I felt a lonely man's desire to be understood. And I was unwilling to spurn my only ally—my only friend. With some difficulty, I murmured, "Name it."

"You have spoken of 'dooms.'" She sounded parched as dust. "Your auguries have revealed that more than one calamity gathers toward Indemnie. What do you fear will fall upon us? What do you fear so extremely that you seek to oppose my mother's wishes?"

I was unable to meet her gaze. Speaking to the stained floor, I replied, "They are two. I have performed auguries beyond count, but they do not vary. If we are not enslaved by some power from the east, we will descend to barbarism."

Then I conceded, "It may be that other outcomes are possible, but my small gifts do not reveal them. I am my Queen's Hieronomer. I must believe what I have learned."

There I paused, awaiting protests or demands. I imagined that my companion would wish to know how these catastrophes might befall Indemnie. Indeed, I dreaded such questions. I had no answers that would not cause pain—or occasion disbelief.

But when it came, Excrucia's response was not an inquiry. It was an assertion—or perhaps a recognition. "You have spoken of this with my mother."

"I have." Still I confessed myself to the floor. "Indeed, I hold myself culpable for her present policies," for her manipulations and betrayals, of which her offer of wedlock to all the barons was only the most recent example. "The machinations which now beset Indemnie did not commence until I began to perform my tasks as Her Majesty's augur."

To my surprise, Excrucia favored my accusation with scorn. An angry oath compelled me to face her.

"Fie, Mayhew! My mother's deeds and policies are her own. You merely **exercise** your gifts. You do not determine the use to which she **commits** your scrying."

Confronted by my companion's ire, I did not disclose what was in my mind. I might have said, My Queen acts as she does because I have made her afraid. But I had given a young girl too many burdens. I did not desire her to bear more.

Also, as I have said, she was far from dull. I could trust that she would infer more than I expressed.

Quietly I replied, "She is more than your mother, Excrucia. She is our rightful ruler, charged with sovereignty because we have no other means to live as we do. If we do not understand her, we must nonetheless place our faith in her. We must do so especially when we do not understand."

Had Inimica Phlegathon deVry not foreseen that her daughter would require a bodyguard? I had not done so much, though I had bathed my hands in lakes of blood.

While I watched, Excrucia strove visibly to contain her indignation. After a moment, she retorted, "As you say." Then she rose to her feet, concealing her visage in her hood once more. More calmly—or perhaps more drily—she added, "I will speak with Vail." A heartbeat later, she continued, "And I will ask my mother what gain she finds in policies that can only sow discontent, if they do not provoke worse. I will ask her to account for the attempt on my life."

She startled me. Indeed, she frightened me. Yet she also prompted me. Without pause for consideration, I returned, "If you would dare so much, dare more. Ask her if she has spies among the baronies. Ask her if she has learned of intended betrayals, of impending rebellions."

As the girl turned to depart, she repeated only, "As you say." Then she was gone.

Her manner baffled me. She was my Queen's daughter, therefore proud. At the same time, she was ashamed to be perceived—indeed, to perceive herself—as plain and dull. Therefore she was humble. Also she had a private courage that expanded my bewilderment. I could not grasp the workings of her heart.

Yet I fretted over graver concerns when my companion had departed. Did my Queen know of her daughter's alliance with me? Beyond question, Vail knew of it. How could he not? He watched over Excrucia while she slept. Surely he shadowed her every waking step. Thus if his devotion as he saw it belonged to Inimica Phlegathon deVry, he would speak—and I would be lost. But if his post as Excrucia's bodyguard included his loyalty, he might keep silent and name his silence duty. In that event, I might keep my head yet awhile.

He had outfaced his monarch's ire in the aftermath of the

attempt on Excrucia's life. Perhaps, albeit indirectly, he would do as much for me.

My Queen's solstice ball remained some fortnights distant, yet while I floundered in uncertainty, apprehension, and wasted blood, events within the Domicile—indeed, movements throughout the realm—appeared to quicken. Inimica Phlegathon deVry forbade unions which one baron or another had approved. She encouraged marriages which the immediate families had declined to countenance. She dismissed contentions which pertained directly to her rule over Indemnie, preferring rather to meddle in matters which properly belonged to individual baronies—matters such as grazing rights and access to timber. Thus she stirred the pot of discontent, usurping the prerogatives of the barons while undermining her own authority.

Such seeming quirks and misjudgments disturbed me in my laborium, but did not impel my Queen to summon me, either for counsel or for eavesdropping. Other events, however, were more fraught. One such I heard described in converse with scullery-maids and servers and an occasional household guard in the lower eating hall of the Domicile. For a time, the hall was rife with talk that another attempt had been made on Excrucia's life.

This was not reported to me by my ally herself. She was occupied elsewhere, perhaps commanded to tasks or ceremonies by her mother, or perhaps restricted to the sanctuary of her chambers. I did not see her. Therefore I knew nothing of her own heart and life, certainly nothing of her efforts at my behest. However, the tale as I retrieved it from overheard snippets, direct queries, and flagrant exaggerations went thus.

In the aftermath of the first attempt, my Queen and Vail augmented their caution. Several of the household guards were placed at Vail's disposal. Increased entourages escorted Excrucia's movements. And either Her Majesty or Vail foresaw that the girl's food must be tasted—a precaution which would not have entered my head, but which events proved necessary. Some ten days after our discussion of Indemnie's need, Excrucia's taster fell violently ill. Fortunately he did not perish, though my Queen's physician declared poison without hesitation. Alive, the stricken taster offered a degree of guidance to Vail's investigations. Within hours, the source of the poison was traced to a flask of wine intended for Excrucia's sole use, she being partial to it. The wine steward and several serving-maids and boys were put to the question. After what some called minor flogging and others described with shudders as crippling torment, one of the younger maids admitted responsibility. Persuaded by her lover, whom she named as the scion of a family in service to Baron Jakob Plinth, she had added a powder both tasteless and potent to Excrucia's wine. The reason given to the maid—so rumor proclaimed—was a desire to end the rule of the Phlegathon deVrys for the good of the realm. Baron Plinth was widely considered censorious enough to nurture that ambition.

So much was hearsay rather than confirmed knowledge.

Thus I felt entitled to my doubts. Jakob Plinth was known to be dour, stern, strict in honesty, and uxorious to a fault. Among the barons, therefore, he was the man whom I was least inclined to suspect, despite his disapproving acceptance of his sovereign's proposal. When I had recovered from my alarm on Excrucia's behalf, I concluded that the use of a man putatively attached to Baron Plinth was a ploy to deflect attention from the true traitor.

Who then remained to accuse? Praylix Venery I discounted. He would not keep his own secrets—and could not keep another's. And Quirk Panderman spent his days irredeemably fuddled by drink. As for Glare Estobate, he was wrathful enough to strike any blow, yet I judged him too blunt for subtle treachery. By such reasoning, my suspicions fell on Thrysus Indolent, who had revealed the nature of Inimica Phlegathon deVry's marriage machinations to Baron Estobate.

However, my every search by augury for the truth failed. In such matters, I relied chiefly upon chickens. Being simple creatures, their entrails were easily interpreted by such gifts as mine. And to a scrying eye, the light they shed, being likewise simple, promised illumination. Alas, their minds were too simple for my purpose. Lacking awareness, they also lacked subtlety. I had it in my heart to forewarn my Queen, but I found myself unable to confirm my suspicions—or, indeed, to deny them. Though I stewed in intestines, small organs, and worry until I feared that my mind would boil, I learned nothing not already known to me.

Doom from within Indemnie. Doom from the east. And the policies of Inimica Phlegathon deVry subverted hope with every passing day. They subverted mere comprehension. She had encouraged me to sacrifice a child—a *child*—but that I would not do. For that reason, I positively required an understanding of alchemy, and of *chrism*. Also I required spies to counsel me when hieronomy could not. Yet I had none. Therefore I was dependent on Excrucia for further aid—and she was now too closely sequestered to attend me.

Frustrated beyond endurance, I felt the walls of my laborium crowd close around me until I labored for breath and a foul sweat stood on my brow. When I could no longer suffer the littleness of my domain, I took to wandering the servants' halls where my presence was permitted, seeking scraps of gossip, rumor, complaint, and speculation concerning events beyond the Domicile—hints which might serve to relieve me. Also I ascended and descended endlessly the passages within the walls, aspiring to some glimpse of my Queen's dealings—or of her daughter's circumstances. However, I found no ease until a handful of days had passed. Then I was nearly toppled by alarm when the jangle of a bell summoned me once again to attend upon Indemnie's ruler unseen.

Now I did not trouble to compose myself. When my knees had recovered the strength to support me, I flew like a demented bat for the nearest of the Domicile's hidden stairs.

As before, I found Her Majesty in the opulent chamber which served as her public boudoir. As always, the meretricious bed and furnishings fostered a feigned suggestion of private comfort, indeed of private pleasure. On this occasion, however, I came belated to my post behind the tapestry which concealed my entrance. My Queen's visitor had already effected his entry.

Before Indemnie's sovereign in all her regal splendor and—as I deemed it—lusciousness stood Baron Thrysus Indolent.

He was a lean man, slight of stature and homely of visage, yet his lack of ordinary attractions, such as regular features, fine hair, and well-formed limbs, was contradicted by the perfect elegance of his attire, which conveyed both great wealth and unassuming modesty in equal measure. In addition, his manner expressed a supreme assurance inexplicable in a man utterly out-shone by his monarch. As for his eyes, they had demons dancing in their depths, mirth and scorn and appreciation and multiple intentions obliquely commingled. Taken together, his manner and his gaze presented him as a man quick as a fox, sagacious as an owl—and hypnotic as a serpent.

I considered it fortunate for the realm that my Queen's own assurance, penetration, and subtlety were in no way diminished by the challenge of Baron Indolent's presence.

They must have exchanged moments earlier the requisite courtesies of such an occasion—inquiries regarding health, personal satisfaction, and so forth. While I strove to master my labored breathing, they continued their colloquy.

"My lord Baron," my Queen now said with no more than the most delicate hint of tartness, "your entrance is peremptory."

She might have said *presumptuous*. "I did not summon you. Nor is this the hour when it is my custom to receive my subjects."

Only then did I recognize that I had no notion whether the time was day or night. I had been entirely consumed by fretting.

"Your Majesty," he explained, "I came when I was informed of the attempt upon your daughter's life. I confess, however, that I did not travel in haste. I am not precipitate in such matters. The circumstance demanded thought. Nonetheless I am now before you, hoping as any loyal subject must that you will profit from both my tidings and my counsel."

Inimica Phlegathon deVry gifted the man with a smile to melt stone, had stone either heart or loins. "And do you conceive, my lord Baron, that I am in need of tidings or counsel?"

"Certainly you are not, Your Majesty," he replied, his assurance undimmed. "Yet I will wager my head that you will be glad of both."

"Then do so," she returned with an air of graciousness that belied her command. "I am unaccustomed to intrusion, both upon my person and upon the affairs of the realm."

"I will, Your Majesty." His own smile conveyed the curious impression of a pounce held in reserve. "To comply, however, I must first speak of Baron Venery."

My Queen awaited him with amusement on her lips and flames in her gaze.

"It will not surprise you, I think," Thrysus Indolent continued, "to hear that he has spoken of your proffered hand—the same hand which you have offered to me. As you are doubtless aware, Praylix Venery is a treacherous friend—and an invaluable foe. His mind knows nothing that his mouth does not speak. If the other barons remain ignorant of your proposals, it is only because they do not heed him.

"For myself, I am untroubled. I comprehend your gambit, Your Majesty, and consider it wise. Also I am confident of your eventual determination."

My Queen lifted a flawless eyebrow. "Are you indeed? Then you are as discerning as I have always deemed you."

Baron Indolent nodded. "A question," he ventured, "if you will permit it ere I say more. May I trust that you have proposed wedlock to each of the barons—proposed, and been accepted?"

While I strained to hear underlying significances, her manner revealed only that she remained secure in the effect of her loveliness—or perhaps in her comprehension of the Baron. "Trust what you wish," she replied, unconcerned. "My policies are my own." A moment later, she deigned to add, "The character of Praylix Venery is known to me."

Her visitor's glances appeared to flash. "Then I will say no more on the matter," he conceded, calm as moonlight. "Rather I will hazard another query. Have you been made aware that both Baron Plinth and Baron Estobate are raising armies?"

I found myself unable to draw breath despite my recent exertions.

My Queen again lifted an eyebrow. "Are they indeed? And if they are, what is that to me? Doubtless they intend to assail each other over some petty affront. I will be displeased—but I will not forbid them to shed each other's blood."

"I believe otherwise, Your Majesty," returned the Baron promptly. "I believe that they will unite their forces to assail *you*."

"Ha!" Her scorn betrayed no taint of doubt. "They are not men enough for the attempt. They have not the daring."

Thrysus Indolent advanced a step. He held up a hand to caution her as though he had cause to suspect that he might be overheard. In a lowered voice, he avowed, "You discount them too readily, Your Majesty. They are both wrathful men, albeit in divergent fashions, and wrath may drive them to a daring which would daunt ordinary courage." Before his sovereign could interrupt, he continued, "Also when I speak of raising armies I do not refer to Indemnie's customary motley of peasants and pitchforks. Rather I speak of trained men well armed and armored, with fine sabers and halberds in their hands, helms of iron, and hauberks of boiled leather. I speak of a hundred such men at Glare Estobate's command, and nearer one hundred and fifty obedient to Jakob Plinth's will.

"Such numbers may appear small, but they are too great for the lesser purpose of avenging some petty affront. Indeed, there is no purpose in the realm large enough to justify such force— no purpose other than to overwhelm the Domicile itself. Estobate and Plinth mean to put you to the sword"—he paused long enough to underscore his assertion—"Your Majesty."

My Queen's smile now held less of ravishment, more of calculation. "My lord Baron, I admire your certainty, though it may mislead you. Let us suppose briefly that your imaginings are not mere vapor. I have studied ancient treatises on warfare, and I know my house. Two hundred and fifty men however trained and armed cannot carry the Domicile, though my guards number no more than a score. Such *armies* cannot breach my walls."

Thrysus Indolent shrugged as though the issue were trivial. "They have no need to breach your walls, Your Majesty. They will starve you out. Sources of water you have, but your stores of food cannot endure without the isle's largesse."

In response, my Queen's shrug mocked her visitor's. I was scarce able to credit my ears as she answered, "Then I must urge you, my lord Baron, to raise an army of your own. Quirk Panderman and, yes, even Praylix Venery must do likewise. You will all need an abundance of men trained and armed. If you do not commit them to my defense, you will require them for your own. When Jakob Plinth and Glare Estobate have put me to the sword, as you suggest, they will turn on *you*. They must, lest you become the blade that bites their backs."

Though I was badly shaken, I did not miss Thrysus Indolent's reply. His act of surprise—indeed, of alarm—might have appeared genuine, had it not been contradicted by his ready grin and eager gaze. "Then I am lost, Your Majesty," he claimed without visible discomfort. "We are lost. I am no man for warfare. Panderman cannot concentrate, and Venery cannot rule his thoughts. If you do not assuage Plinth and Estobate—if you do not find some means to deflect their wrath—Indemnie itself is lost."

And still he conveyed the sense that he was prepared to pounce—and that he had not yet done so. He must, I thought in a scramble of words, he must have felt certain that his sovereign had already been apprised of raised armies and wrath. He must be confident of her spies. Therefore— I endeavored to swallow my heart. Therefore he must also recognize that her air of uninformed unconcern was mere charade, a masque performed to lull his deeper purposes.

A dangerous man, this Baron. His purposes were too deep for my shallow penetration. Why did he pretend to accept her pretense that she was blind to her own peril? What gain was there for him in the revelation of known secrets? In sum, why was he *here*?

For her part, however, my Queen was neither daunted nor doubtful. "Nonetheless," she stated with some asperity, "it must be done. If you do not caution me against Baron Plinth and Baron Estobate frivolously, it must be done. If you do not provide for my defense or your own, I must conclude that you give no credence to your own suspicions.

"And in *that* case, my lord Baron, I must also conclude that you have yet to name the true purpose of your presence."

Still Thrysus Indolent did not hesitate. His assurance acknowledged no rebuff. With a conspiratorial air—the air of a man who commonly spoke so as to foil eavesdroppers—he answered, "Your Majesty, your discernment may misguide you. I remain confident that I have not judged Baron Plinth and Baron Estobate unjustly. Yet I have no cause to question the worth of your spies.

For that reason, I surmise that you seek to divert yourself at my expense. Thus I have no means by which to demonstrate my loyalty, both to you and to Indemnie, other than by still greater daring. I have spoken honestly. Hoping to sway you, I will hazard a more perilous honesty."

"Then do so," she instructed him, now without graciousness.

Though he held her gaze, his eyes appeared to continue their dark dance as he pounced at last. "Your Majesty, I am responsible for the recent attempt upon your daughter's life."

"You?" There my Queen betrayed true surprise. "Not Jakob Plinth?"

Indolent made a dismissive gesture. "Baron Plinth's rectitude condones no subterfuge. He is blameless. Yet I do not scruple to assert that I also am blameless. Or rather, I will assert that my purpose in the attempt was not blameworthy."

Outfacing her scrutiny, he said, "Your Majesty, I state my case thus. Turmoil afflicts Indemnie. So much you will surely acknowledge. But any turmoil that endangers you must also imperil the succession. Therefore no good will come of our efforts, should Baron Venery, Baron Panderman, and I exert ourselves for our own protection—or should we fail in yours—unless your daughter is worthy of rule—aye, and *proven* worthy. *That* was my purpose."

While my Queen studied every shift of muscle, every fleeting expression, every intake of breath, Thrysus Indolent presented his defense.

"By various means, none in themselves honest," he admitted

as though he sought to appear innocent as water, "I made arrangement that a unique powder be mingled with your daughter's wine, for her preferences are well known." So saying, he confessed—albeit indirectly—that his own spies were as skilled as hers. For myself, I began to fear his more so. "For those whose blood holds no admixture of our distant ancestors' gifts, this powder might well prove fatal. However, I did not fear that outcome. Your daughter is your daughter. A portion of her blood is yours. And on one of mixed blood, my powder would inflict no more than a fleeting distress. To one of pure blood, however, my powder would occasion no conceivable discomfort. Rather it would provide a pleasing elevation of the senses. A pleasing elevation of *life*, Your Majesty.

"I sought no harm to your daughter," he avowed. "I desired only to prove her worthy of command over all the realm—and to do so covertly so that she, and you, and Indemnie might have no cause to fear a subsequent public demonstration. And I did not speak to you ere I risked my test because—" He made a show of chagrin and honesty. "Well, because, Your Majesty, I had no wish to incur your displeasure unnecessarily. I could imagine that you might take my head without heeding my reasons.

"Sadly"—now he feigned regret, though he could not mask his more private anticipations—"I did not foresee the expedient of a taster. Also I was but recently informed that an earlier attempt had been made upon your daughter's life. Had I know of *that* treachery, I would not have undertaken my own small machination.

———

"Your Majesty, my ignorance of that earlier attempt accounts for the insistence of my present wish to speak with you. Now I await your mercy—or your ire, should you deem my purposes blameworthy."

I could not fathom him. To the extent that his defense was honest, his ploy appeared comparatively harmless—certainly less fatal than a knife in the night. Yet his credibility, suspect at best, was undermined by an air of satisfaction that he did not trouble to conceal.

And my Queen clearly thought as I did, though her insight surpassed mine. "Indolent," she replied, her voice a silken blade, "I find truth in few of your fine speeches, cause for offense in many. However, your observation that Indemnie is in turmoil is simple fact. And my keen desire to put *you* to the sword—to have you beheaded after much torture—will achieve only an increase of turmoil. For that reason, and for that reason alone, I will not heed the counsels of my ire. Be careful now that you do not sway me against my better self. I will have truth or blood.

"What cause justifies your doubt that my daughter's lineage is pure?"

Oblivious to her threat, or perhaps merely unalarmed by it, the Baron positively gleamed. "The simple fact, Your Majesty," he replied at once, "that your daughter's father was murdered. *His* purity cannot now be examined."

"And you call it *credible*," she retorted like a woman stung, "that I would endanger the succession by bedding a man lacking the requisite heritage?"

Thrysus Indolent shrugged again. As though he considered his rectitude the equal of Baron Plinth's, beyond doubt or aspersion, he answered, "I call his death murder. So much is commonly known. But more knowledge is needed, and there is none. Do you ask me to imagine that a woman who offers marriage to five barons would scruple to bed *any* man who chanced to appear desirable?"

Tension filled the boudoir until the very lamps appeared to flicker. The insult of his retort filled my bowels with tremors. As for my Queen, her tone hardened, and a dire fury burned in her eyes. "You dare to provoke me? I perceive now that you are certain of my restraint, as you have been from the first. However, your cunning betrays you. Alter the terms of your query. Do you imagine that a woman who did not scruple to shed her daughter's father's blood would fear to shed yours?"

So plain a threat might suffice to unman any of the barons, yet Thrysus Indolent's daring did not falter. "Answer my question, Your Majesty, and I will answer yours."

Briefly I imagined her voice raised to summon guards. However, she did not call out. Rather her manner became both resigned and rigid.

"My lord Baron," she announced in a tone of extreme self-mastery, "I will not partner with you in this gavotte of deception and falseness. Stripped of its obfuscations, your defense rests upon Indemnie's turmoil, which I have chosen to call simple fact. I will have one simple fact from you to counter your affronts.

———

"You assert that a *unique powder* in my daughter's wine would serve to gauge the purity of her blood. Name that powder." Unbidden, the word *chrism* came to my mind, though I could not account for it. "If it has no name," she continued, "tell me of its composition, its preparation. I will suffer no further hazard to my daughter until I have tested the efficacy of your powder upon myself."

The man had pounced. Now he acted a dignified reluctance. "Your Majesty, I cannot. That secret is not mine to reveal. You must glean the knowledge you seek from another. You will not have it from me."

Thus he pretended honor.

With sweetness and venom commingled, my Queen countered, "Not to save your head? Not to spare yourself the attentions of my torturer?"

Did I perceive a suggestion of concern in the Baron's mien? I could not be certain of it.

"If I must experience agony and death," he offered with seeming hesitancy, "now is as good a time as any, and better than some." Then he rallied his assurance. "However, I am confident that you will not harm me. You dare not. Were your threats more than mere vapor, *four* barons would have no recourse but to rise against you. And when you were slain, the condition of your daughter's blood would not suffice to ward her. My fellow barons would see your line entirely ended."

I repeat that Baron Thrysus Indolent was a dangerous man. Only now did I begin to grasp the magnitude of the peril that he presented to my Queen, and to the realm. His innocence—and indeed his honor—I discounted altogether. Yet I could not dismiss his appraisal of *armies*. I had heard a multiplicity of threats, some perhaps imagined, some certainly feigned. Nevertheless the danger of armies had substance.

"Enough, my lord Baron." On the instant, Inimica Phlegathon deVry became imperious and calm. Though she did not condescend to raise her voice, her command was unquestionable. "You may depart. We have acknowledged the absence of scruples. You will feel no surprise, then, that I do not scruple to conclude that Baron Plinth and Baron Estobate ready themselves for war at your instigation. Now be gone while you remain able to obey."

Thrysus Indolent appeared to contemplate some protest. If he did so, however, her abrupt quiet dissuaded him. Apparently he had discernment enough to recognize that he was not the only dangerous personage present. Making a hasty leg, he withdrew like a man both routed and jubilant.

For some moments, there was silence in the chamber. I heard only the clenched wheeze of my own breath and the hard labor of my heart, nothing more. After a time, I began to suspect that my Queen meant to withdraw as Baron Indolent had done, with no word for her alarmed Hieronomer. Then, however, soft as a whisper, she spoke my name.

"Your Majesty." Trembling, I emerged from my covert. Yet when I stood in her presence, I found that I had lost my voice. I had witnessed Inimica Phlegathon deVry in a variety of moods—

some or most admittedly dissembled—but on no other occasion had I seen her forlorn.

To my sight, her air of lonely bereavement only served to make her beauty more ineffable.

She did not glance at me. Rather she considered some private vista of loss or ruin. In a small voice, as though I were not near enough to hear her, she murmured, "I have erred, Mayhew. I did not foresee Indolent's boldness. You are now aware of matters concerning which I have sought to preserve your ignorance. Your gifts are thus made useless to me."

"Your Majesty." Her distress prompted me to a boldness that would have eluded me under any other circumstance—a boldness entirely unlike Baron Indolent's. "My gifts have been useless for some weeks. I have made many attempts and shed much blood, yet the outcome of my scrying remains unaltered. For that reason, my efforts as your Hieronomer serve no further purpose." She had encouraged me to sacrifice a child, but that I would not do. Even to spare my head, I would not. The horrors of having once studied the entrails of a stillborn infant remained present to me. "Yet the possibility remains that my understanding will prove of some worth.

"May I question you, Your Majesty?"

Still she did not direct her gaze upon me. Like a woman embattled within herself, she remained silent a while. When she replied, her tone was frayed. "Speak, Mayhew. I fear that I have been made blind. I see no harm in you."

At another time, I might have answered that she saw none

because there was none. Now, however, the urgency of the occasion pressed me to persist in daring.

As though I were certain of myself, I said, "You have spoken of turmoil. I have spoken of rebellion. It is plain now that the turmoil is of your own making, and that therefore the threat of rebellion has acquired substance. Your Majesty, I wish to comprehend the policy that inspires you to provoke the barons."

As she turned toward me, the force of her regard caused me to quail. "Provoke?" With that word, and with those that followed, she gathered strength. "I have done more than *provoke*, Mayhew. I have positively *lashed* those weak men. I require them to set aside their complacence. They luxuriate in it, and their self-indulgence will ensure at least one of the dooms which you have foretold.

"Mayhew Gordian, I must have war. For the sake of the realm, Indemnie must have civil war."

I gaped indecorously. In one respect, her assertion answered me. It accounted for her many contradictory dealings, with the barons as well as with her lesser subjects. Yet in another and deeper form, it defied my explication. I could imagine no measure by which war was preferable to peace.

I must have croaked a protest, though I did not hear myself. My Queen's smile now resembled the glare of a headsman's axe. "I repeat so that you will heed me. Mayhew, *we must have civil war*. If I am deposed, I will not regret my loss. If I am slain, I will not fault my foes. Indemnie *must* have war."

Swallowing consternation, I contrived to ask, "Why?" I felt

myself gasping to ascend an endless stair into an abyss of darkness. "Your Majesty, *why?*"

"*To reduce the population.*" The frustration and ire in her voice was such that a lesser woman might have rent her hair. "We must have bloodshed, *quantities* of bloodshed, lest we fall to the curse of Indemnie's prosperity.

"We live too easily, feed too easily, multiply too easily. For the present, no subject of this realm knows true *want*. Even the most vacant of our people—those lacking in wit enough, or vitality, or will to engage in constructive effort—do not also lack food or shelter or garments.

"Yet our population *grows*, Mayhew. It *doubles*. With every generation of Queens, it *doubles*. In a short space of years—a time which I am now able to foresee as clearly as you—true want will begin. It must. We are blessed by bounty in every form, but that kind fortune has become a curse because it does not extend to *land*. We have not *space* enough, neither for our people nor for the crops to sustain them.

"And when true want begins, it will end as you have foretold it. Those with less will grow jealous of those with more. Jealousy and hunger will fester into ire. Eventually that ire will catch its spark, and then Indemnie will burn with revolt—not the rebellion of barons unendurably provoked by their sovereign, but the savage and indiscriminate conflagration of *want*."

Eyes aflame, she pronounced, "Civil war will *cull* us, Mayhew. It will be bloody and regrettable, but in some measure it will be *restrained*. It will be limited by the commands—by the will—of the barons. They do not crave absolute decimation. Even Indolent does not. Rather their assaults on me, and upon each other, will reduce our populace without altogether destroying civil order.

"The revolt which I fear will put an end, not merely to our present ease, but also to any prospect of future relief. Inevitably Indemnie will become an isle ruled by brigands and butchers, and our descent into barbarism will be complete.

"I *must* have civil war. As matters stand, our prosperity is a moldering corpse draped in the finery and vestments of a banquet. Only blood-letting can hope to restore us."

Hearing her, I felt that I could not see. Her assertions struck me as though I had inadvertently gazed at the sun. Did she call herself blind? I was more so.

"Your Majesty," I breathed like a man made craven in an instant, "I did not understand. Now I cry your pardon. I will do so on my knees if I must. Dooms I scryed for you, but I did not grasp the nature of the burden that even one doom would compel you to bear."

By her own dealings, she was lost. Nevertheless by that means she sought to drag Indemnie back from the brink of a worse catastrophe.

And she had made no mention of ships from the east. Yet now I guessed her deeper designs. Beyond question, she searched the seas in all directions for habitable lands. Should they be discovered, the need for war might be averted. To meet the failure of that hope, however, she had conceived another expedient. She now imagined that by preventing one doom she might thereby diminish another.

An isle accustomed to disciplined war and restrained killing might be able to defend itself against enslavement.

But while I pleaded with her with my eyes and my empty hands, Inimica Phlegathon deVry turned from me. "You did not understand," she replied as though she had no interest in my concern, "because I did not wish it. There is no fault in you. Remain my servant. Resume your auguries. Your gifts may yet catch some gleam of a salvation that surpasses my apprehension."

Doubtless I should have withdrawn at once, overwrought as I was. Yet one query remained in my mind, placed there by Thrysus Indolent. Having already presumed so much, I hazarded an end to her forbearance.

"Your Majesty—" My voice caught in my throat, but I goaded myself to swallow the obstruction. "How did you select the man who became the father of your daughter?"

She sighed, and her burdens appeared to settle more heavily on her shoulders. In a wistful tone, she answered, "My mother taught a strict adherence to the Articles of Coronation. However, I was a willful girl, determined that my actions should not be constrained by either hieromancy or statecraft. I chose whom I chose, thinking myself ready to defy the cost.

"As I came to know the man, however, I discovered him oblivious of the larger world. He heeded neither the restrictions nor the perils of his place in my bed. Also it was not in his nature to remain silent when he wished to boast. Therefore I deemed it certain that he would one day inform his family or his comrades that he was my lover, and that by so doing he would put both them and the realm in jeopardy.

"Slew ended his life at my command. Thereafter I became willful for other purposes. Perhaps they will prove more worthy than a girl's self-gratification."

So saying, Inimica Phlegathon deVry left the chamber. As she departed, however, her every step was eloquent to me. As though her strides were language, she informed me that she could not be certain of Excrucia's lineage. It was possible—indeed, it was probable—that my friend and ally's veins held an admixture of ungifted blood. She would have failed Baron Indolent's test, and was as lost as her mother.

Thereafter the days passed in growing unrest within the Domicile. Rumors of *armies* spread as though a shaft of lightning had struck the heart of the house. Whispers of *war* and *siege* were everywhere, though none knew who the foe might be. Flustered serving-maids and cooks blundered about their tasks, heedless of their own deeds. My Queen's more personal servants and counselors ran hither and thither, to no visible effect. Groaning wains bore foodstuffs of every description through the great gates, unloaded their cargos indiscriminately, and hastened away in plain flight. Calls went out to every nearby town, village, and hamlet for physicians and herbalists. And in the Domicile's courtyard, as well as atop the walls, Her Majesty's two captains commanded their mere score of men—a group from which Slew and Vail were conspicuously absent—in a frenzy of unwonted training and unfamiliar instruction. The Domicile—so the captains insisted ever more hoarsely—might be well defended, were the guards but willing enough, and ready in their deeds, and quick with the knowledge of their duties. Yet the residents of the house were not comforted by such exhortations. We were accustomed only to peace. The prospect of battle, with its attendant maimings and death, filled us with dismay.

Nevertheless my Queen's solstice ball drew closer, and she would have no slack or slovenly preparation for her festivities. Though her household servants fretted and trembled and indeed wept as they labored, they were granted no respite in which to multiply their fears. The Domicile's Majordomo was at all times a shrill harridan, but she well understood that those under her rule must not be permitted to dwell on matters over which they had no sway. Also she knew that Inimica Phlegathon deVry required perfection for *this* ball above all others. Therefore the Majordomo drove her forces with a fever to match the urgency of the guards' captains.

And still I received no word from Excrucia. I caught no glimpse of her, though I haunted the secret passages of the house with the diligence of a man obsessed, having as a servant no admittance to—or indeed knowledge of—the more public halls and chambers. Some weeks now had passed since she and I had discussed history and lineage, *chrism* and the Articles of

Coronation, yet of the efforts which she had promised at my urging I had no tidings. As the threat of armies and the prospect of the ball approached, I was as lost as she—and far less significant. I had gleaned all that my gifts offered, and had now no occupation other than to nurture my dismay. Indeed, I had not worth enough to merit attempts upon my life, while twice more assassins had endeavored to end Excrucia's. In consequence, Slew had joined Vail for her protection—and I survived my days in untroubled safety, knowing only that my sole friend still lived.

Indemnie's dooms drew near while I served no more purpose than the croaking of a storm-crow.

Fortunately—I mean that it was fortunate for my remaining sanity, if for no other cause—one law was immutable. Change ruled every circumstance, for good or ill. The ball was no more than a fortnight distant when I returned to my laborium from my meaningless peregrinations and encountered Vail at my door.

A tall man, muscled and broad, he dominated my slightness. Stooping, he gripped the shoulder of my robe so that I could not draw away from his mouth at my ear. In a hasty whisper, he informed me, "Her Highness awaits you. Do not tarry to speak with her. Do not acknowledge her presence. Much depends on the pretense that she witnesses nothing, knows nothing.

"The command that you asked of her did not suffice to compel compliance. For that reason, Slew obtained Her Majesty's authority. He brings a visitor. They will arrive at any moment."

At once, he opened my door and thrust me inward, then withdrew, closing the door at my back.

As I reeled in both body and mind, I endeavored to scan my chambers. Such was my fright that I did not immediately discover my friend. After a moment, however, I found her seated in the farthest corner of my workroom, concealed by shadows and a dark cloak, the hood of which prevented any glimpse of her features.

Well, I thought as I sought for calm. Well. Did she depend upon a mask of ignorance? Her caution I did not comprehend, but I could well believe that she had good cause. As I did also. Slew had made my Queen aware of her daughter's alliance with me.

Obedient to Vail's command, I did not address Excrucia. Rather I took a stool facing the door and seated myself, pretending nonchalance with poor success. Naturally I was curious to know the identity of my visitor. Also I wondered at the apparent need for secrecy. More than the answers to such queries, however, I wished to know how my Queen would respond to my dealings with Excrucia. Did my friend's mother now condone our efforts together? Or had I now incurred our sovereign's wrath?

While I gnawed my uncertainties, a knock sounded on my door. Ere I could shift my limbs or my voice to respond, Slew's thick arm swept the door aside, and my visitor was ushered inward.

As did Vail, Slew wore no livery to distinguish him from a

common laborer. Only his great strength set him apart. And only the quickness of his gaze hinted that he was alert to every peril. Unhesitating, he brought his companion to stand before me. Behind them, Vail closed the door again, remaining in the outer corridor himself to stand guard over my encounter with an individual whom I did not recognize.

He was by a hand's width taller than I, and clad as I was in an unadorned black robe, though our apparel differed as to cleanliness. His appeared freshly scrubbed and pressed as though for a stately occasion. Indeed, his hands and face were pink with washing, and his groomed hair was enclosed by a circlet of dark iron. In addition, his bulk emphasized my leanness. He was of a size to command more than ordinary attention, corpulent to the point of obesity, with plump hands, fat thighs, and a barrel torso. The heavy flesh of his cheeks bulged into trembling jowls, and that of his brow sagged to give his eyes a perpetual squint.

"Brother," he began at once in a voice that rattled with catarrh, "I do not know you. I was encouraged to imagine that I would meet with Her Majesty Inimica Phlegathon deVry, to whom my allegiance belongs. Instead I find myself in this lowly and noisome chamber. I see by your furnishings and filth that you are a hieronomer. In that, we are brothers, though I hold our kinship in small regard. More than that, I do *not* know.

"Explain, Brother. I am impatient to resume more worthy tasks."

Ere I was able to master my surprise at his address, Slew answered him in a threatening growl. "He is Mayhew Gordian,

Her Majesty's Hieronomer. He desires speech with you. More than that you do not *need* to know."

This was an expression of loyalty that exceeded my expectations. While I strove to steady myself, however, and my visitor wrestled with an alarmed indignation, Slew continued.

"Hieronomer, you wished to speak with an alchemist. This is Opalt Intrix, held in *large* regard by others of his ilk. Among them, he is considered an adept of iron."

Well, I thought again. Well indeed. I had asked of Excrucia that she summon an alchemist, and now both Vail and Slew supported her desires—with Her Majesty's consent. For the first time as my Queen's Hieronomer, I was gladdened by Slew's presence. His service to Excrucia strengthened me.

An adept of iron? I knew too little of alchemy.

With what assurance I could muster, I spoke at last. "Brother Intrix, be welcome. Though your reluctance is plain, I am pleased by your arrival. I find that my service to Her Majesty requires a greater knowledge of alchemy than I have the good fortune to possess. It is my hope that our Queen's desires will inspire you to satisfy my queries."

"What queries?" Opalt Intrix's demand was a loose rasp. "This lout"—he indicated Slew—"invoked Her Majesty's authority. Now I am inclined to doubt his use of it."

"He is her man," I replied with a semblance of equanimity. "That must suffice to content you."

The alchemist appeared to consider the prospect of refusing

Slew by plain strength. After a moment, he repeated more warily, "What queries?"

I rubbed my hands together to disguise their trembling. "Let us begin, Brother Intrix, with alchemy itself. As all know, it is vital to Indemnie's prosperity, capable of great feats for the benefit of the realm. But what precisely does it *do*? What is its power? How does it serve the needs of our Queen, the barons, and the isle?"

"Do?" My unwilling visitor snorted his disdain. "It grows. More *precisely*, it causes growth in any form of mindless matter. It causes crops to flourish in once-barren soil, thereby bringing fertility to the soil itself. It expands stones to any desired shape and size, if the stone itself is apt for its intended purpose. It makes trees of shrubs. From trees it fashions forests. It will bring forth purity from tainted water by increasing any small portion that chances to be clean until the taint is diluted to nothingness."

He fascinated me. Clearly Indemnie's life had been made viable by alchemy. "And iron, Brother?" I inquired. "You are an adept of iron?"

"Iron also," he conceded with some bitterness. "From the ore, iron can be grown for any use when the mold necessary for that use has been prepared."

Thinking I knew not what, I asked, "Is the mold required by alchemy?"

Opalt Intrix sighed, a man vexed by a fool's inquisition. "It is required by the need for a particular shape. Lacking a mold, the iron will retain its first form as it grows."

Unable to explain myself even to myself, I continued my queries.

"What does it signify that you are deemed an adept?"

Now my visitor answered more readily. My interest appeared to touch his vanity. "Any alchemist may apply his gift to any material. However, the purity of the blood varies. Also natural inclinations and talents vary. Each alchemist must discover the best use of his gift. For myself, I am named an adept, and am held in considerable regard, because my abilities pertain to iron.

"The growing of iron, like that of stone, is considered of especial worth because both iron and stone are more malleable than any material able to live and grow without the application of alchemy. Such plants as grasses, shrubs, and grains may be grown with comparative ease. It is their nature to grow. Consequently they can only be denied their natural shapes by warping, or by some other distortion. Iron and stone have no natural shape. Therefore they have no use unless they are simultaneously increased and molded for some desired purpose.

"Some generations past, the purest alchemists of their time labored for a decade to create the many blocks of granite which became this edifice." He glanced at the walls around him. "They were true adepts of stone. For that reason, I esteem their memory." In this assertion, he may have been sincere. "Iron is a laborious material, but it is not as arduous as stone."

Altogether he filled me with a sense of wonder which I could ill afford to indulge. After a moment's consideration, I turned to a new heading.

"Clearly, Brother Intrix," I observed, "the abilities of other alchemists, like your own, are wide-ranging and remarkable. Is it conceivable that an alchemist may turn his gifts to hieronomy?"

My visitor shrugged heavily. "The gift is the gift." He did not trouble himself to meet my gaze. By such signs, he expressed a profound disinterest. "Only purity, talent, and character vary. What is hieronomy but an attempt to expand discernment itself, albeit by external means? Yet the uncertainties of the future are both subtle and extensive. They thwart even an expanded discernment. Alchemists prefer tangible tasks, ones which may be effectively achieved."

He piqued me despite his manner. By external means? With an eagerness which I endeavored to conceal, I pursued my interest.

"Brother Intrix, given that the alchemists of Indemnie are capable of such wonders, I must wonder why they cannot perform similar miracles with men."

The adept shrugged again, plainly wishing himself elsewhere. "I know not. *We* know not. We are certain only that any flesh possessed by a living mind cannot endure the effects of alchemy. Even the beasts of field and forest perish if growth is attempted upon them.

"Some among us surmise that any mind—even that of a beast—cannot suffer its own increase, which must affect that mind as warping affects a tree. For myself, I have no opinion on the matter. It has no pertinence to my own labors."

So saying, he appeared to dash a hope that I had not expressed. Nonetheless I was not dashed. His elucidation—however grudgingly granted—sufficed to heighten an excitement which might come to serve as hope.

Yet I did not pause to contemplate my own thoughts. Striving to unsettle my visitor, I stated bluntly, "You spoke of purity of blood, Brother."

He gazed at me with unconcealed exasperation. "Is even *that* unknown to you? I refer to *lineage*, to inheritance from the first families of Indemnie. Are you not gifted? Are you ignorant of your place among your kind? Your knowledge of history is scant indeed if you are unaware that those families were forsaken upon this isle because their gifts were feared. That alchemists— and hieronomers," he conceded ungraciously, "do not now command this realm is of no significance. In our forgotten homeland, we learned that our lives are both more valued and less at hazard when we do not rule."

"A wise policy, Brother," I replied, pretending a fatuous equability. "Fortunately my further queries will not transgress its bounds. Hearing you, I am made aware that the alchemists of Indemnie are capable of much which lies beyond my poor comprehension. Pardon, if you will, an inquiry which may surprise you. Being capable of so much, are you also able to expand our isle itself? Can the alchemists of Indemnie at work together create more *land*?"

For a moment, he stared as though he confronted a madman. Then he coughed a harsh laugh. "You wander in your wits, Hieronomer. Have you considered the *magnitude* of the labor you suggest? If you crave more land—why, I know not— we cannot simply spread earth over the seas. The isle itself must be increased upward from its foundations in the depths of the ocean—depths, I hasten to add, which have not been fathomed, and which may well lie leagues beneath the waves. Such labor is not the work of one lifetime, or of several. Generations beyond number might pass ere a hundred alchemists, or a thousand, increased Indemnie's land by as much as an acre."

In response, I laughed with better grace than he. "Then let that thought be forgotten. It was indeed as ill-considered as you have deemed it. I am humbled by your better apprehension."

Resuming my efforts to unsettle him, I again altered my heading. "As an adept of iron," I remarked, "you, Brother, and others of similar gifts must have been in considerable demand recently."

Of a sudden, the alchemist's manner became wary. "Why do you say so?"

I offered my own shrug, watching him narrowly. "Baron Estobate and Baron Plinth have armies. Their soldiers are well-supplied with swords and helms of iron."

There Opalt Intrix hesitated. Briefly he appeared to reconsider his desire to challenge Slew's strength—or perhaps the strength of Slew's authority. If so, he must have concluded that he could not out-match my Queen's man. His shoulders slumped in resignation.

"Then I must confess that the demands of the barons have indeed been considerable. But of their purposes I know nothing. I care only that I am valued." A moment later, he averred, "My allegiance belongs to the pure Queens of Indemnie."

His emphasis upon purity urged me to draw inferences which I could not then examine. Believing that I had disturbed his composure, I chose rather to pursue my advantage. "That being said, good Brother Intrix," I continued as though my inquiries were the ordinary and predictable outcome of his answers, "I must now ask *how* alchemy is performed. My service to Indemnie's present pure Queen requires an understanding of the preparations, methods, and materials necessary to your gift."

"Ha!" His expostulation rattled in his chest, the cough of a man who would have preferred to bring up his lungs. "You are a fool indeed if you imagine me fool enough to disclose my knowledge to *you*, gift-kin though you may be."

Ere I could reply, a dirk appeared in Slew's fist. With his other arm, he clasped my visitor's shoulders. His blade he rested on the loose flesh of Opalt Intrix's throat.

Slew's instant support both startled and steadied me. Relying upon it, and encouraged by the alchemist's quick fear, I addressed Opalt Intrix in a cautioning tone.

"Yet you must do so, Brother. You must do so for your life, if you will not for your rightful sovereign. Slew may have a flaw or three in his nature, but hesitation is not among them. Indeed, he may be entirely innocent of scruple. If you will not answer,

Indemnie will lose an adept of iron—and the loss will be scantly grieved."

"No!" the man protested. "I *must* not! The secrecy of our knowledge preserves our lives. More, it wards those who lack our gifts. Our knowledge will prove fatal to all who attempt its use without the aid of our blood. Disclosure will cost *lives*, Brother, and not only among the alchemists who nurture the realm's prosperity!"

"Nevertheless," I insisted, reassured by the man's urgency. "On this matter, Opalt Intrix, I will not relent. However, to appease your fears, I will vow upon my own blood that your secrets will not be shared beyond this chamber. We are not Baron Venery, Brother. We are able to keep our own counsel."

"It is certain," growled Slew, "that I am. I can seal my mouth as easily as I can shed your life."

"What of—?" The alchemist's scrubbed hand indicated Excrucia's shadowed form.

Of her I had no doubt. "My word binds our silent companion."

Still he strove to muster some protest that I might heed. Twisting his throat away from Slew's blade as best he could, he pleaded, "Yet the essence of my secrets is known to you." His catarrh appeared to choke him. "You are aware that gifted blood is necessary. I have spoken of the role of natural inclination and talent. What more do you desire?"

"Preparations," I repeated. "Methods. Are incantations needful? Are there rituals which must be performed?"

"Paugh!" In his desperation, he coughed phlegm and scorn. "Does hieronomy rely upon incantations? Do you enact rituals here, in the privacy—the *secrecy*—of your laborium?"

The revelation that I sought now trembled upon his tongue. I had only to provoke its utterance, knowing that my own small gift depended solely upon itself. I had no use for incantations and rituals, and was now assured that he had none.

"Brother Intrix," I replied with an air of nonchalance that pleased me, "I am not altogether as ignorant of history as you suppose. I have discovered that when our ancestors first endeavored to live upon this isle, barren as it then was, their alchemists lacked one material required by their gifts." Then I allowed my years of loneliness and ire into my voice. "I am *aware* that our ancestors would not have survived their abandonment without the scrying of hieronomers to discover that one material." Harsh as a scourge, I said, "I demand of you only that you *name* it. For my Queen's sake, I must know by what means the gifts of alchemists are transformed from illusion to effect."

Still Opalt Intrix closed his mouth. Beneath their flesh, his jaws knotted as though he intended to remain silent forever.

Lifting my shoulders in a last shrug, I nodded to Slew.

At once, he set the point of his dirk and pressed until blood began a ready trickle from the alchemist's jowl.

Swift panic glared in my gift-kin's eyes. His mouth appeared to open of its own accord. His thick lips flapped as he cried, "It is *chrism*, you fool! A natural ore, and rare. A catalyst! The deeds of alchemists require only blood and talent and will and *chrism*."

There an instant of elation overcame me. Though I was myself as fearful as my victim, and held in far less regard, I had achieved a portion of my purpose—perhaps the most vital portion. I now needed only one further disclosure from the alchemist, no more, and my use of him would be complete.

Ere I could master my exultation, however, my door swung open, and I sprang immediately to my feet. There was but one personage in all the realm to whom Vail would have granted admittance.

With the light of my candles glittering in her eyes and a heave of haste in her bosom, Inimica Phlegathon deVry entered my chambers.

That she was fraught with wrath was plain. That she was of a mind to claim heads—mine first among them—seemed probable. Yet I had come far in her name, and now found myself disinclined to falter. With an exertion of will, I resumed my seat. This was my laborium, and I intended to preside over it.

"Your Majesty," I said as though her arrival had been agreed between us—as though my posture upon my stool were not in itself an unpardonable affront—"we are speaking of *chrism*." Though I trembled, I held to my purpose. "Opalt Intrix has just informed us that it is vital to the deeds of alchemists—and that it is fatal to all who do not share the blood-gift of our ancestors. I was about to inquire whether it may be used to test those who lay claim to pure lineage."

With her finery and loveliness—with what I must call her splendor—my Queen by her mere presence caused my workroom to appear soiled and tawdry, a place where unsavory deeds were performed by a despicable man. Yet she addressed no word to me. Briefly she glanced at her daughter hooded and cloaked in the corner. Her gaze rested for a moment on my tables, no doubt marking the absence of fresh blood. Then she turned to confront Opalt Intrix and Slew.

"Slew Immordson," she began, "I give thanks daily for your service. Now I do so again that you informed me of this gathering, and that you remained to stand guard on my behalf. Had you not asked in my Hieronomer's name for authority to summon an alchemist, I would not have granted it. And had you not informed me of my Hieronomer's alliances, I would not have allowed this inquisition to proceed so long in my absence. I will not sully your loyalty with promises of reward. Know, however, that my gratitude is yours."

To this comparative effusion, Slew replied with no more than a blunt nod. If my Queen's thanks either pleased or irked him, he gave no sign.

To all appearances, she expected none. Rather she shifted her attention at once to the alchemist.

"And your answer, Opalt Intrix?" she inquired. "Can this *chrism* be employed as my Hieronomer suggests?"

In reply, he stared as though he beheld his life in ruins. Sweat beaded upon his brow, and his mouth attempted words for which he had no voice. He had spoken easily enough of *allegiance* and *pure Queens*. Confronted by Inimica Phlegathon deVry herself, however, he appeared lost in fright.

Frowning, she uncoiled a silken ire studded with barbs. "Do not think to refuse me, Alchemist. In matters that concern your life and your secrets, my rule is supreme. You have a supply of this *chrism* upon your person?"

From the depths of his self-regard, Opalt Intrix summoned a timorous nod.

She allowed him no pause for reflection. Holding out her hand, she commanded, "I will have it now."

His dampness and pallor were such that I feared he might faint. It was fortunate for his dignity, then, that he remained standing. With quaking hands, he opened his robe, reached for a hidden pocket, and drew forth a leather pouch of a size to fill the palm of my hand.

"A lifetime's worth, Your Majesty," he gasped thinly. "It is potent. Be sparing."

Taking the pouch from him on the instant, my Queen untied its neck and peered within. "A powder," she observed, doubtless for my benefit. Dipping one finger inward, she withdrew a few fulvous grains. When she had granted me a moment to regard them, she lifted her finger to her mouth and licked it.

"Tasteless," she pronounced it—and after an interval during which her gaze appeared to absent itself, "Pleasurable."

As though such actions were common between us, she offered the pouch to me.

There I found myself as frightened as the alchemist. I had prepared neither my expectations nor my resolve for such a test. I had scant confidence in my lineage. My gift—such as it was—had not manifested itself in my immediate family, or in any of my relations. Nevertheless I recognized at once that both my service and my life depended upon my response. And during the space of a heartbeat I realized that I desired this test. If I wished to know how I might contrive to serve Indemnie as well as my Queen, I must first know myself.

In the corner, Excrucia had risen to her feet. However, she did not advance toward me or uncover herself.

After a moment's hesitance, I accepted the pouch. Emulating my sovereign's air of certainty, I used the tip of one finger to shift a minute portion of *chrism* from the pouch to my tongue. Then I closed my eyes to await the outcome.

When I opened them again, I met my Queen's gaze. "Tasteless," I assented. More I could not say while an urge to gag choked me. When the impulse had passed, however, and I had swallowed a measure of bile, I was able to confess, "And sickening. Distinctly unpleasant." In a limping tone, I added, "Fortunately the sensation is brief."

Masked by shadows, Excrucia resumed her seat like a woman collapsing.

Two mysteries were thus revealed. We now knew the nature of the powder with which Baron Indolent had indirectly tainted Excrucia's wine. And I had confirmed that my blood lacked sufficient purity to forestall Indemnie's dooms.

In addition—a thought that occurred to me belatedly—I had discovered that Excrucia was concerned for my well-being. Previously I had gauged that she had allied herself with me because my queries interested her, and perhaps also because she desired some use for her days that was not constrained or defined by her role as her mother's daughter. To believe that she valued my life for its own sake demanded an effort of which I had not then been capable.

For her part, Inimica Phlegathon deVry derived conclusions with a celerity that I could not match, and reached decisions as swiftly. To all appearances satisfied by my replies, she turned again to the alchemist.

"Opalt Intrix," she commanded with the imperious calm of a monarch who had no cause to fear disobedience, "you are dismissed. Return to your labors. Say no word of our exchanges in this chamber. For the present, I have no further need of you."

The alchemist's mouth opened and closed without issue. Another man might have offered some protest. This man may have wished to plead for the return of his *chrism*. But if his voice declined to serve him, his wits remained adequate to estimate the perils of his straits. Assisted by Slew's hand upon his shoulder, he jerked a bow. Without daring to raise his head, he backed toward the door, which Slew opened to expedite his departure.

When he was gone, my Queen stood silent a moment. Then she said in a musing tone, as though she spoke only to herself, "Now I comprehend Indolent's ploy. By testing my daughter's blood, he sought to determine whether she would suffice to command the support of Indemnie's alchemists in my absence. They would be loath to stand against a successor of pure lineage. But should her blood fail of purity, he could hope to win some or all of them to his cause, and my rule would be at an end."

So much I now understood. Seeking to comprehend more, I ventured cautiously, "Other attempts have been made as well, Your Majesty. Are they also Baron Indolent's doing?"

"No." Her reply was a snap. "Indolent is too subtle for such crudeness. Plinth has honor, Panderman is besotted, and Venery's mouth betrays every intention. The instigator is Estobate. He aims high. My daughter's death would end the Phlegathon deVry line. Thereafter he conceives that he would supplant me, either by marriage or by force of arms, and the line of the Estobates would begin.

"He is deluded. He does not grasp—though his prompter Indolent does—that he cannot rule Indemnie without the fealty of alchemists and augurs."

I did not contest her assertion. It conveyed conviction. Rather I dared to suggest, "Then, Your Majesty, we must speak further of alchemy."

It was in my mind to urge the formation of an army for the Domicile's defense. Such an endeavor would require quantities of iron to match the equipage of Baron Estobate's men, and of Baron Plinth's.

But the force of my Queen's eyes—indeed of her entire manner—as she turned on me froze my thoughts in my head. She appeared to shout with rage, though in fact she spoke quietly.

"Must we, Hieronomer?"

I confess that I quailed before her—or I did so until I saw

that Excrucia had again risen to her feet. Whatever my friend's emotions may have been, her effect upon me was one of supplication. For her sake—or for ours—she appeared to ask of me that I stand firm.

By small increments, I squared my shoulders, straightened my spine. As well as I could, I faced Inimica Phlegathon deVry.

"You know this, Your Majesty." My voice was a dry husk in my throat. "Throughout its history, Indemnie has relied upon alchemy. By the transformations of alchemy, we have become what we are. Without it, we cannot become more—a deed which we must accomplish, lest our dooms prove beyond our strength."

Such boldness threatened to unseat my reason. However, my Queen did not respond as I anticipated. Still quietly, though she was rife with wrath, she inquired, "Throughout its history, Hieronomer? I had not known you so learned. Where have you found time to immerse yourself in study? The state of your laborium suggests neglect for the tasks which I require of you."

To this query, I had no direct reply. I could not answer honestly without naming Excrucia, and I had already earned her more than enough of her mother's ire. Fear for her inspired me to a still greater boldness.

"Your Majesty, you digress. The *how* of my learning is without import. Only alchemy signifies. If we do not grasp its uses, we cannot turn it to our needs, and we will not long endure."

Again my Queen's response mocked my expectations. In a tone of ice and harsh winds, she demanded, "*We*, Hieronomer? *I* rule here. Our fate is *mine* to determine."

Her manner might have caused Thrysus Indolent himself to falter. In Excrucia's presence, I did not.

"*We* indeed, Your Majesty. I am your servant. Your needs, and Indemnie's, are mine as well. My scrying serves no further purpose. My best efforts discern no future which I have not previously beheld. Yet my desire to be of service remains. For that reason, I have interested myself in alchemy."

"*Enough*, Mayhew," she commanded, speaking yet more softly. I saw what I took for a glitter of dampness in her eyes, and for a moment her lower lip appeared to quiver. Ere I could be certain that she had betrayed so much access to her heart, however, she tightened every aspect of herself. Now stone of eye and compressed of mouth, she repeated, "Enough."

While I gazed at her, and feared her, and sought to conceive some appeal that she might heed, she stepped close to me. Gripping my arm, she positively lowered her mouth to my ear. In the barest whisper—and yet distinctly, so that her words could not be mistaken—she breathed, "I have urged you to sacrifice a child for my sake. Do you name yourself my servant? Will you defy me in this?"

Standing as we were, I could not observe her mien. I could glance only at Excrucia's tense apprehension and Slew's cruel strength. For reasons of terror rather than of privacy, I was able to muster no more than a wisp of sound.

"I will. Take my head if you must. I will sacrifice my life for you, and for Indemnie, but I will not shed that of a child."

Briefly Inimica Phlegathon deVry appeared to slump. Holding me with one hand, she braced the other on my shoulder as though she lacked will to stand. However, her lapse was momentary. As self-command returned to her limbs, I strove to ready myself for death.

Still she did not release me. Her mouth remained at my ear. Soft and chill as the exhalation of a grave, she informed me, "Then I will demand more of you. Much more when the time requires it. Do you imagine that I have not consulted other hieronomers? Other augurs of every description? Catoptromancers, astrologists, interpreters of dreams? Do you suppose that I myself cannot scry?" *The gift is the gift*, and her blood was pure. "You have a gift which others do not, though your inheritance lacks purity. From this moment, you will undertake every effort and perform every deed that your service demands.

"Inform my daughter that my trust in her is absolute."

While I struggled to comprehend her, staggered as I was by the realization that I had been spared, she left me. Swiftly she departed the chamber, taking Slew with her.

Thereafter I gaped at the iron of my door until relief and dismay overcame me, and I measured my length upon the floor.

L ater I found Excrucia on her knees at my side, shaking my arm and whispering my name, and I understood that I had lost consciousness. My daring in my Queen's presence had exceeded my small firmness of character.

However, the sight of Excrucia's visage had an alchemist's power to transform my weakness. Seeing her unhooded, with a luxury of tresses beside her face, a sweet mouth, and open fright in her eyes, I had good cause to marvel that any man deemed her plain. And good cause also to rally my wits, for I apprehended that her mother had revealed much that disturbed her, much of which she had been ignorant of.

For a moment, I was nearly overcome by a desire to kiss my friend and ally—an affront as unpardonable as remaining seated before Inimica Phlegathon deVry. Fortunately I had now sufficient presence of mind to recall that I was merely a servant. Rather than risk further insult to the line of the Phlegathon deVrys, I offered Excrucia a smile which I intended as reassurance. Then I made shift to regain my feet.

Briefly my laborium appeared to reel, altered in every dimension by the aftermath of Opalt Intrix's disclosures. However, Excrucia held my arm until my walls and tables and drains regained their familiarity. Thereafter I was able to stand unaided, and to bow as I should, albeit somewhat unsteadily.

"Accept my thanks, Your Highness," I pleaded in a shaken voice. "Excrucia. Friend. Your kindness exceeds my worth. I implore you to believe that I express my gratitude so poorly because I have no words adequate to the fullness of my heart."

The moisture in her gaze was more explicit than her mother's fleeting weakness—explicit in that she made no effort to conceal it. "Oh, Mayhew," she replied like a woman shuddering, "what have you done? When you asked to speak with an alchemist, I did not foresee— And your daring—! I feared for your life, Mayhew! What did my mother say to you? I could not hear. It must have been terrible indeed to strike you down."

To calm her, I cautioned wryly, "A breath, Excrucia. You must breathe. As I must.

"I could not have imagined that Her Majesty would enter here under any circumstance, and certainly not as she did. Her every word and deed surprised me utterly. As to her private commands, however, they were not terrible." Deliberately I suppressed any mention of a child's life, or of my desperate defiance—or of my sovereign's unvindicated faith in me. "For reasons that I cannot fathom—though I suspect that they are a matter of deep policy—she did not address you. Yet her words to me were intended for you.

"She instructed me to assure you that her trust in you is absolute."

"Oh, truly?" Excrucia's response was acid. "If trust she feels, she demonstrates it ill." More anxiously, she continued, "You must speak of all that you have discovered. And I must confess that I have gleaned little.

"But first—" Her gaze dropped to the floor, where Opalt Intrix's supply of *chrism* rested. "First I must test my own lineage."

Ere I could attempt to dissuade her, she stooped to claim the pouch.

In truth, I was not certain that I wished to dissuade her. Much depended on her blood—much more than on my own gifts.

For a few heartbeats, she merely held the pouch, gauging its weight of import in her hand. Then she did as her mother and I had done, dipping one finger inward to transport a few tawny grains to her tongue.

Her quick moue of disgust supplied her answer while I strove to draw breath. With some difficulty, she swallowed. When she spoke, her parched tone was underscored with bitterness. A dark scowl distorted her brow as she passed the *chrism* to me as though the pouch itself had become repugnant to her.

"It appears that my father's blood will win no allegiance to my cause."

Defying the Articles of Coronation, Inimica Phlegathon deVry had slept with a man ungifted—had slept with him until her womb quickened, and then had commanded his death to mask her disobedience.

I felt the blow that Excrucia had received. I could not deflect it. Its force was too great. My Queen spoke of *trust* when in effect she had betrayed her daughter from birth. Now I feared that Excrucia would believe that she must hide her face wherever she went.

Like a man compelled, I took my friend in my arms and held her until the first impact of her dismay had faded.

Thereafter I brought a stool near and urged her to sit. Seating myself, I shifted my own stool so that my hands might touch her if my heart could not. "Excrucia," I said softly, a wan effort to appear soothing, "you have suffered a hurtful loss, and a worse disappointment. Your distress is plain. Let us speak of other matters for a time. Perhaps they will serve to ease a portion of your pain."

She did not meet my gaze. Rather she studied her hands in her lap, where they gripped and twisted each other as though they were writhing. After a moment, however, she replied with a slight nod.

"May I assume," I began, "that you have spoken with your mother, as you proposed? Must I assume that you were given no satisfactory account of her dealings?"

To my relief, my query provoked anger when I had feared a further dismay. "Satisfactory?" she returned like a woman with gall in her mouth. "I was given no account at all. Our exchanges did not extend to the subject of spies. They proceeded no farther than the question of provoked discontent and attempted murder. Speaking sweetly—sweetly!—she assured me that such matters need not concern me. Unaided, I would grasp them all too readily when I became Indemnie's Queen. For the present— she *said* this to me, Mayhew!—she preferred that I remain a girl, innocent of trouble. Then I was dismissed. And from that day to this, I was made a prisoner in my home, my every step guarded, my every deed watched, my every word overheard. And all no doubt reported to my loving mother.

"I cannot describe my delight when Vail informed me that

he would contrive a visit here. I have been *stifled*, Mayhew. I felt an urgent desire to speak with you. Yet more than that, I burned to draw a breath which served no purposes but my own.

"And now I learn that my presence here was *arranged*. Even with you, I serve no purposes but my mother's."

She was my Queen's daughter and heir. Her bitterness ran deep. Clearly she had no use for her mother's assertion of trust.

And I felt as she did. The betrayal of Excrucia's birth cast a pall over her life. It might well bring about its premature end. For her sake, however, I assumed a contrary stance.

"Perhaps," I ventured hesitantly, "you would do well to view the conditions imposed upon you in another light. Imagine, as I must, that your mother has spoken no honest word to you except that her trust is absolute. Should that avowal be truth, it alters the meaning of her conduct.

"The attempts upon your life justify your comparative imprisonment. And her refusal to include you in her counsels may be explained by a desire to spare you the taint of participation—of implied consent—in her ploys and false dealing. If she does not relieve you of trouble, or indeed of peril, she *does* relieve you of complicity.

"Events may prove her refusal no small gift."

Though Excrucia did not lift her head, I pursued my theme.

"As for her involvement in Opalt Intrix's coming, and her own arrival, they may be seen as mitigated both by her consent to your presence and by her subsequent unwillingness to acknowledge it. Her policy in this has enabled all that you have discovered here—indeed, all that you may yet discover. At the same time, she denies that you play any part in her machinations. She will not reveal that you have heard her. The alchemist cannot, for your identity was well concealed. And Slew and Vail will say no word to contravene her wishes."

I saw tears fall to mark my companion's hands with woe. To my mind, the drops were liquid jewels, as honest as sapphires and rubies, yet as eloquent as sobs. Nevertheless I did not pause.

"Excrucia, hear me. It is conceivable—is it not?—that your mother seeks to provide for you a singular freedom. Can you not hope that she desires you to determine your own course—and your own loyalties—independent of her policies, which she deems the necessary consequence of her willfulness with your father? If by her conniving she gains naught else to Indemnie's benefit, the ruse of your innocence may do much to preserve you."

To answer her mute weeping, I insisted, "If what I say defies credence, allow me to disclose what I have learned since our last meeting. Perhaps it will sway you to reconsider your mother's conduct."

Still she did not raise her gaze to mine. Shrouded by her tresses, she inquired, forlorn as a wail, "Do you serve her still?"

Feigning assurance, I replied, "I do. When you have heard my tale, you will understand my resolve to do what I must for my Queen."

I feared Excrucia's silence. In her own fashion—a form entirely unlike her mother's—she shared Her Majesty's power to damn me, in my own sight if not in the realm's. I could not conceive how I might endure my life without Excrucia's friendship. Without her aid and support as well as her quick mind. It was fortunate for me, therefore, that she did not hold me long in suspense.

"Speak then, Mayhew," she answered, a low breath of sound. "There is no one else to whom I can turn for comprehension or kindness."

Altogether she filled me with a wish to shed my own tears. However, I perceived clearly enough that this moment was not an occasion to indulge my personal distress. In the past, she had blessed me with her courage. Now she required a comparable benison from me.

"While you have been imprisoned," I began, "I have not. I have witnessed—and indeed have been told—much that has shaken my understanding to its foundations."

With such concision and accuracy as I could muster, I described my Queen's audience with Baron Indolent, excluding nothing. Certainly I did not neglect to mention her belief that he had incited both Jakob Plinth and Glare Estobate to raise armies. I related my own efforts to confront my Queen—my efforts and their outcome. I explained the Domicile's preparations for war—which in turn explained the increased urgency with which Excrucia had been guarded. And when I had said so much, I endeavored to outline my own conclusions, both those of which I was certain and those that were simple conjecture.

Throughout my exposition, my companion did not speak. However, her head lifted slowly, and when her gaze found my face her eyes were free of tears. As I fell silent, she struggled to find words for her incredulity.

In a tone trenchant enough to draw blood, she demanded, "She goads the realm to civil war because she calls such conflict *preferable*? She believes one form of warfare or another inevitable because we *prosper*? She believes Indemnie doomed by no greater threat than *prosperity*?"

I felt as Excrucia did. Though I now grasped the isle's plight as my Queen viewed it, I could not conceive that no other answer than war existed. Nonetheless I continued to defend her.

"There is also the peril from the east that I have descried. Your mother's dealings strive to counter both hazards. A realm prepared for civil war may suffice to counter a sea-borne foe."

I did not repeat my earlier assertion that Inimica Phlegathon deVry reasoned as she did because I had forewarned her, that all of her policies were derived from my auguries. Excrucia had countered my claim during our previous exchanges. Nevertheless I knew that the courses which my Queen had chosen rested entirely on my service to her. When the bloodshed began, the fault would be mine.

Yet how else could I have performed my duty? I had exercised my gift honestly. And I had tested and tested and yet again tested my scrying, hoping thereby to discover some misjudgment in myself, some error of interpretation which might undermine the import of my counsels. My blood was not pure. Surely therefore my gift was likewise tainted. Still my mistake—if mistake there was—had eluded me.

Having found none, I had now no other path than perseverance.

For a time, my companion regarded me with a gravid admixture of scorn, disbelief, and bewilderment. Yet she remained her mother's daughter, incisive of mind and prepared for hazard. When at last she spoke, her words conceded much.

"I will consider the dangers of prosperity. And I will measure my mother by the forces arrayed against her as well as by her role in inciting those forces. While I do so, do you require further aid? I can accomplish little, guarded as I am, yet I will attempt whatever you ask of me."

Grateful that she did not altogether spurn me, and thus compelled to truthfulness, I replied, "At present, Excrucia, I have no needs that you do not meet. My fears concerning my Queen and Indemnie are many, yet my greatest fear is that I have sacrificed your friendship."

She made a dismissive gesture, her mouth twisting as though I had uttered foolishness. "Then you need fear nothing. My mother speaks of *trust* to no apparent purpose. I am not her. My trust in *you* is absolute."

At first, I stared at her openly, scarce able to credit my hearing. Almost at once, however, my gaze fell to the floor in relief and shame. "You humble me," I answered like a man broken. Her mother's voice was in my mind. *Then I will demand more of you. Much more when the time requires it.* "Indeed, you terrify me, though such is not your intent. If I do not fail your trust, a day will come—or so I fear—when I will feel driven to ask far more of you than you have yet given."

There she rose to her feet as though her sufferance were at an end. In a tone once again arid and distant, she informed me, "Should that day come, I will confront it forearmed by your concern."

Briefly she rested a hand like a pardon on my shoulder. Then she turned to the door.

Her departure left a hollowness that resembled expended weeping in my chest. My Queen had said, *Will you defy me in this?* And I had dared to reply, *I will.* Still Excrucia had declared her trust absolute. Her plight was as lonely as mine, and as fraught. Yet my life had been spared, though with the promise of future demands beyond my strength. *Her* life held no prospect of a comparable forbearance.

Therefore I shunned tears and self-sorrow. I banished cowardice from my heart. In the name of Excrucia's trust, if not of Inimica Phlegathon deVry's, I flung myself into motion.

Much had been altered within me, as it had within my only friend, and conceivably within the breast and purposes of my Queen. Grim with haste, I sought some sign that might betoken other alterations.

I was my sovereign's Hieronomer, was I not? What other service remained for me to perform?

From the chamber where my supply of chickens, piglets, lambs, and other such small beasts were kept cooped and ready—a supply regularly replenished by one of the Domicile's lesser servants—I selected a bristling rooster at random. Holding its wings pinned, I bore it to the nearest of my sacrificial worktables. There I wrung the rooster's neck, taking care only to spill no drop of blood. Deft with long practice, I plucked feathers enough to expose the flesh from gullet to tail. Then I dropped the still-warm corpse to the table. Rather than arrange it for my convenience, I briefly busied myself selecting and sharpening a suitable blade.

When I returned to the table, I did not hesitate. Glancing at my victim only long enough to ensure that I did not slice my hand, I turned my head away. Deliberately negligent, I made one untidy slash to open the whole of the body.

Such negligence was vital to hieromancy, as it was to other arts of augury. Its purpose was to foil the augur's natural impulse to impose an artificial and therefore misleading interpretation upon the scrying—the impulse, that is, to obtain a desired result rather than an honest one.

Having performed my cut, however, I did not immediately turn to consider my sacrifice—to examine the splash and texture of its fluids, the condition of its organs, the twisting of its entrails, and so forth. For a time, I found myself transfixed by my hand.

I could not release my blade. Whether by some form of cramping, or by some unfamiliar effect of the blood which had drenched my hand to the wrist—or perhaps by simple dread—I had lost command of my fingers. They would not unclose.

Some moments passed as I stared at my hand as though it had performed an action personally abhorrent.

I did not understand.

Nonetheless paralysis was as distasteful as bloodshed. Suddenly vexed, I stabbed the blade into my table with force sufficient to break my grasp. Then, unwilling to consider the import of my unaccustomed helplessness, I turned at once to regard my handiwork.

All was as I had interminably discerned it. An awkward loop of the intestine *there*, a curious eruption of blood *there*, an apparent necrosis of the liver and bowel *there* and *there*. Such signs may have conveyed naught to one ungifted, but to a hieronomer they were as eloquent as language.

As they had ever done, they spoke to me of barbarism and slavery.

So disappointed was I—so disgusted with my impure lineage and inadequate sight and overcome mind—that moments were lost ere I glanced at the rooster's heart and saw it still beating.

The creature was dead. I had slain it with my own hand. More, I had savaged its corpse. Yet its heart beat on.

As I stared dumb-struck, the heart ceased its labor. No further blood pulsed from its severed channels. Nonetheless I had seen it. I had *seen* it.

Thereafter some considerable time appeared to vanish. When I returned to myself, I understood that I had witnessed another in a sequence of unforeseen alterations. Though I was strangely reluctant to consider its significance, I found myself convinced that it expressed a further alteration in me.

In the days that followed, I grew ravenous for tidings, though none were forthcoming. Of activity the Domicile housed a frenetic abundance. One of the guard captains shouted himself mute striving to train some ten or twelve conscripted servants and villagers while the other lashed men familiar with their duties through an arduous iteration of drills for the defense of the house. The Domicile's gate-facing courtyard and walls were crowded from dawn to dusk with exertion, oaths, and sweat. Yet those who labored within the huge edifice were no less driven, and their tasks did not commence at dawn or cease at dusk. Cooks and scrub-maids prepared tables, vessels, utensils, and ovens to produce a vast array of pastries, roasts, confections, and the like. Wains arrived almost hourly to supply the grains, meats, sugars, ales, and wines required by Her Majesty's feast. Chamber servants hastened to ready accommodations for a considerable surfeit of guests. Menials on their knees polished the stone floors of the feasting-hall and the ballroom to an improbable luster, while others took down every tapestry and rolled every rug to beat them clean of dust, and still others waxed every wooden surface. Altogether I could not venture beyond my laborium without finding myself in the path of rushing servants harried by the Majordomo's tongue.

Nevertheless rumors there were in comparable abundance, all believed, none verified, and most contradictory. None of the barons proposed to attend their sovereign's festivities. All of them would come accompanied by their entire households. Excrucia had been seen in the kitchens, or abroad among the halls. She had been gaoled in a tower where none beheld her other than those who conveyed her meals, tasted every dish, and bore away her trays. My Queen herself was everywhere and nowhere. And at all times there was talk of armies. All or few of the barons had mustered forces. All or few intended contests of strength or blood with each other. Men-at-arms were marching even now to crown their ruler's solstice ball with a display of allegiance—or to lay siege against Her Majesty—or they made haste elsewhere to oppose foes striking at distant coasts. My Queen intended her ball as a welcome for those foes, but also as a reward for the barons who drove Indemnie's enemies from us.

Yet of the actual movements of armies—or indeed of ships—I gleaned naught to appease my hunger. Nor did I learn aught of Excrucia or her mother. Where every possibility was averred, none inspired credence. Seven days remained until the ball, and then five, and still I had neither outlet nor relief for my anticipations and dreads.

On the fourth day, however, a knock sounded on the iron of my door. When I opened it, heart leaping, I found myself staring at Slew with his arms laden.

To my sight, he had the look of a headsman. The manner in

which he discarded his burdens at my feet resembled the fall of an axe.

While I gaped in open befuddlement, he essayed my chamber, the tables devoid of victims, the stains of old blood in the wood. No doubt he noted the blade driven into a plank of one table. I had not thought to remove it.

Seeing that his arrival had deprived me of language, he indicated his bundles with a slight twist of one hand—the same hand with which he had caused a dirk to appear at Opalt Intrix's throat. In a tone of veiled amusement or scorn, he pronounced, "Livery."

I managed a croak. "Livery?"

"You will attend," he informed me, "among the household guard."

Peering at his burdens, I saw now that they were the attire and weapons of a guard. A halberd and dirk lay atop a rough-spun hooded cloak as black as my own garments. Boots with iron studs in their soles were there, coarse pantaloons of the same dark fabric as the cloak, a finer surcoat—black also—that may have been silk, an ornamental helm little more than a band for the brow. In addition, I recognized the style of the belt chased with silver. And I gazed agog at the hauberk of boiled leather, a hauberk such as the Domicile's defenders wore, emblazoned in silver with Inimica Phlegathon deVry's coat-of-arms, which was an emblem of a dove with its wings outstretched to both shield and be supported by five pillars representing the barons.

Still gaping, I inquired hoarsely, "Her Majesty wishes me to stand the walls?" The notion was absurd. I knew nothing of such duties—or of such weapons.

"Her Majesty," replied Slew, his tone still veiled, "commands your attendance at the ball."

"The *ball*?" There I met the man's ungiving gaze with my astonishment. "Her Majesty commands me to attend the *ball*?" A notion as ludicrous as defending the house. I was merely her Hieronomer, a servant. I had no place among my Queen's festivities. "Disguised as a *guard*? For what purpose?"

My visitor granted me a small shrug. "Entertainment."

Enter*tain*ment? I endeavored to bleat the word aloud, but my voice had forsaken me. Did she require me to perform like a harlequin for her guests?

There Slew took pity on me. "*Your* entertainment," he explained. "And perhaps enlightenment. Your only task will be to mingle and hear. Attired as a guard, you will encounter no interference. Nor will you be accosted with queries or conversation. You need only move about and give heed and bear your weapons"—briefly he bared his teeth in a humorless smile—"as a man who understands their uses."

His teeth, I observed with some disgust, were as yellow and clotted as a dog's.

Nonetheless I felt an urgent impulse to plead with him. I craved a more forthcoming explanation. However, the sight of his teeth and the memory of his dirk encouraged the recall that he was Inimica Phlegathon deVry's instrument of murder, not her privy counselor. And I had learned that her dealings commonly resembled whims—fanciful words and deeds calculated to conceal her true purposes. I would gain no further insight from Slew, for in all likelihood he had been accorded none.

With an effort that caused tremors in my knees, I straightened my posture and lifted my chin to gaze more directly at my sovereign's bodyguard. Though my voice lacked true self-mastery, I managed a measure of firmness.

"Accept my thanks, Slew. Inform Her Majesty that I will obey her commands with considerable interest."

Returning no better answer than a grunt of disdain, the man withdrew, shutting the door at his back.

Well, I thought while I attempted to calm myself. Well. Had I desired further alterations within the conundrum of Indemnie's dooms? Had I been so reckless? Well, then. Here was one that searched me to the core of my private desires. And while I felt confident that I would make a poor showing as a guard, I began to guess at my Queen's motive for this apparent whim. Somehow—though I could not imagine how—my plain defiance had persuaded her of my loyalty. And I had heard her speak of her underlying purposes. Granted, therefore, the freedom of the ball, I might well come upon some oblique remark or chance reference which would prove more reliable than the host of rumors festering within the Domicile. And if I acquired some noteworthy hint or insight, my Queen could trust that I would disclose it.

If I could but avoid dropping the halberd, or cutting myself with the dirk loose in its sheath, or wandering in my wits, I might discover some better form of service than hieromancy.

The gift is the gift, Opalt Intrix had declared when I had inquired whether an alchemist might attempt hieronomy. *Only purity, talent, and character vary.* From such assertions, I deduced—though my reasoning stood in a quag of uncertainties—that a hieronomer might likewise attempt alchemy. *Alchemists prefer tangible tasks*— Did they indeed? Then I required only a tangible task when the crisis or opportunity with which my Queen had threatened me presented itself. A tangible task—and the strength of will to hazard its completion.

Hardly knowing what was in my mind, I felt certain only that failure would cost hundreds or thousands of lives. In truth, it might bring about the dooms which I yearned to avert. Still I did what I could to ready myself for a bold and nameless deed that would doubtless exceed my abilities, flawed as they were by imperfect lineage, ignorance, and various defects of character.

However, my ability to fret over possibilities without form or substance was not limitless. For perhaps a day and a half, I gnawed to no good effect on thoughts too vague to be named intentions. Thereafter I endeavored to emulate the practicality of alchemists. Donning my unfamiliar livery—a poor fit, but I did not trouble to amend it—I secreted both my commandeered pouch of *chrism* and my best blade under my hauberk, then practiced withdrawing both as swiftly as I could manage. The trick, as I discovered at once, was to do so without either spilling the powder or cutting myself. At first, I was clumsy beyond sufferance or use, having no gift of grace or fluid movement. With repetition, however, I became marginally more adept. And when I could endure no more, I rested for a time, ate a meal provided by one of the Domicile's serving-maids, drank a substantial quantity of wine, replaced the emptied tray outside my door, and resumed my efforts to acquire dexterity.

The day before the ball dawned to gusting winds and mountainous thunderheads. In the distant east, a storm gathered, baleful and rife with omens. Yet it did not strike the isle. While the winds persisted, the clouds themselves drifted apart as though they had lost interest. Toward evening, they renewed their resolve, again seething toward us with condensed malevolence. Then, however, they frayed away once more, seemingly dispersed by the relentless—if somewhat unsteady—winds.

Heartened by such imprecise auguries, I left my chambers clad as myself and accosted the first serving-maid whose path intersected mine. Assuming an imperious air that little resembled my customary demeanor, I instructed her to inform Vail that I wished speech with him. To ease her over-stretched nerves, I added that my desires could be relayed by any of Her Highness' guards, should Vail himself be unavailable. Then I sent her on her way.

Thereafter I spent a portion of the evening sampling the Domicile's disquietude, hoping to find it as changeable as the weather. In that, however, I was disappointed. A dread more explicit than the forecasts implied by winds and weather crowded my Queen's habitation. When I judged that I had allowed time enough for my wishes to reach Vail's ear, I returned to my laborium.

Some hours later, my useless impatience was rewarded with a knock at my door. Hastening to admit Vail, I found the same serving-maid there, trembling as though she feared for her life. "Your pardon, Hieronomer," she blurted in a scramble of alarm. "Vail replies that it is impossible. Her Majesty requires him."

While I scowled my dismay—which no doubt resembled wrath in the girl's sight—she fled. Thus I was left with naught but my own thoughts to ready me for the morrow.

They augured only a blank and uninterpretable peril.

As though echoing my doom-drenched mood, the morn of my Queen's ball was met with massive thunderheads driven toward the isle by a harsh easterly. Yet the threat of storms remained in abeyance, withheld by some vagary of weather. Nevertheless a fever of haste gripped the Domicile, though only the last preparations remained to provide a vent for the Major-domo's ire. Servants ran they knew not where to complete uncertain tasks. The household guards sharpened their blades and oiled their leathers with a look of madness in their eyes. Chamber-maids made a flurry of unnecessary cleaning in the apartments and bedrooms assigned to Her Majesty's guests, while cooks and their underlings verified again and again that they would not be tardy in welcoming arrivals with refreshments and treats.

And the guests came, some with the dawn, others soon thereafter. No doubt they had eyed the thunderheads, and had concluded that they required immediate shelter more than they desired dignity after their various journeys. From the vantage of an oriel overlooking the wide flag-stoned courtyard or bailey which lay between the gated walls and the solid bulk of the house, I watched their arrivals.

First to enter the Domicile was Baron Jakob Plinth with a modest entourage including only his wife—a curious choice, considering that his sovereign had offered to marry him—his five daughters, their immediate servants, and no guards. Of his reported army there was no sign. However, the western vistas below the Domicile on its eminence were complicated by numerous hills, any one of which might serve to conceal from sight hundreds or indeed thousands of men. How he proposed to signal his forces, should he determine to strike, was a nice question for which I had no answer.

To all appearances, however, such queries did not trouble Inimica Phlegathon deVry IV. Cloaked against the wind, and smiling at the prospect of civil war, she greeted Baron Plinth with perfect grace in the courtyard. A model of courtesy, she spoke kindly to his wife—a slim woman no longer young clinging urgently to her husband—then addressed each of his blushing daughters by name. Thereafter she delivered the Baron and his people to the Majordomo, who sweetened her manner to emulate Her Majesty's example as she assembled an escort to guide the Baron and his party to their apartments.

Throughout the encounter, Baron Plinth's manner was at once dour in the extreme and scrupulously correct. By no hint of voice or demeanor did he suggest that he had an army within call. Nor did he deign to acknowledge that any subject of doubt or contention lay between him and his monarch. The only sign of his stance toward Her Majesty's policies was the firmness with which he supported his wife as he followed the Majordomo inward.

An hour later, Baron Praylix Venery approached the gates, surrounded by ten men-at-arms and perhaps twice that many seeming courtesans. Him also my Queen greeted with exquisite politesse, ignoring the obvious affront of his guards while exchanging warm badinage with his women. To his sovereign's courtesies, he replied with a surplus of effusion, simultaneously proclaiming himself innocent in the affairs of the realm and implying that he had much to relate at a more private moment. However, Her Majesty consigned him and his company to the Majordomo without offering him an occasion for his secrets.

Plainly disconcerted, and more than mildly irked, he entered the Domicile speaking volubly to all within reach of his voice.

Hard on Baron Venery's heels came Baron Quirk Panderman. Eschewing some more traditional entourage—apart from a man known to me only as the Baron's companion in drink—

he brought with him teams of drovers to manage five wains laden with tuns of wine. To my Queen's studious warmth, he responding by declaring his resolve to share his finest vintage with Her Majesty's guests. When his wains had been unloaded, and his drovers dismissed, he entered the house reeling, accompanied by the Majordomo's ill-concealed disgust.

Toward noon, Baron Glare Estobate approached on his horse, no doubt delayed in his wonted haste by the inconvenient detail that his cadre of soldiers—a band of twenty men armored, helmed, and armed—marched afoot. By this time, rain had begun to fall. Though the clouds that released it glowered, heavy as a warlord's wrath, the rain itself was little more than a drizzle. It might have resembled a spring shower, kindly and nourishing. Flailed by the chaos of winds within the bailey, however, it stung with the force of small insects. Nevertheless my Queen strode out to meet the Baron as though she were inured to such discomforts. Her only concession to the wet was the hood of her cloak.

Baron Estobate's men did not enter. He left them erecting tents and making camp on the slope below the walls while he rode inward alone. Dismounting before his sovereign, he stood scowling as servants led his horse to the stables. Then he proffered a brusque bow. "In the *rain*, Your Majesty?" he demanded, a man affronted to be greeted thus exposed—or perhaps discomfited by her willingness to stand humbly among the elements.

"For one of my barons?" she replied in a tone that affected

fondness. "I have done as much for Baron Panderman. I will do so much and more for you, my lord Baron."

Now visibly uncomfortable, he performed a second bow, one considerably improved. "Then, Your Majesty," he growled in return, "I must encourage you to seek shelter. Such weather is unkind to women."

Still fondly, she countered, "Yet what of your men, my lord Baron? They will find no relief from the coming storms in their rude camp, and surely no pleasure also. I would welcome all to my festivities. May I not welcome them as well?"

Hearing her, my ears fairly burned. She invited armed and armored men—surely the Baron's advance force—into her house? Where they would have the freedom to betray her hospitality at any word from their lord? With stealth, they might contrive to unbar the gates, thereby at a stroke rendering moot the Domicile's arduously prepared defenses. Yet Inimica Phlegathon deVry offered her welcome as though neither Glare Estobate nor any conceivable army wielded power sufficient to disturb her composure.

For his part, the Baron's eyes appeared to bulge in his head, and his jaw dropped. When he forced his mouth to close, I imagined that I heard the grinding of his teeth. To his sovereign's gracious smile he returned only silence for some moments. When he spoke at last, it was with the sound of a man humiliated—and denied satisfaction.

"My men," he announced, "will do very well where they are.

Their purpose here is to watch over the tranquility of Your Majesty's ball. I will not alter their duties, or transgress upon your kindness, by housing them within your walls."

He may have feared that they would be murdered in the privacy of their bedchambers. Or perhaps he merely felt unmanned by my Queen's impenetrable intentions. In either case, he plainly saw the folly of attempting to match wits with her. Having declared himself, he sealed his mouth. As soon as she conceded with a promising sweetness, "As you wish, my lord Baron," he strode past her to enter the house, leaving her to follow or remain at her pleasure.

Ere she left the courtyard, she cast a glance directly at my vantage some levels above her—gazed toward me as though she had known from the first that I stood witness. Distinctly she nodded like a woman who had fixed my fate in her mind. Then she passed beyond my sight, returning to the shelter and warmth of her home.

Well, then. My Queen had often commanded me to overhear her private encounters. I chose therefore to believe that she approved my presence now. Were I mistaken, I could do naught to unmake my error.

For an hour thereafter, the drizzle became a downpour, a deluge freed from the storm's earlier restraint. When the rains had pummeled the Domicile for a time, however, apparently seeking to damage the very flag-stones of the bailey, the dark seethe overhead parted strangely, allowing the sun to shed its beneficence over the house once more. To left and right, south and north, fierce rainfall streaked golden by sunshine still beat upon the slopes and hills, yet above us stretched a swath of the sky's clearest azure.

Almost at once, vapors began to coil and sway upward from the drenched stones. They rose in questing tendrils and wreaths until the sun dismissed them. And through these mists came riding Thrysus Indolent, last to arrive of the barons.

He had the air of man who had never in life felt the touch of rain or discomfort. Even the hair of his uncovered head appeared undampened.

He entered the courtyard accompanied by no other entourage than half a dozen seeming bodyguards. They were plain-clad men heavy of arm and wary of eye, with sabers at their hips and dirks at their belts. No insignia—indeed, no form of livery—marked their station. Yet their formation around the Baron made manifest their purpose.

As my Queen strode forward to give greeting, parting the mists by her presence, Thrysus Indolent and his men dismounted in near-flawless unison. With the efficiency of much practice, the men delivered their horses to the Domicile's ostlers. Only then did their formation open so that Baron Indolent could emerge to meet his sovereign.

To Her Majesty's welcome—as warm as any, and as impervious to bafflement or insult—the Baron replied with an elegant and apparently gratified bow that nonetheless conveyed a suggestion of mockery. "Your Majesty," he declaimed, "I have come eagerly to your ball, anticipating much of pleasure, and more of interest. I hope that you will indulge an exposed man's caution by extending the hospitality of your house to include my companions."

Ere she answered, she gazed at each of his bodyguards in turn as though committing their visages to memory. Then she said, "They are most certainly welcome to enter my house and attend my ball, my lord Baron." After a brief pause to emphasize her words, she added, "Provided that they attire and comport themselves as guests rather than as ruffians."

To this, he returned an easy chuckle. "They will surely do so, Your Majesty. Indeed, they have come both prepared and strenuously instructed to do so." He, too, paused for emphasis. "However, they will not set aside their weapons. Speaking freely, Your Majesty, I confess that I fear harm to my person." His manner did not suggest fear. "Certainly not from any member of your household," he assured her. "Your hospitality has ever been immaculate, a comfort to even the most timid of your subjects. Yet I have been made aware that Jakob Plinth is wroth with me. As for Glare Estobate, he is at all times wroth with everyone. And Praylix Venery is readily misled by false counsel. I am discomfited by the prospect of a blade in my back while I enjoy your festivities."

My Queen nodded as though she had expected some such peroration. "Then be at ease, my lord Baron," she replied. "Your companions have my leave to retain their weapons. This ball and its pleasures are *mine*"—she stressed the word slightly—"and I will countenance no harm to any of my guests."

There Baron Indolent proffered a second bow deeper than the first. "You are at all times the very model of graciousness, Your Majesty."

So saying, he nodded to his nominal companions. Bowing in their turn, they resumed their formation around their master as he led them, positively bristling with delight, past his sovereign into her house.

At his back, thunderheads closed above the Domicile once more. The rains resumed their vehemence. Distant thunders growled in the east, promising lightnings that were for the present blocked from sight by the high roofs of my Queen's habitation. To my mind, they announced that the crisis of Inimica Phlegathon deVry's efforts to preserve her realm had now truly begun.

Much of the afternoon was spent in a mad rush of activity that I did not trouble myself to observe. Fleeing for shelter beneath the rainfall, more guests arrived in great numbers. Respected merchants, large landholders, prosperous fishmongers, notable mine and timber mill overseers, and no small count of their less recognizable relations entered the house, bringing with them every marriageable maiden and eligible bachelor to whom they could lay claim. And for this multitude, the multitude of my Queen's servants scrambled to provide attendance. Cooks, serving-men, and chamber-maids were run off their feet. Much care was required for the finery of the guests, and much effort for their refreshment. Indeed, some fools had set out from their homes already clad in their most splendid attire, and for them the laundries and clothes-presses and seamstresses labored double to repair the soilure of travel in forbidding weather.

Of all this flurry and even desperation I was aware, albeit indirectly, yet I gave it no heed. Having repaired to my laborium, where quiet reigned despite the storms and frenzy above me, I donned my assigned livery, concealed my pouch of *chrism* and my hieronomer's blade within the hauberk, and hefted my unwieldy halberd. With my Queen's heraldry bright on my chest, I practiced pacing my floors in a grave, unhurried manner—practiced, that is, managing my halberd without either tripping my own feet or harming those guests who would soon surround me. At intervals, I confirmed that my pouch and blade had not shifted inconveniently in their coverts. And when I had achieved a modest confidence that I would not fail Her Majesty through plain blunder, I departed my chambers to seek some vantage among the Domicile's secret passages.

By my reckoning, my Queen's call would not summon her guests to feasting for another hour. The ball itself would not commence until two further hours had passed. First, therefore, I sought some forgotten spyhole which would permit me to observe one party of guests or another in their last preparations. Thereafter, having no place at the feast, where all the guests in their seats would be both observed and effectively sequestered among their immediate companions, I proposed to watch as well as I could for movements and gatherings in the now presumably deserted regions of the house. Further, I must confess that I hoped for some glimpse of Excrucia. My fondest and most foolish wish was to snatch some moments of converse with her ere the ball began.

In these latter desires, I was frustrated. Indeed, I gained naught beyond an increase of both weariness and anxiety. In the first of my purposes, however, I found a measure of success. Treading narrow corridors which I had not previously explored, I encountered a series of chinks in the wall. They were widely spaced for some distance, and each provided a view into the common or sitting room of an apartment prepared for one of my Queen's most honored guests, the five barons and their immediate families or companions.

For a moment, however, I did not enjoy my advantage. Slew was there ahead of me, and his presence checked me. I thought to withdraw at once, yet I was forestalled. Taking note of my arrival, he gestured a command to advance.

Thus condoned, I set my eye to the nearest spyhole, though Slew stood at the fourth.

Within I saw Baron Plinth seated rigid as my halberd in an armchair with his fists knotted on the rests. Beside him sat his wife, leaning close to him and whispering urgently. Indeed, she appeared to seek some private boon or course of action that he sternly denied. Unfortunately her words were inaudible to me.

In a cluster apart, the Baron's five daughters chattered together, both flustered and eager, seeming younger than their years. Yet they were all attired as available women in search of husbands. Their gowns, though not elaborately expensive, displayed considerable attention to both provocation and modesty.

As I was unable to divine the subject of contention between the Baron and his lady, I moved on.

At the next chink, I did not linger. It granted me a glimpse of Baron Panderman and his companion as they waved flagons about, singing ribald songs with strenuous enthusiasm. In the interval since their arrival, they had amended their raiment but not their conduct, and one glimpse of them was more than I required.

At the third spyhole also, one glimpse sufficed for me. In the common room, I beheld Baron Venery and several of his women in various states of undress apparently seeking to exhaust themselves ere the more public festivities began. Grimacing to myself— perhaps because I had no acquaintance with such sport—I approached Slew.

I had learned to share my Queen's beliefs. Indemnie's prosperity was an edged blessing.

At Slew's post, a single glance through the chink justified his attention. This sitting room had been provided for either Glare Estobate or Thrysus Indolent, though which I could not determine, for both were present. And they were alone. Every door to the apartment's bedrooms was shut, as was that to the outer hallway.

That they were engaged in intense converse was plain. Unfortunately Baron Estobate stood with his fists on his hips and his back to the spyhole. Though his posture and manner suggested ferocity, his voice did not reach me.

However, Baron Indolent faced the wall behind which I regarded him. Though he endeavored to comport himself as a man poised for grim hazards, the eagerness in his gaze was as distinct as his words.

"And I repeat, my old friend," insisted Thrysus Indolent, accompanying his speech with gestures of placation, "there is no cause to be precipitate. All is in readiness. Any premature act will harm our designs. You need only await the signal, and events will transpire as we have prepared them."

Glare Estobate barked some demand, to which his companion replied with a shrug. "Who can say? We have readied ourselves for a variety of eventualities. Only the stars know which will first occur. That woman herself may provide an occasion, if our allies do not."

With ill-concealed impatience, Baron Indolent continued, "Should some clearer sign fail us, however—" He raised his right arm before his companion. At his wrist, the ruffles of his shirt, pale burgundy in color, showed themselves beyond the deeper purple of his brocaded coat sleeve. There among them peeped a corner of purest white muslin. "I will contrive to drop my handkerchief where you cannot fail to see it. That will be our signal in the absence of a better one."

Baron Estobate's reply was guttural in the extreme, yet I heard—or perhaps only imagined—the word *fireworks*.

The smaller man flapped a dismissive hand. "My friend, you are too fretful. My men have already secreted themselves near the walls, or at high western windows. The blaze of their missiles cannot be doused by mere rain. Upon command, our summons will brighten even these louring heavens."

At my side, Slew muttered some obscenity to which I gave no heed. The exchanges within the sitting room consumed me.

For some moments, Glare Estobate spoke in his harsh low growl. When he fell silent, Thrysus Indolent answered with an air of sadness, "On that point, I confess myself uncertain. Good Jakob Plinth is as predictable as sunset and moonrise. That woman, alas, is not. Her whims and gambols outstrip my foresight. They baffle the very stars. Should she proclaim or reveal nothing to sway Plinth's rectitude, he will stand with us. His given word is his law. As you know, however, his word was not given without provisos. Beneath his ire lies a staunch desire to remain that woman's subject. If she contrives to strike an appeasing note upon his honor, he may bend at last to his shrew-wife's counsels—and bend at a moment untimely for our purposes.

"Nevertheless I am comforted by the knowledge that his forces await the same signal which commands your men." There Baron Indolent grinned. "Even Jakob Plinth in a transport of rectitude cannot countermand our missiles if he does not live to do so."

The sound of Baron Estobate's gritted laughter chilled me. I had imagined a plethora of challenges from the barons, some honest, others feigned. Yet I had not conceived that a relish for plain murder might determine Indemnie's fate.

However, Thrysus Indolent was not chilled. Briefly he and his comrade in treachery clasped each other's arms. Then, grinning, the smaller man took his leave. Muttering darkly, Glare Estobate turned to one of the apartment's bedrooms. Thus he passed from sight.

My knees wobbled as I withdrew from the spyhole. While I leaned my weakness on the opposite wall, small blots swam in my sight as though I had neglected breath. I had learned too much to master myself quickly. For that reason, a moment or three fled from me ere I recognized that Slew stood before me like a man poised for killing.

"Gather yourself, Hieronomer." His low snarl was a slap. "We must act swiftly. Will you bear what we have heard to Her Majesty?"

Reeling inwardly, I stared up at him. "Without her summons? How?" I meant, How could I convey that my need to speak with her was urgent? With the feast close upon us, and no other man in martial livery present, she would be walled off with servants and guests, beyond my immediate reach. I would have to persuade one or several of her overworked attendants to deliver my message. "You have her ear. You must contrive to speak with her."

Through his teeth, Slew swore at me. "I cannot. I have no time. I must find and end those men who hold Indolent's signal missiles, and they will be well hidden."

"No!" I blurted without pause for thought. "Do not!"

Upon the instant, Slew's demeanor became as fatal as a dirk at my throat. "Not?" he demanded. "Do you also betray Her Majesty, Hieronomer?"

"*No*," I insisted, panting. "No. Never. I serve her with my life. But you must *think*." I struggled to do as I urged him. "There is much to consider. The failure of their signal will warn those barons that they are discovered. That in itself is of little concern. Yet Her Majesty, Slew—"

I beat upon my brow with my fists, striving to impose a measure of coherence on my thoughts. "She is *aware* of armies, Slew. She is *aware* of Indolent's conniving with Estobate and Plinth. She has drawn the barons to her for some purpose that will serve Indemnie. And treason within the realm is not her sole consideration. She has cause to fear other foes, foes against which ready armies are her only defense. If those armies are not summoned—"

Slew cut me off. "*What* foes?"

I could have wept in frustration. "I know not. I cannot name them. I cannot account for them. Yet I have *seen* them. A darkness in the east seeks to enslave us. How, I know not. *Why*, I

know not. Nonetheless I am certain of it. Two dooms await
Indemnie, and treachery is not the greater. Even proud, clever,
despicable Thrysus Indolent may set aside betrayal when he is
threatened with slavery."

In the gloom of the narrow passage, Slew was no more than
a looming threat to my sight. With a twitch of his fingers, he
might snap my neck. His instant dirk might open my throat
ere I saw it move. Yet I held his bitter gaze without shrinking.
The crisis of my service had begun, and of my Queen's reign,
and of Excrucia's life. It could not be answered by cowardice.

Slew paused there a moment. He desired haste, however, and
did not delay himself with rumination. Abruptly he announced,
"I will speak with Her Majesty. I will report your counsels. This
choice must be hers."

At once, he strode away, leaving me slack-limbed. In my brav-
est dreams, I had not imagined myself able to withstand a con-
frontation with Inimica Phlegathon deVry's most trusted dealer
of death.

After a time, however, I recalled that this passage held no
further interest for me. Also I no longer conceived that I might
spy upon covert movements within the Domicile. Doubtless
Baron Indolent's men were even now in their hiding places,
silent and ready. No entourage had accompanied Baron Estobate past the gates of the house, and concerning the Barons
Panderman and Venery I had no cause for suspicion. As for
Baron Plinth, I was confident of him to this extent, that he had

no war-like minions among his company. He would not thus expose his family to peril. Their safety depended upon his scrupulous detachment from Thrysus Indolent's immediate machinations. In addition, I imagined that my Queen would not thank me for conniving against—or, indeed, for addressing directly—that stringent man on her behalf.

By such reasoning, I gave myself leave to concentrate on a search for Excrucia.

In that quest, to my dismay, I failed utterly. I carried no map of the house in my head, and the turnings, cul-de-sacs, and branches of the passages and stairs multiplied my disorientation. Being unable to determine my own location within the Domicile, I could not gauge where I might be in relation to any of the towers where the object of my heart might be imprisoned or guarded. In simple truth, I was too ignorant to find my way.

Time passed while I scurried here and there to no purpose, a mouse lost in the maze of the walls. At this hour, the feast had surely begun. Ere long, I would be expected in the ballroom— and I was no longer confident that I could retrace my path to more familiar regions.

Fortunately I stumbled by chance into the passage which had often admitted me to my Queen's public boudoir. Thereafter I knew my immediate route. Well before my appointed appearance, I reentered the servants' corridors several levels below my Queen's festivities. Now I required only the flustered indication of a serving-maid and the curt nod of a butler to direct me until I gained the ballroom.

———

That hall was vast beyond my preconceptions, high of ceiling and long in shape—a space of size sufficient to accommodate all of Her Majesty's guests' and many of the Domicile's servants' dancing. If rugs had previously warmed the stones of the floors, they had been removed to facilitate the steps of gavottes and allemandes. Around the walls were an abundance of chairs and divans to rest those who did not dance, or to provide respite for those who did. At each end of the hall, hearths which I might otherwise have entered upright held flames fed by logs like the boles of trees, blazing to dispel the residual chill of so much stone, and also of the storms which even now assailed the house. Ornate sconces high in the walls supported ponderous lamps to augment the illumination. Banners as large as rooftops hung from the rafters to display the heraldry of the seven Queens of Indemnie and the five barons. And at one end of the hall, between the hearth and the wall, a score or more of chairs had been arrayed for the musicians, some of whom had already gathered to unpack and tune their instruments.

Though the guests were yet to come, I was not the first man in livery to arrive. Nor was I the last. When all had gathered, eight guards who could ill be spared from the Domicile's defense attended the hall. Two stood to open the massive doors of graven mahogany which would admit the feasters to the ball. Four watched over smaller doors that no doubt provided access to the more private conveniences of the house. Several other doors marked the walls, but these were intended for the use of the servants and did not require men to open and close them. Thus two guards—or three, if I included myself—were left free to wander where they willed. Their nominal duties—and mine, at least by appearance—were to intervene in altercations between men in their cups, to assist guests overcome by excessive indulgence, and to aid those who suffered some mishap in the intricate dances. In addition, I had my own singular instructions. And all of us served the tacit purpose of reminding the guests by our presence that they were ruled by Inimica Phlegathon deVry.

The demeanor of the guards at this time was casual in the extreme, nonchalant or disgruntled according to their individual perceptions of the Domicile's straits. At intervals, they treated me to distrustful glances. Soon, however, the last of the musicians arrived. And when they had taken their places, settled themselves, and begun to play a soft introit, the Majordomo entered. At once, the guards assumed postures of correct attention. Thereafter neither they nor the Majordomo—nor, indeed, the musicians—regarded me at all.

As I have remarked, the Majordomo was ever a shrill harridan, a veritable harpy of supervision and meticulous effort. On this occasion, therefore, I was surprised to see her resplendent in a dowager's finery, all cuffs and ruffles, laces and skirts, necklaces, earrings, bangles. Her colors were royal purple and demure ecru, and to her lips she had positively nailed a pleasant smile. Briefly she scanned the entire hall with a glance both cursory and penetrating. Then she clapped her hands as though she imagined that she had not yet gained our heed.

In a voice carefully modulated, she announced, "The ball of Her Majesty Inimica Phlegathon deVry IV begins."

So saying, she stepped aside. Obedient to her signal, the guards opened the hall's formal doors. Amid a confused clamor of conversation and eagerness, the first of my Queen's revelers arrived.

So high within the house, I was able to hear the muffled rumble of thunder and the softer thrash of rain until the accumulating noise of the guests masked other sounds.

First in order of precedence, though not of entrance, came Baron Jakob Plinth with his wife and daughters. Within the general swirl of skirts, gowns, and badinage, Thrysus Indolent entered, having claimed the arm and companionship of a maiden unknown to me, a young woman much exposed by her raiment. Behind him followed Baron Panderman and his comrade, both with their legs splayed to preserve their balance. At their backs strode Baron Glare Estobate alone, glowering like a man who would have preferred to expend his energies among slatterns or sheep. And last came Baron Praylix Venery in the midst of an escort of women whom he pleased—or perhaps merely piqued—with a spate of gossip and rumors, some or most no doubt scurrilous.

Ahead, among, and behind the barons walked or scampered the throng of my Queen's other guests. All had presumably been formally introduced at the feast. Now they eschewed such niceties in their anticipation of dancing, courting, and other forms of excitement. They entered with a bare minimum of dignity, talking, laughing, or complaining together as though they expected the ball to be the summit of the year—or perhaps of their lives entire.

Honesty compelled me to confess, if only to myself, that I had never seen the like. The village where I had been reared had evinced no desire for such doings. And since entering my Queen's service, my experiences had been restricted to the serving regions of the house, the secret passages, and my laborium. Some few trysts among the serving-maids and scullions had ill prepared me to comprehend the energies which goaded these revelers to their present fever of attraction and repulsion, modesty and concupiscence.

Now I could not imagine a mask better suited to disguise traitors and conceal betrayal.

As though to confirm my observation, thunder sounded through the ceiling, a blast of force sufficient to disquiet the high windows.

When most of the guests had gained the hall, the musicians ceased their playing. Decorum dictated that the ball itself could not commence until Her Majesty commanded it, and she had yet to appear. In her absence, the guests milled about, expanding their presence to fill much of the ballroom, entertaining themselves with quips, persiflage, and assignations, and supplying their eagerness with goblets of wine delivered by a flotilla of simply clad serving-maids. Prompt to my duty, I began to circulate among the flows and eddies of the gathering, taking what I hoped was unobtrusive care to remain within hearing of Glare Estobate and Thrysus Indolent. My two comrades in livery also wandered here and there, but they paid no apparent heed to any particular coterie of guests.

Within that press, the Majordomo was conspicuous by her withdrawal. She stood apart with her back to the wall near the musicians, observing everything, acknowledging nothing. No doubt she, like the guests, awaited her sovereign.

For my part, I awaited Excrucia. I had begun to fear that her mother would forbid her presence. Indeed, I deemed it probable that Excrucia had not partaken of the feast. How could my Queen be certain that one or another of her foes would not again stoop to poison? Yet the necessity of a taster would have been an intrusive reminder that the safety of the Domicile was an illusion. It would have consorted ill with Her Majesty's private intentions.

Remembering my duty, however, I also remained alert for some indication of the sign that Baron Indolent had discussed with Baron Estobate—the sign that would launch their treachery.

Without forewarning, the Majordomo again clapped her hands, and at once the musicians struck up a regal announcement. As one, the guests turned toward the great doors.

At the entrance to the hall stood Her Majesty Inimica Phlegathon deVry and her daughter, Excrucia.

As ever, my Queen outshone all other women in beauty and

splendor. In a gown of palest green designed in every detail to emphasize both her lush womanliness and her royal stature, she accepted the accolades of her subjects, smiling with the beneficence of a summer sun. A choker of diamonds encircled her neck, ornamenting her loveliness with dazzles. From her ears hung rubies like drops of the earth's blood, while the emerald set within her royal coronet enhanced the auburn luster of her tresses. Altogether she was more than a woman—more, indeed, than a sovereign. She was an icon of every blessing that provided Indemnie with wealth, prosperity, and independence.

Yet her arrival won no more than a glance from me. My gaze was fixed upon Excrucia, for I had never before beheld her so bedizened, so simply and yet so elegantly clad, or so entirely desirable.

Her only ornaments were the net of pearls in her hair and the bracelets of sapphire at her wrists, embellishments too unassuming to detract from the startling effect of her raiment. Where every other woman present wore some variation of a gown—dresses that both offered and withheld their charms—Excrucia was attired from neck to toe in a fitted silken sheath of deepest cyan, a garment that appeared to shimmer with every movement. However, it was neither forbidding nor austere. A slit from collarbone to navel teased the eye, while similar cuts on either side below her waist revealed enticing glimpses of her legs. So clad, she was farther from *plain* in my sight than any living creature.

And for the brightness of her gaze I had no adequate language. I knew only that it entranced me utterly. The lost and grieving girl with whom I had last spoken was gone, hidden away at her mother's command—or by her own resolve. In that girl's place stood a woman neither humbled nor self-doubting. I had long known her intelligent, insightful, humorous, studious, concerned, courageous, even severe, but until that moment I had not known her ravishing.

When my Queen was content with the approbation of her guests, she made a gracious show of presenting her daughter, a gesture that earned fresh appreciation from the assembly of men and women, gallants and maidens, all openly astonished. Thereafter the Majordomo gave a new command to the musicians, who at once launched themselves into a lively air that pleaded for dancing. Within moments, half or more of the guests were twirling each other around the hall, while those too elderly, infirm, or captious to be seduced by such pleasures withdrew gradually to the walls, some standing to observe the dancers, others resting their bones in the chairs and on the divans.

Among the dancers none was more prominent than Baron Panderman, whose unsteady bulk remained upright only because one luckless maiden or another supported it. However, Baron Venery with his shrill laughs and jibes challenged his drunken peer for notice. In contrast, Baron Indolent glided discreetly across the floor, graceful, elegant, and full of self-appreciation, with his young woman obviously charmed in his arms. Solitary in a corner, Baron Estobate glowered at the proceedings, while Baron Plinth sat without visible emotion beside his wife on one of the divans.

My Queen herself did not dance. Playing the part of a distinguished hostess, at once too grand to be approached and too modest to offer herself, she floated apparently at random among her guests, smiling at all, engaging with none. Excrucia, however, was immediately swept away by a sequence of ambitious swains, each seemingly bent upon claiming her as his own.

For my part, I continued to wander as I had been instructed. By a strict effort of will, I prevented my eyes from following Excrucia wherever she went. My duties were serious in all sooth, and I schooled myself to attend them seriously. Therefore I assumed the pose of a mere emblem, a symbol of my sovereign's rule, and pursued my purpose with a grave tread, neither pausing to overhear nor neglecting to give heed. Yet whenever my gaze chanced to encounter Excrucia, she returned it with an air of awareness—indeed, with a distinct nod—as though she knew my mind and wished me to understand that she was prepared for whatever I might require of her.

With the passing of time and music, waltzes became intricate patterns of bows and sweeps for which I had no name. At other moments, younger participants pranced to the strains of gavottes, joined by their elders only when the musicians offered more stately allemandes. If Thrysus Indolent or Glare Estobate engaged in any conversations more private than common courtesies, I did not observe them, though I often paced near them.

Altogether the ball offered no hint that it might at any moment degenerate into disaster.

Nevertheless my apprehension grew with the lateness of the hour. My Queen had yet to announce the outcome of her many proposals of marriage. Indolent and Estobate had indicated that they awaited only some nameless sign to launch their betrayal. For differing reasons, Baron Plinth also no doubt waited, though his demeanor acknowledged no possibility of impatience. Thunder grumbled in the hall with increasing ferocity, and at every clap and burst, Her Majesty glanced aside as though in fright quickly concealed—as though she anticipated a fearsome intrusion that only she had foreseen. Yet nothing untoward occurred.

Having no other outlet for my suspense, I assumed the temerity to step so near to Baron Indolent that our shoulders brushed. He did not appear to notice me. His attention was on his companion, his eyes feasting openly on her scarcely constrained bosom. When I moved beyond him with no murmur of apology to attract his regard, I held crumpled in my fist a square of white muslin from his sleeve, the handkerchief that he had intended as a last signal for Baron Estobate if all others failed.

Childishly proud of my daring, I gazed for a moment at my Queen as though I sought her approval. However, she did not take note of my appeal—and in any case she could not know what I had done. Rather her attention was fixed across the hall on the Majordomo. Apparently she desired that woman to meet her stare.

Almost immediately, the Majordomo did so. Turning to the musicians, she gestured for silence.

They halted their efforts in mid-strain. Many of the dancers stumbled as though they had been upheld by the music and could not manage their feet without it. Others exclaimed in surprise, while some over-excited youths shouted for the music to resume. Then, a few at first, the rest in a sudden rush, all eyes turned to Inimica Phlegathon deVry.

At that moment, a blare of thunder struck with such force that the entire ballroom shook. Thick as mist, dust drifted down from the rooftrees.

So startled was I that several heartbeats passed ere I understood—well, anything at all. In a daze, I saw my Queen flinch outright. I saw Baron Estobate run instantly from the hall. I saw Baron Indolent wheel from his companion—wheel not to pursue Glare Estobate, but rather to approach Her Majesty. Obliquely I perceived that Baron Plinth had leaped to his feet and now followed Thrysus Indolent toward my Queen, apparently seeking to forestall his fellow conspirator. Yet I comprehended naught until the realization found me that no natural thunder conveyed such deep destructiveness. No thunder of the world had the power to disturb the solid stone of the Domicile.

From some distance, Jakob Plinth shouted, "Matrimony, Your Majesty! We must speak of your demeaning proposals!"

Nearer at hand, Baron Indolent called, "Your games are at an end, woman. Now every truth will be revealed."

Yet my Queen gave no heed to them, or to any of her guests.

Her gaze studied the ceiling, and in her mien and posture I beheld that which I would not have believed possible for her. She radiated plain dread.

Behind her, chaos reigned as every reveler clamored for comprehension. What had gone awry, they knew not. They knew only their monarch's fear—and perhaps Plinth's demands or Indolent's assertions. Such things herded them toward confusion as though they were cattle.

A second blast distressed the stones. It had the sound of an explosion—a sound that called to mind the ruin of houses.

Suddenly over the tumult of the guests came a shout from the Majordomo. In a voice stentorian as a trumpet, she commanded, "Clear the hall! Return to your rooms! You must all leave the hall and seek shelter in your rooms!"

For no more than a moment, her words silenced the clamor. Then consternation resumed with renewed urgency. "*Matrimony*, Your Majesty!" insisted Baron Plinth. "You have dealt falsely with us!" Yet the loud dismay of the gathering muffled his outcry. If Baron Indolent spoke again, I did not hear him.

The guards at the doors had left their posts, hastening toward their sovereign. One contrived to intercept Jakob Plinth's rush. With the barest minimum of courtesy, the guard redirected the Baron toward the main doors. For my part, I strove to block Thrysus Indolent's path, but too many flustered or indignant revelers intervened. Fortunately another guard succeeded where I failed. This man did not scruple to grasp the Baron's shoulders and thrust him aside from Her Majesty.

Again the Majordomo raised her shout. "Clear the *hall*!" she repeated. "Be orderly! Return to your rooms!"

Some of the guests complied. Others elected to dither. A few apparently preferred fainting.

A third booming crash resounded from the walls. Now the uncertainty of the guests became a frenzy of departure. Some fool yelped, "The house falls!"—an unthinking outburst that served nonetheless to goad the more recalcitrant members of the throng into motion. Obstacles cleared themselves from my path, and once again I saw my Queen clearly.

She no longer regarded the ceiling. Nor did she betray any lingering residue of dread. Rather she fixed her gaze upon me, imperious in her self-command, and sure of her courses. "Find Excrucia," she instructed me distinctly. "Bring her to me."

Confident of my obedience, she turned at once to a near-by guard. "Summon Slew. Summon Vail. There is betrayal among us."

Stricken of eye, the man forced his way from the hall through the panicked mob of guests.

No less prompt, I flung myself to a new heading against the current of fervid departures. The guests were a great many, and I could not scan the hall effectively while they interrupted my view. Fortunately I was aided by Excrucia's dramatic raiment. Off to one side, I caught a glimpse of deep cyan, a flash of leg. At once, I shouldered a matron aside, insinuated myself through a cluster of frantic maidens, and blocked an ash-visaged gallant with my halberd, which I then cast from me. In a moment, I contrived to catch Excrucia's wrist, halting her amid the press of fleeing limbs and bodies.

She was not panicked. Indeed, she did not appear to know fear. My unexpected grasp merely startled her. When she turned to me, her expression offered nothing more than her endearing frown of concentration.

"What transpires, Mayhew?" she inquired with such calm— or perhaps with such focused discipline—that I was scarce able to hear her. "Does the house fall? Are we betrayed?"

"Yes," I gasped, meaning both, Yes, we are betrayed, and, Yes, the house of the Phlegathon deVrys falls. However, I had neither breath nor clarity for a fuller reply, and in any case much that I might have said was little more than speculation and instinct. Warfare and barbarism from within the realm. Enslavement from the east. Instead I panted merely, "Her Majesty requires you. She will explain when she can."

To this unsatisfactory response Excrucia gave no more than a firm nod. Without delay, she joined my efforts to brunt a path through the diminishing crowd.

I was hardly aware that I still clutched her wrist. I knew only that I was determined not to be parted from her.

Harassed by the Majordomo, the greater portion of the guests had now shoved or squeezed their way from the ballroom, occasionally trampling the fallen. With the assistance of the guards, the lash of the Majordomo's tongue and the compulsion of her voice drove the rest before her. Among the distraught, only Thrysus Indolent declined to be dislodged. Baron Plinth with all his family had been expelled. By the expedient of tripping one guard, however, and slapping another aside, Indolent succeeded at advancing toward Her Majesty despite the last flurry of escapes.

"I warned you," he snapped as he drew near, "as clearly as I dared. Your reign has been madness piled upon folly. I could endure no more. *Indemnie* could endure no more. Your heedlessness requires this outcome."

Her Majesty did not deign to respond. She spared no more than a glance for the Baron's self-righteousness. Her regard was fixed on Excrucia. As I urged my friend and ally forward, my Queen scrutinized her daughter, apparently assuring herself that the young woman was unharmed. Then in an iron voice as though she addressed the hall rather than any single person, she demanded, "I have summoned Slew. I have summoned Vail. Where are they?"

As though called into existence by his sovereign's need, Slew appeared in the formal doorway. Parting the last of the guests by plain strength, he came to Her Majesty. Without preamble or courtesy, he said, "Vail follows. We were delayed by distance."

Shaking her head, my Queen dismissed any possible explanation or apology. "You discovered the men holding Indolent's signal missiles?"

The fact that the Baron could hear her caused her no visible concern.

"We did," Slew answered.

"You left them unharmed?"

"As you commanded. Trusted men keep watch on them."

"Are they aware that they are watched?"

"I think not. We have been soft and wary."

"Good. We must trust that your men will also be wary of Estobate. He has fled to ready his forces." Her Majesty spared one more glance for Thrysus Indolent, perhaps gauging the shift of emotions across his mien. Then she instructed Slew, "Bring him." A disdainful toss of her head indicated the Baron. "We cannot delay. Vail must follow as he can."

Shifting her regard to Excrucia—and to me—she made her wishes explicit. "Accompany me. We will gaze upon this threat."

Immediately she strode from the hall with Slew at her side. The man's brutal grip on his prisoner's arm elicited a gasp from the Baron, who then elected submission rather than resistance.

For the briefest moment, Excrucia and I shared a gaze of bewilderment and resolution, though I must confess that she was both more bewildered and more resolute than I. Thereafter we hastened in her mother's wake.

Still I held her. I found, however, that I no longer gripped her wrist. Somehow we had entwined our fingers so that we might hold each other.

Of our shared clasp she appeared unaware. I was altogether too conscious of it.

Though we moved at a swift pace through halls unfamiliar to me, I guessed our destination without difficulty. High on its outward sides, the Domicile was surrounded by walled balconies as wide as avenues. It was customary—so I had been informed—for high-born men and women to walk there in pleasant weather, relishing the various vistas or each other. To the east, of course, lay only waves and water, the featureless expanse of the sea. To both south and west, the Domicile on its height overlooked sparsely inhabited hills and valleys, some punctuated with copses, small fields, and hamlets, others not. To the north, however, the balcony provided a broad view of the town which the first Queen had named Venture, the town which manned, tended, supplied, and entertained Indemnie's principal harbor. There fishing vessels, pleasure craft, and two-masted schooners plied the waters, though at night—and in such weather—all would be safely secured at the many piers that served the docks.

Some incomprehensible bombardment from the west may have been possible, perhaps by catapult. We had cause to believe that one or more armies camped hidden in those valleys. Nevertheless I dismissed the notion. To my knowledge, all Indemnie possessed no engines of war capable of delivering the blasts which had shaken the ballroom. In addition, the terrain there was inconvenient for any assault, lying so far below the house. By such reasoning, I felt confident that my Queen aimed for the northern balcony. If she feared some new *threat*, it would only be visible to the north.

Another thunder-like crash sounded at a greater distance. Halls led to stairs, to further halls and yet more stairs. Excrucia strode at my side with her jaw set and her brows knotted. For my part, I chose to number my blessings rather than to question my boldness. I could readily believe that never again in life would I enjoy such intimacy with my companion. Therefore I elected to treasure it while it endured.

The next blast caused the stones beneath my feet to lurch. It was nearer, louder, more ominous. I heard—or perhaps imagined—shattered rock falling to smite the waves at the base of the Domicile's seaward cliff. Then a broad entryway to the balcony appeared before us. For the space of no more than a heartbeat or two, I wondered whether Inimica Phlegathon deVry clad in her festive splendor would dare exposure to the storm. Then with a snort of derision I dismissed the notion. No deluge, however wind-whipped and punitive, would daunt my Queen on the occasion of her reign's betrayal.

True to my expectations, she hastened into the open air and proceeded directly to the balcony wall so that she might gaze out over Venture.

Fortunately the downpour had lessened during the ball, though the winds and lightnings had not. Through curtains of rain and acrid gusts of strange smoke, the other observers and I were able to descry the harm wrought upon the town—and the cause of that harm.

Mere fathoms beyond the longest piers, a tall-masted ship black as night lay at anchor. At first, wiping my eyes repeatedly, I perceived only that this vessel was half again larger than any ship built on the isle, and that its outlines were unfamiliar in ways difficult to name. But then a long jet of flame streaked the rain, an appalling boom echoed the storm's thunder, a shipwright's merchantry near the wharves flew apart in splinters and fire, and my gaze was drawn to examine the foredecks of the intruding craft more closely.

There I beheld five massive devices, apparently of iron, with heavy tubes jutting from them. Attended by teams of sailors or marines, these devices were rolled back and forth, and their tubes raised or lowered, presumably to adjust their aim. One of these had been set facing the Domicile with its tube angled higher than the others. While I gaped at it, the tube spoke flame and fierce concussion. An instant later, some projectile struck the cliff below the house—far below. Stone and fire sprang from the impact while our edifice trembled as though gripped by a momentary ague. Yet I saw no indication of damage, felt none. The smoke of some eruptive many times more violent than the powder which carried fireworks aloft passed through the rain to sting my eyes and nostrils.

The other devices did not trouble themselves to hurl malice at our unattainable eminence. Rather they delivered cruel imprecations and ruin to various regions of the town.

There their destructiveness was terrible to witness. Entire buildings were torn apart. Merchantries, stables, warehouses, pubs, inns, chandleries, garment and sail makers, residences, houses of entertainment, all were helpless before the blasts. People ran everywhere, some then trampled by squalling horses, others impaled by or buried under debris. They, too, were helpless. No event in Indemnie's history had prepared them to confront such a catastrophe.

Swallowing bile, I understood that the enemy vessel was entirely capable of reducing the whole town and much of its inhabitants to rubble and charred meat in a matter of hours.

Excrucia had released my hand to brace herself upon the wall as though she feared that she might plunge to her death. Rain-matted hair veiled her mien. I could not guess what dreads filled her mind, what fates she considered. Rainfall had soaked her raiment, causing it to cling more intimately to her form—a sight which I might otherwise have coveted, but which I now ignored. If she feared for herself, I feared for her more.

Too much alarmed for any other word or movement, I turned to my Queen—and was taken aback by the individuals assembled around her.

Four guards were there. Them I had expected. And I was not displeased to see that Slew still clenched Thrysus Indolent's arm painfully. But I was surprised by Baron Panderman's presence. Hulking like a bear, he stood with his back to the wall of the house, a glare of madness or drink in his eyes. Near him was Baron Plinth, rigidly outraged, and undiminished by the drenching of his face and apparel. He appeared to be awaiting speech with his sovereign. And Vail also had arrived. His habitual erect carriage had deserted him. He stood somewhat hunched to one side before Her Majesty as though he sought to protect the long cut streaming below his ribs. Red stains gathered in the pools surrounding his boots.

In the entryway, the Majordomo barred all others from the balcony.

As I turned, Inimica Phlegathon deVry did the same, putting her back to Venture's devastation. In appearance, she reflected the carnage of the town. Her elaborate tresses had become sodden tangles, and her coronet sat askew. All her jewels had surrendered their brilliance to the rain. The former magnificence of her gown resembled a bitter defeat, drooping precariously from her shoulders as though to deny the effect for which it had been created.

Yet she remained regal withal, imperious in her posture and her hard gaze, chin and head held high, anger flashing. For Jakob Plinth she spared one brief glance, for Quirk Panderman another. When she spoke, she addressed Vail.

In a tone to pierce the rain, she observed, "You are wounded."

With a small wince, Vail replied, "That Estobate is skilled with a blade."

"And the man himself?" inquired my Queen.

Vail bared his teeth. "Dead."

She frowned. "That will stir up his forces." Then she shrugged. "It was necessary." Continuing to ignore the barons present, she asked, "Are you able to serve me still?"

Vail held his grin. "Pity the man who hinders me." A moment later, however, he sagged. "But I cannot draw a bow."

To this admission she gave no apparent heed. Instead she demanded of all who stood within earshot, "Tell me of those fiery engines. What are they? How can they be silenced?"

I positively gaped when the only response came from Baron Panderman.

"They are cannon," he rumbled without courtesy or circumspection. "They use the same powder that we use for fireworks, but much concentrated. The powder sends an iron ball from the barrel. Some or all of the balls are hollow, filled with the same powder, and supplied with fuses. They burn what they do not break."

There he appeared to recall that he addressed his sovereign—reminded, perhaps, by her frank stare. Ducking his head, he added more softly, "My house has documents. Records. The oldest describe cannon. Our lost homeland had them.

"I did not read the records. They were read to me by a scribe. It is an old custom of my house. I find it soothing." A moment later, he mumbled, "Your Majesty."

My Queen dismissed his defects of etiquette. "Are we able to devise such engines ourselves?"

Now Quirk Panderman squirmed. "If I understood my scribe, the principles are simple. We make fireworks. We shape iron. Therefore we can produce cannon. But the design, Your Majesty—"

Baron Indolent cut him off. Pleased despite his pain, Thrysus Indolent interjected, "It will be a laborious undertaking. You have not time enough. When that vessel has reduced Venture, its soldiers may storm the Domicile, aided no doubt by smaller cannon, ones more easily transported. Or the vessel may depart for other harbors until all have been reduced. Then other vessels may come, bringing men sufficient to conquer us at their own pace.

"You are done, woman. Abandon all thought of resistance. You must surrender now, ere more of what you presume to call your subjects perish."

My Queen met his gaze with wrath in the set of her jaw, yet she did not grant him a reply. In a whetted voice, she called, "Baron Plinth!"

That man advanced a step, upheld by grim rectitude. "Your Majesty?"

"My lord Baron," she said as though she had no doubt of him, "you will muster your forces—and those of Glare Estobate, if you can—to Indemnie's defense."

"I will, Your Majesty"—the man's tone was a match for hers—"when you have given a satisfactory account of your marriage proposals."

The rainfall continued to dwindle during these exchanges. Lightning still flared overhead, though it was passing with its thunderheads to the west. I was able to observe my Queen more closely as she sighed. Though she may have wished to do so, she did not attempt to impose her will. Instead she bowed to the exigencies of the occasion.

"I proposed wedlock to my five barons," she confessed without remorse, "intending matrimony with none. By that expedient, I hoped to provoke traitors to expose themselves. You have witnessed the success of my ploy. Indeed, it succeeded beyond my expectations. That vessel could not have come upon us as it has without the guidance of a traitor.

"Should you challenge my methods, I care not. Should you think to question my motives, however, you must first consider the cost of your choices."

Two or more of the enemy's cannon blared with one voice. Another distinct tremble passed through the house. Concussions and fires made wreckage elsewhere. As the rain faded, the screams of people and horses reached the Domicile.

Almost at once, I perceived that Baron Plinth's inflexible demeanor disguised a comprehending mind. He neither struggled within himself nor harassed my Queen with further inquiries. He permitted himself no more than a brief silence. Then he replied, "By your leave, Your Majesty, I will now hasten to my forces, that I may lead them in the defense of the Domicile."

His sovereign forestalled his departure with the lift of one finger. "The defense of the Domicile must be delayed. For the present, my lord Baron, you must aid Venture. Do not expend your forces against our foe. Rather do your utmost to rescue townsfolk."

As she spoke, a light caught Jakob Plinth's eyes—a reflection of conflagration in the harbor, perhaps, or a spark of respect. Saying only, "At once, Your Majesty," he bowed and was gone.

Briefly I studied Thrysus Indolent, hoping to catch some sign of consternation. Despite my Queen's manner, however, and Baron Plinth's response, Indolent's mien revealed only satisfaction and anticipation—as much of both as the hurt done to his arm allowed.

With Jakob Plinth's leaving, Inimica Phlegathon deVry now turned to me.

Stone of eye and tight of mouth, she said, "I have warned you, Hieronomer. One refusal I permitted. I will not countenance another. Here you will counsel me according to your gifts.

"What must I do to end this carnage?"

When I had declined to sacrifice a child, she had replied, *Then I will demand more of you. Much more when the time requires it.* The moment of crisis was upon me—surely the last crisis of my life—and I was unprepared for it.

Yet not as unprepared as I felt myself to be. In the interval between my encounter—and my Queen's—with the alchemist Opalt Intrix, I had learned much. At a calmer moment, I might have said that I had also come to understand much. Indeed, I had considered much that would have been inconceivable to me scant fortnights ago. When I realized that Excrucia had come to my side—when I felt her hand rest on my shoulder as though she had determined to share my straits—words came to my lips, words half unbidden and no more than vaguely apprehended.

"Your Majesty," I answered in a croaked and cracking voice, "you must do nothing. I will do it."

"How?" she snapped at once.

Fright dimmed my sight. She confronted me as though through a greying mist. The blasts of cannon struck directly at my heart. With Excrucia at my side, however, I did not fail to continue.

"I will descend to Venture and approach the vessel under a flag of parley. When I stand before the captain of our foes, I will persuade him to desist. I will persuade him to name his terms, for truce if I can, for surrender if I cannot."

"How?" my Queen repeated with some ferocity. "Why will he heed you?"

Desperately I wished to turn aside from my purpose, yet I could not. "Alone, he will not. In his eyes, I will be naught. Yet I believe that he *can* be persuaded." In a rush, I endeavored to explain. "What is his purpose here? I have foreseen enslavement. One vessel cannot achieve that end. Harm it can do, terrible harm. But it cannot impose submission. Even an assault upon the Domicile cannot. Our people are too many, and the men under Baron Plinth's command are ready.

"Should that ship be the vanguard of a greater power, it must await reinforcement. If it is merely a scout, it must depart to summon aid. In either case, its captain will have much to gain by parley, a large victory at small cost. The only difficulty will be to assure him that I speak with your authority.

"For that reason," I said, though my heart quailed and my throat was thick with fear, "I will be accompanied by a hostage, a personage of sufficient stature to confirm that my voice has weight and substance. By that demonstration, I will gain his heed."

Now Inimica Phlegathon deVry nodded. "A clever ploy, Mayhew," she conceded more softly. "I will be your hostage. I am

Indemnie's Queen. My shoulders must bear the burden of Indemnie's peril."

Too quick for courtesy, I retorted, "*No!*" Then I recalled myself. With greater care, I said, "Your Majesty, you must not. You are necessary *here*. Your sovereignty must rally our defense. For that task, none other will suffice. You must remain Indemnie's Queen whatever the outcome of my efforts may be."

Hearing me, her ferocity returned. Once again, I had refused her. Yet she did not gainsay me. Still more softly, as though she dreaded my response, she asked, "If I am not your hostage, whom will you hazard? Who among our personages of stature will consent to accompany you, certain of imprisonment and confident of death?"

There I turned from my Queen to regard Excrucia.

She did not glance at me. Speaking only to her mother, she announced, "I will do it." Though her voice was small, it was also firm, unshaken at its core. "For Mayhew, and for you, and for Indemnie, I will do it."

"An ideal choice!" bleated Thrysus Indolent in mockery. "Holding your daughter against you, that captain will be sure of his success."

For that rejoinder, at least, I was prepared. "He will also be sure that I speak for Her Majesty."

My Queen gazed at her daughter with droplets streaming from her eyes as though she wept rain. Of her emotions she gave no other sign. I saw—or perhaps merely imagined—

considerations of one sort or another scud like stormclouds across her sight. In her reckless youth, she had bedded a man without regard to his lack of gifted blood. At her command, her daughter's father had been murdered. I could only guess at her thoughts until she spoke.

Sounding strangely stricken, as though something within her had cracked, she said, "Some escort you must have. I will not consign either you or my daughter to that horror"—a twist of her head indicated Venture—"unguarded."

Given a choice, I would happily have preferred fainting. Sadly, I had already announced my own doom. For a moment, I rubbed at my eyes, striving to wipe the dimness from my vision. Excrucia's fate I now held in my hands—hands which had not been formed for great deeds, but rather for shedding the blood of small creatures. Should I fail, my sole consolation would be that I would be slain while my only friend remained imprisoned or enslaved.

"By your leave, Your Majesty," I contrived to reply, "I will have Vail and Slew. No larger escort will serve my cause. They will suffice."

For an instant, my Queen showed her teeth as though she meant to spit an obscenity at my head. At once, however, she mastered herself. To Slew and Vail she merely nodded, committing her daughter and me to their care.

While the four of us left the balcony, she returned to her study of Venture's ruin. Her hands she propped on the wall, perhaps hoping to steady or suppress the trembling of her frame. Yet her shoulders betrayed her. They shook as though she were overcome by wrath or woe.

Holding aloft a halberd with Thrysus Indolent's white handkerchief tied to its blade as a flag of parley, Slew and Vail accompanied Excrucia and me from the Domicile on horseback. Slew himself bore the standard, for Vail could not. In addition to his saber and dirk, Slew had shouldered a longbow and a quiver of arrows. Leading us, he rode like the herald of a mighty force of arms, with his gaze fixed upon Venture to seek out the safest passage.

In contrast, Vail sat hunched in his saddle. At every third or fourth jolt, a thin gasp broke from him. His only weapon was his dirk, and I doubted his strength to wield it. Yet he rode with his jaw set as though he dared any foe to believe him weak.

I had been on horseback no more than twice in my life. I bounced and flailed in my saddle like a sack of grain loosely filled. Fortunately Excrucia was an accomplished horsewoman, and she glided more than rode with a supple cloak for warmth fluttering from her shoulders. At intervals, she turned toward me, perhaps to confirm that I had not unhorsed myself. When I met her gaze, she smiled like a woman born for daring.

Again fortunately, the rain had ceased. Slashing winds had driven the storm from the headland, leaving clear skies, a bright moon, and multitudes of stars overhead. Though I understood none of my mount's movements, I was able to trust that it saw its road clearly enough to avoid mishap.

More swiftly than I had imagined, we neared the outskirts of the town. At some distance—a distance greater than it had appeared from the vantage of the balcony—the black vessel continued its bombardment as though its supplies of balls and powder were infinite. Across the whole of the east, burning merchantries, warehouses, inns, and residences flung flames that dimmed the stars, giving the very moonlight an infernal cast. Already we had passed small clusters of men, women, and children, all fleeing for the presumed sanctuary of the Domicile. Soon we encountered throngs of refugees, most cradling wounds or each other, some burned beyond recognition. One and all, they were too stunned with loss and pain to ask succor of us. Among the fire and concussions of their homes, their livelihoods, their futures, they had exhausted their capacity for terror. Now they merely ran, expending the remainder of their lives or their wits in flight. What hope remained to them, they fixed upon the Domicile and Inimica Phlegathon deVry.

Slew drew us aside. Standing in his stirrups, he peered into the west. Then he informed us, "I see no sign of armies. They are too distant. They must march hard and long to reach the town if they hope to find any of its folk alive."

"A generous gesture," Vail muttered, "but wasted. Better to defend her house."

I believed that my Queen's commands to Baron Plinth served

more than one purpose, but I did not speak my thoughts. Our mission demanded haste—and yet the prospect of wending our way through Venture's wrack sickened me to the marrow of my bones. While I flinched, however, Excrucia touched my arm. She nodded to indicate her comprehension, then smiled to demonstrate her willingness. Thus encouraged, I swallowed my nausea and urged Slew to proceed.

With more alacrity than I knew how to endure, Slew Immordson led us among the storms of fire and destruction that were Venture's death-throes.

At every moment, I expected to be struck by a fatal ball, or by its explosion, or by the wreckage it wrought. In my mind, I saw myself become a smear of blood and meat on the cobbled streets. Evidences of similar fates lay everywhere. I beheld an appalling number of mangled corpses—a number matched only by the maimed and dying. I rode haunted by screams, and endangered on all sides by wind-lashed pyres, and near blinded by heat. Excrucia had grasped the edge of her cloak and drawn it across her face, leaving only her eyes uncovered. Of her, I knew only that she wept. Vail, however, reacted in another fashion. He now rode erect, straight as the shaft of a halberd, and in his slitted eyes and clenched jaws I saw a rage of such intensity that the wound in his side was forgotten.

As for Slew, the sight of his back revealed naught except concentration. Turning this way and that, choosing one street rather than another for no reason that I could discern, he led us ever closer to the wharves and the attacking vessel.

Through carnage and devastation, we went onward until I guessed that we were near our goal, though our foe remained blocked from my sight. There I called Slew to a halt. In Vail's hearing, and in Excrucia's, so that they would know my needs, I spoke to my Queen's bodyguard.

"I cannot gauge whether what I ask is possible. That you must determine. But I hope that you will now part from us to seek some concealed vantage from which you can observe us. The difficulty is that your covert must be within bowshot of that vessel's foredeck.

"I will bear our flag of parley. It will persuade our foe's captain to take us aboard his ship." If it failed to do so, Excrucia's presence would succeed. "With Vail, we will gain the foredeck. There we will attempt some form of negotiation. If I am then permitted to depart, you will know that my efforts have succeeded. If I am altogether spurned, however, I will drop my halberd. By that sign, you will know that we require an instant distraction.

"My hope is that you will send a shaft into the chest of some foeman upon the foredeck. If you cannot strike at the captain himself, or at the man who speaks for him, any other will suffice. But you must be able to use your bow accurately at a considerable distance.

"Tell me now if what I ask is possible. Otherwise I must consider a more hazardous distraction."

By *more hazardous*, I meant *more easily anticipated*. More easily thwarted. I depended upon the confusion that an unanticipated attack would cause.

While I spoke, Slew betrayed no reaction. Briefly he studied me as though he doubted neither his skill nor his success, but only my true intent. Then he released his halberd to me.

"Venture lacks elevation," he replied. "I must have higher ground. There is a path that ascends partway up the cliff below the Domicile. It is used to watch for returning vessels when the seas are perilous. There I will be able to do as you ask."

An instant later, his tone and manner changed. Abruptly he became the man who had murdered Excrucia's father—a man who did not balk at bloodshed. "Be warned, Hieronomer," he said in a bitten voice. "If you intend betrayal, my second shaft will find *your* heart."

At that, Excrucia flinched. She poised herself to expostulate. Ere she could find words for her protest, however, Slew wheeled his mount and rode away, running hard for the south and the cliff.

She flung a look of fright at me—or perhaps it was an appeal for reassurance. Yet she did not utter her query, and I did not answer it. So craven was I that I could not name my intent, even to myself.

When I had secured my grasp on the halberd, and had confirmed that my pouch of *chrism* and my hieronomer's blade remained hidden within easy reach, I urged Vail to lead us onward.

The man replied with a grin as ready for killing as Slew's threat, but he did not hesitate. First trotting, then cantering, he took us toward the docks.

Over the roar of cannon and flames, the smash of balls and the fall of timbers, Excrucia contrived to make her voice carry. Doubtless Vail heard her, yet her challenge was for me alone.

"Betrayal, Mayhew? You?"

My need to offer some reply was as great as her need to receive it. "Never!" I shouted though I quavered. "I will serve Her Majesty and you and Indemnie with my last breath!"

Staring at me, her eyes grew wide. Surely she had already surmised that my peril was more immediate than hers. She was too valuable a hostage to be blithely slain, whereas I might well be deemed mere dross. Now she appeared to consider less obvious dangers. Indeed, she appeared to consider that I had chosen her to bear the greatest cost of my designs.

So softly that I was scarce able to hear her through the tumult, she replied, "I will have you or nothing, Mayhew Gordian. If you mean to cast away your life, I will cast mine with you. I will not remain to be imprisoned while you are lost."

Altogether she compelled me to consider that she—like Slew and Vail—like Inimica Phlegathon deVry herself—knew my last secret.

Spurred by alarm, I struggled to envision some expedient that would spare her. However, I was too much afraid to reason clearly.

Also I had no time. While I belabored my mind in a bootless effort to exceed its bounds, we passed among the few remaining structures and cantered onto a wharf in plain view of the black ship at anchor.

For a moment, I froze in my seat, stricken motionless by the sight of the huge vessel with its cannon protruding from its foredeck—and by the sudden knowledge that my small gifts and smaller wits could serve no worthy purpose against so puissant a foe. Until Vail barked my name, making a command of its humble sounds, I did not recall myself enough to hold my halberd high and wave its flag of parley from side to side, demanding notice—or pleading for it.

So convinced was I of my littleness that I expected no response. Indeed, I saw none, heard none—no men at the foredeck rails, no shouts across the water. For that reason, I was shocked by Vail's nonchalant announcement, "The cannon do not fire."

Forgetting to flourish my flag, I gaped around me. For a time, I held my breath, certain that the bombardment would resume on the instant. Yet the tubes did not utter their jets of flame. No horrid thunder resounded from the unruly seas. No exploding balls crashed into Venture's heart. An unearthly silence deafened the harbor—unearthly and fatal. Long moments passed ere I was again able to discern the shrieks and wails of Venture's people at my back.

Vail stood in his stirrups. Excrucia pointed. "There, Mayhew," she panted. "There." Yet I saw nothing, understood nothing. I only listened as she breathed, "They lower a longboat. They will take us aboard."

Now I remembered to hold up my halberd.

Black against the black ship, the longboat remained invisible to me until it entered the glare of fires upon the water. Then I was able to descry it—a longboat indeed, three oars to a side, six men at the oars, and four more armed and armored in the stern. These four remained standing despite the heave of the seas and the strong sweep of the oars, a feat which they achieved by bracing their legs against the thwarts.

Straight as an arrow, the longboat came for us, bringing with it a doom that I had chosen for Excrucia as well as myself—and perhaps for all Indemnie.

When Vail dismounted, clutching briefly at his side, Excrucia and I joined him, she lightly, I with trembling legs.

At once, I took Vail's arm. "Hear me," I urged, attempting command. "Should my efforts fail—should I drop my halberd, and Slew succeed—you must save yourself at any cost. We will endure our fates. You must bear our tidings to Her Majesty. She must know all that you will be able to tell her."

He spared no more than a grunt for my instructions. His gaze remained fixed on the approaching longboat. When he nodded, I could not determine whether he indicated assent or mere comprehension. He may have wished only to direct my attention toward our foes.

The great vessel was not distant, and the longboat was swift. With quick proficiency, the rowers shipped their oars, caught the side of the nearest pier, and secured their craft. Thereafter they returned to their seats while the four soldiers or marines disembarked. The heavy rise and fall of the waves caused them no apparent awkwardness.

The four marched toward us with their blades drawn, cut-lasses keenly curved. Seen by moon- and firelight, their raiment was motley. Two wore chain sarks that flapped against their knees. Another had a turban on his head, a shirt open to the navel, and voluminous pantaloons. Only the fourth was clad in what might be styled a uniform—a fitted breastplate of bronze, leggings of silk, and high boots much abused. In addition, the men were variously groomed. The individual in the turban wore a shrubbery of beard to cover much of his chest. One of his comrades had a moustache oiled and waxed to sharp points. Another was clean shaven. The man in uniform had neglected his whiskers for some days. Altogether they resembled brigands more than men-at-arms.

Nevertheless their discipline was plain. As they gained the wharf, they fanned out to encircle us with their blades. Only when we were surrounded did the uniformed man speak.

In a voice thickly accented, he announced, "You are now our prisoners. If you seek parley, you must convince our captain to hear you. If you have some other purpose, we will cut you down." After a pause, he added, "We may find a better use for the woman."

Excrucia met his gaze as though to defy him. Nevertheless she closed her cloak around her and held it tight.

Angered by this threat to my friend and ally, I overcame my fear with an attempt at hauteur. "We do seek parley. We have made our purpose plain." I waved my halberd. "You will treat us courteously until your captain has heard us. Thereafter you may learn to regret your rudeness."

Vail's brief glance hinted at approval. Excrucia's gaze held firm on our foe's spokesman.

My reply was greeted with coarse chuckles and guffaws, but our captors offered no further threats. The spokesman answered only, "Follow me," and turned away.

Encouraged by cutlasses, Vail, Excrucia, and I obeyed.

Soon we were upon the pier—and sooner still, Vail dropped into the wave-tossed longboat. That movement wrung a groan from him, though he mastered his pain quickly to assist Excrucia. For my part, I contrived to step from the pier and land on the floorboards without pitching myself overboard. A moment later, our captors embarked, now guarding us fore and aft. At once, the near-side oarsmen cast off, unshipped their sweeps, and joined their fellows rowing us headlong into the high tumult of the seas.

When the longboat had been hoisted onto its hanger, and we had made shift to gain our feet aboard the ship, our escort accompanied us to the foredeck. There we found ourselves placed near the foremast at no great distance from the infernal bulk of the cannon. Piled near the mast and the rails were the usual equipage of a large vessel, chiefly massive hawsers coiled almost to my own height, ranks of belaying pins, and anchor-chains, but also long troughs lined with iron balls for the cannon, and iron-bound casks which doubtless held explosive powder.

All along the rails and before the forecastle, men as motley as our guards studied us in silence—sailors, soldiers, marines, I knew not what. Most regarded us with an admixture of open animosity and glazed disinterest, though a small number appeared to regard us as freakish curiosities. All, however, were armed with cutlasses, and some bore dirks and truncheons as well.

No one among them spoke.

At my side, Excrucia surveyed the assemblage with her head held high and her eyes clear in the moonlight. Near us, Vail hunched over his wound, clamping one arm there to constrict the flow of blood, and breathing in low hisses through his teeth. While I searched myself for courage, I scanned the men, seeking one with an air of authority, one who stood somewhat apart from his fellows. However, I found none. To my eyes, they were all and none captains, as leaderless and incapable of restraint as a rabble poised for frenzy.

Prompted by a glare from Vail, I raised my voice. "Who speaks for this vessel?" I had come for this, had I not? I had chosen this doom. Why, then, did I falter? "Who will parley with me?"

From somewhere that I failed to identify, a voice that rasped like the cut of a saw commanded, "Disarm them."

At once, the uniformed member of our escort approached us.

Ere he could demand or claim our weapons, Vail tossed his dirk aside, then swept his free hand down his length to indicate that he could not have concealed a blade, had he wished to do so. My dirk I also discarded, clinging only to my halberd with its flag—my promise of peaceful intent. As for Excrucia, she remained with her cloak closed around her. Her gaze dared the guard to lay a hand upon her person.

He considered her for a moment, then dismissed her with a shrug. Clearly he did not fear harm from a woman. In his clotted accent, he stated, "I will have that halberd."

Now I did not raise my voice. Rather I spoke quietly, as though I were certain of myself. "You will not," I said, "when you have considered that we are visible to those who defend my Queen's redoubt atop the cliff." A twitch of my head indicated the Domicile on its eminence. "While I hold the flag of parley, they will hope that some cessation of hostility may be attained."

Laughter greeted my words, and the man before me declared, "We do not desire cessation."

"Then you are a fool," I retorted. "If my halberd is taken from me, we will be at war. You will be opposed by every man, woman, and child of our isle, and when you have conquered it—should you prove able to do so—you will find that it has been made useless to you, its people slain, its wealth destroyed."

At this rejoinder, the guard glanced aside. Apparently receiving some sign that escaped my notice, he shrugged once more, bared his teeth at me, and withdrew.

The shaft of my halberd I held with whitened knuckles. My

palm and fingers were now slick with sweat, and I feared that my grasp would slip.

Still concealed, the same rasping voice suggested, "Announce yourselves."

With a flick of his fingers, Vail indicated a place to my left, but I did not turn. Facing the forecastle and the guards who had escorted us, I proclaimed, "I am the voice of Her Majesty Queen Inimica Phlegathon deVry IV, beloved sovereign of this isle. While I hold the flag of parley, my words are hers.

"With me are—"

The man with the rasp interrupted me. "And you are? Give us your name."

I spotted him now, a hulk of a man among others at the rail, yet I could not discern his features or his raiment. He stood in the shadow of the forecastle, and those nearby had placed themselves to mask him in part. For some reason, either caution or mockery, he did not put himself forward. Therefore I continued to address the forecastle.

"I have no name of stature. Here I am naught other than my Queen's voice. I stand before you only because I am trusted. If you have some particular interest in my parentage, you must seek among the corpses when you have destroyed the isle."

Receiving no response, I resumed my announcement. "With me are Her Highness Excrucia Phlegathon deVry and Vail her servant. She is daughter to Her Majesty Inimica Phlegathon deVry, who offers her as hostage to assure you that I speak as I have been instructed. Her Majesty will honor every word that I utter in her name."

Apparently satisfied—or perhaps merely curious to regard Excrucia more closely—the hulking man now left the partial shelter of his comrades. When he had taken three or four long strides, he passed out of the shadow, and I saw him clearly.

He was a head taller than Vail upright. His arms were bludgeons, and his chest a hogshead thick with muscle. By no detail of garb was his rank indicated—except, perhaps, by the golden band that secured the long plait of his beard. Two cutlasses dangled from his belt. Though his eyes were porcine, bulging in their orbits, they were quick and discerning. However, the feature that most drew my notice was his mouth.

It resembled the maw of a beast that fed on flesh. His lips by moonlight were the precise darkness of blood, and when they opened, they revealed red-stained teeth and a tongue the fatal hue of a serpent's.

Five paces from us, he stopped, bracing his fists upon his hips like a man accustomed to reprimanding children. Briefly he gazed at me, and at Vail. Then he fixed his pronounced regard on Excrucia.

With a nod of his head rather than a more seemly bow, he informed her, "Your Highness, I am Riddance Glave, captain of this vessel and commander of the forces that besiege your home. At a better time, we will speak of many things, you and I. You will tell me much that your mother's *voice*"—he sneered the word—"will not. I make no claim that you will enjoy our exchanges, but they will give me pleasure enough for both. For the present, however, I will hear your mother's little spokesman."

For a moment, he grinned at the swift flush that darkened Excrucia's cheeks. Then he turned to me.

"What of the lady's servant?" he demanded, a scrape of sound that abused my hearing. "He is too coarse to be believed in that role. You meant to say that he serves *you*."

I could not honestly assert that I had forgotten fear. Nonetheless his address to Excrucia provoked an unfamiliar extreme of ire in me. Therefore I held his gaze as though I intended threats.

"He does not," I replied. "Perhaps I should have said that he has been Her Highness' bodyguard. Now, however, he serves Her Majesty. He has been commanded to witness all that transpires here, and to vouch for my conduct.

"Also he has been strictly warned to inform you if I depart in the smallest particular from Her Majesty's wishes."

This bald falsehood I ventured in an attempt to increase Vail's worth to our foes. Thereby I hoped to improve his ability to escape should the need arise. However, I had not prepared my companions for this ploy. It brought a familiar frown to Excrucia's brow, a frown both parched and endearing. Taken by surprise, she concentrated to guess my intent.

At the same time, Vail astonished me by adding, "I have no other purpose. You see that I am incapable of attack or defense." With a grimace, he shifted his arm to display his wound weeping blood. "Yet I am devoted to Her Majesty, and to Her Highness. I obey their commands."

Ignoring Vail, Riddance Glave considered my words—or perhaps my manner—for a time. Then he showed his teeth in a grin entirely unlike that with which he had insulted Excrucia, a grin suggesting that he would cheerfully set his jaws in my throat.

"Very well," he conceded harshly. "Speak, *voice*. I will hear your Queen's pleas for mercy."

I did not flinch. I did not waver. Though I remembered fear, I did not recall uncertainty. "As I have said," I began, "Her Highness is offered as hostage to ensure the verity of my words, and also to encourage negotiation. Though we are not a war-hungry people, we do not lack force of arms. We will defend our isle if we must. Still Her Majesty wishes to know the terms upon which she may avoid further harm to her realm."

The captain returned a laugh empty of humor. "Know then, *voice*," he replied, "that we have come at the invitation of one Thrysus Indolent, a baron among you. He has offered much, and may be given much in return. In particular, he has assured us that your *beloved* monarch is even now beset by revolt. It may well be that she is already dethroned and beheaded, thereby reducing your pretentious airs to the lowing of cattle.

"Our purpose is to rule this land and take what we wish. We have no interest in negotiation. You cannot stand against us."

On the instant, I found that I had much to say, too much to be said at once. Though I was distraught by this further sign of

Thrysus Indolent's betrayal, I was not surprised. Yet I did not understand it. Therefore it was the first of several matters to compel utterance.

"How did Baron Indolent contrive to treat with you? None of his ships have ever returned. You are glib, Riddance Glave. Tell us how your dealings with him were communicated."

He snorted through his beard. "None of his ships that you know. We captured one of his vessels. In its master's cabin, we found letters addressed to some nameless enemy of your isle. They spoke of rebellion. They promised an easy conquest. They described that which we have come to take. They asked a considerable reward—a request that we may elect to honor. And they included charts with the precise location of your isle, of your Queen's residence, and of this harbor.

"When we recounted the prize that Thrysus Indolent offered to our commander, and were given our orders, we conduced further communication by means of fishing schooners dispatched from the Baron's private harbor. Those letters suggested the time of our assault."

Fishing schooners, I thought. The time of our assault. Heated by this evidence of Indolent's farsighted treachery, I retorted, "Then I must inform you that the Baron's tidings have misled you. He is too confident of his cleverness. There is now no revolt. It has ended in disarray. One conspirator has been slain. Another has returned to Her Majesty's service. And Thrysus Indolent himself is her prisoner. You will have no easy conquest."

"I care not," asserted the captain, sneering. "With or without slaughter, we will take what we wish. If your Queen cares aught for the lives of her subjects, she will surrender ere sunrise."

I was conscious of the glare of fury in Vail's eyes. I felt Excrucia's suspended breath as though it were my own. Yet I did not glance aside from my enemy. By the simulated ease of my tone and demeanor, I claimed his attention.

"Such threats," I observed, "are easily bandied about. They are more difficult to effect. How can Her Majesty surrender—how can I advise her to set aside her sovereignty—when you have not named your terms? She must know what she must surrender and what she will be permitted to retain."

In smoldering ferocity, Riddance Glave answered, "Your words waste breath, *voice*." His mouth emphasized each utterance with red vehemence. "There are no terms. When her surrender is absolute, we will determine the use that we will make of her."

Fearing that Vail would abandon restraint—that Excrucia's resolve would fail—I exceeded mere hauteur. I attempted overt scorn.

"Then, Riddance Glave, you are as much a fool as the one who sought to claim my flag of parley. Your threats expose your desires." One vessel could not conquer Indemnie. It *could* not. "You have come because Thrysus Indolent described a prize that you covet greatly. A man in my place must ask of himself, what prize does our isle possess that justifies a long voyage, a fearsome expenditure of supplies which cannot be replenished, and the loss of many lives, both ours and yours? And how does it chance that Thrysus Indolent knew this prize would be coveted by any foe?

"I tell you plainly, Riddance Glave, that open war will destroy as much of what you seek as it does of what you disdain. When you have mastered our isle—if indeed you are able to do so—you will learn that it is no longer worth what you have expended to acquire it."

My foe appeared to expand before me, filling his lungs for a bellow or a blow. However, he had not attained his present rank through a lack of self-command. When he spoke, his tone was raw derision.

"And you are certain of this, little man?"

"I am," I avowed, upheld by my mask of boldness. "I know it by your reluctance to name your terms. If you did not fear to disclose your desires, you would not hesitate to accept the comparative ease of our surrender. You would not prefer the cost of a long and bloody conflict."

In a crimson fume, he demanded, "You dare speak so? To *me*?"

"Having naught to lose," I answered, "I have naught to fear."

"Naught to *fear*?" He laughed as though to display his cruelty. "Do you not *fear* what will become of your precious hostage? Your Queen's daughter?"

By no flaring of gaze or tightening of muscle did Excrucia betray herself. Knowing her as I did, however, I perceived that she was appalled.

Still I clung to my purpose, and to my halberd. "She has

come willing to her plight. She will suffer whatsoever it requires of her."

For a moment, the captain regarded me as though he deemed me deranged. His teeth bit his flagrant lips in apparent bafflement. Was he uncertain? Did he question my boldness—or his own? Did he struggle to contain frank rage? I knew not. I knew only that any flicker of hesitation on my part would undermine my duty. For my Queen's sake, and for Indemnie's, I required Riddance Glave to name his desires.

When he had achieved his decision, he spat his demands at me as though they were drops of blood.

"Then listen well, *voice*. Here are my terms.

"Your Queen will gather together every alchemist who inhabits this isle"—he pointed one thick finger at my heart—"of which I believe that you are one. I will grant her a fortnight to comply. During that interval, I will not cease my bombardments. I will do what I will to your harbors. And when the fortnight has passed, she will surrender her alchemists to me. Then—only then, mark you—we will discuss her abdication and my ascension in some fashion that does not necessitate slaughter."

There I had him. Revealing himself, he also revealed how he might be opposed. I did not believe that Indemnie's alchemists would consent to forsake their sovereign. And while they were not inclined to conflict, either by their gifts or by their long history of peace and respect, they could accomplish much that would aid the isle's defense.

Still I sought more from my enemy. My Queen would need to know the nature of the passion that drove Riddance Glave and his ship against her. She would need to know the *why* of his cupidity.

"I understand," I replied, resuming my false calm. "I will deliver your terms to Her Majesty. Vail will confirm that I have served her honestly." Seeing that the captain was done with me—that he meant to turn away—I hazarded asking, "Yet ere I depart, will you permit one query for my personal edification?"

At once, he confronted me with his fists knotted on the hilts of his cutlasses. "So that you will know what you must say to your fellow alchemists? Tell them *this*, little man. You will learn that they relish it.

"We resemble brigands. At one time, we were. But now we are commissioned rovers committed to an empire bent upon expansion.

"The empire's most recent conquest was your former home-land, a miserable place scarce able to sustain itself. From documents found in archives, we learned that our new subjects had once been prosperous and wealthy—and that their bounty had been provided by the power of alchemy. Yet some madness had overtaken them. Entirely deranged, they concluded that ease and plenty were not desirable. Bounties and power were curses that stifled the spirit. Rather than seek expansion—rather than discover *some* worthy use for their prosperity and wealth, as sane men would have done—your forebears elected to banish their alchemists. You were abandoned here, and the *spirit* of your homeland fell into decay."

As he spoke, he gathered force until his words resembled thunder. "*We* will not decay. We are an empire, and will grow until the world entire is ours. At any cost, we will acquire your alchemists. We will have them so that they may support our greater glory."

Now I was done. I had accomplished my duty. The inference that our foes possessed no alchemists themselves completed my assigned task. With that revelation, as with those that had gone before, my Queen would call herself content. Only my true purpose remained.

Excrucia had said, *I will have you or nothing*. She had vowed to cast away her life. I could not part from her. Nor could I permit Indemnie to suffer a fortnight of bombardment, only to face open war when the captain's terms were refused.

Had I been craven? Through my life, craven? I was not so now. And I remembered Opalt Intrix. *The gift is the gift. Only purity, talent, and character vary*. My heritage, and Excrucia's, lacked purity. Of talent I was uncertain, though I had chosen to believe that resolve might serve in its place. And for character I could rely absolutely on my friend, my ally, my love.

I waited only until Riddance Glave began to turn away, gesturing dismissal as he moved—only until the guards who had escorted us earlier shifted themselves to advance—only until I had caught Vail's eye, and had clasped Excrucia's hand in mine.

Then, with a suddenness that might serve to startle the captain and his crew of brigands, I cast my halberd into the center of the foredeck.

Clattering on the planks, it caught Glave's notice so that he wheeled toward it. Likewise it plucked at the attention of the assembled men. For a moment, every eye on the foredeck was fixed, not on me and my companions, but rather on my halberd as it skidded to rest.

For that moment, I held my breath, waiting—and praying that Excrucia and Vail would remain as still as I.

Then Slew's shaft struck straight into Riddance Glave's back. Spewing blood, he pitched headlong to the deck. After a moment's writhing, he did not move again.

Around the foredeck, consternation reigned. Tumult, yelled curses, and wild rushing surrounded us. Now, however, I did not wait. Indeed, I was already in motion. Within a few heartbeats, some guard or sailor would recover his wits and cut us down.

As I plunged to my knees, I dragged Excrucia with me. Gripping her hand as though it held the meaning of my life, I slapped its back and knuckles to the deck and covered it there with mine. During the instant that our gazes met, she had no time for words. She could only plead with her eyes.

Immediately I looked away. I had to see what I did. Made swift by long practice, I snatched my hieronomer's blade from beneath my hauberk. Raising the iron high, I hammered it down.

Whetted to a precise keenness, it pierced my hand and Excrucia's, and drove deep into the deck, pinning us where we knelt together.

Blood burst from our wounds, hers and mine. It splashed our hands and the boards, formed a pool of augury. In it, I could have foreseen our futures in every detail, yet I did not pause to regard it. Moving still, I withdrew Opalt Intrix's pouch of *chrism* from its concealment and poured its entire contents over my blade and our hands and our blood.

Now I had done all that I could. My gambit would succeed or fail, I knew not which. Indeed, I felt certain that it would fail. How could it succeed? By blood, talent, and character, I was no alchemist. As Excrucia opened her mouth to cry out, I pulled her to me and kissed her—an act of contrition or farewell, but also of longing.

Past her shoulder, I saw that Vail had crouched low, readying himself to spring. Perhaps in the confusion he would be able to effect his escape, as I had urged him to do. My life was now certainly forfeit. Excrucia might be spared, if only to punish her for my deeds, but she would not be relinquished. Therefore Vail's escape was vital.

Excrucia's kiss clung to mine as mine did to hers. Persuaded of failure, I resolved that I would not release her until we were torn asunder.

In the clamor of shouts as another man fell to Slew's second arrow, in the frantic pounding of boots, and in the utter necessity of Excrucia's kiss, I was slow to recognize that the hurting of my hand had changed.

It had become agony.

Compelled, I turned my head to gape at what I had done.

The wooden hilt of my blade had grown too large for my grasp. It increased visibly before me. And the iron of the blade extended itself likewise, growing in both length and girth—but much more in length. From it came screeching sounds like the violent splintering of boards.

For one astonished moment, I was able to imagine that my blade had already penetrated the foredeck—that even now it extended its piercing through holds and compartments until it embedded itself in the next deck—that it might grow far enough to hole the ship. I had supplied my blood and Excrucia's and my iron with a considerable quantity of *chrism*—enough, Opalt Intrix had suggested, for an alchemist's lifetime.

There my moment ended. Agony became excruciation as my iron's growth forced the bones of my hand apart, crushing them against their neighbors until my flesh tore. For the space of a heartbeat, or perhaps two, I screamed with force enough to shred my throat, and Excrucia screamed with me.

Then some heavy impact drove us from our knees, ripped our ruined hands from my blade. As I fell, my head pounded the deck. At once, the forecastle and the coiled hawsers and Riddance Glave's corpse became stars, and the distraught tumult of men faded from the world. I understood that I was dead, and with that realization I was content.

Death, however, was not the oblivion that I had anticipated. It was a staggered jolting that shifted me from side to side. It was the agony of my bound hand. It was cool air freed from fires and blasts. It was the sound of breathing not my own. Also it was the damp cling of raiment that had been immersed in blood, and the caking of salt upon my face, and the sensation that my body had been beaten with clubs. It was the conviction that miracles had been wrought.

Some time passed ere I opened my eyes to gaze upon an afterlife in which I did not believe.

At first, I beheld only the moon riding high above me amid its panoply of stars. The heavens appeared entirely at peace, and as I regarded them, I found that they filled my eyes with tears.

Thereafter more immediate matters claimed my notice. By increments, I recognized that I lay upon a sheet of canvas that had been stretched between two long shafts to form a crude litter. Beyond my head and past my feet, men held the ends of the poles, and their motion resembled running, though I could not determine where they ran. My thoughts were sluggish or hampered, as though the life in my veins had begun to clot. I required long moments to note that the dark shape trotting at my side belonged to Vail.

He appeared heedless of his wound, a detail that bewildered me. As my sight cleared, however, the moon's shining enabled me to discern that Glare Estobate's cut—indeed, the entire lower half of Vail's torso—had been heavily bandaged. He was able to match the pace of my porters because his bleeding had been stanched, because he was inordinately strong, and also because his visage suggested that his dour nature had been transformed by triumph.

Coughing to clear my throat, I endeavored to speak the query uppermost in my mind. Unfortunately that effort caused fresh knives of pain to pierce my hand. Indeed, it caused my flesh to throb from head to foot. I was unable to utter a word.

Vail glanced down at me, then called elsewhere, "Water! Water for Her Majesty's Hieronomer!"

At his command, my porters halted. Various boots and sandals scrambled in the distance. Then a flask was thrust into Vail's hands. Bending over me despite his own hurt, he lifted me so that I could drink.

While I gulped water—bliss to my sore throat—he instructed me, "Do not speak. When we gain the Domicile, you will ask and answer every question." Briefly he looked away, then met my gaze once more. "Her Highness lives. Her litter follows yours. Her hand has been bound. She is unconscious and pale, having lost much blood, but I do not fear for her."

Again I attempted to form speech. Again I failed.

Nodding as though he knew my needs, Vail gestured for my porters to resume their trek. Now, however, they bore me more slowly so that he could walk at my side in less discomfort.

"You will be pleased to hear," he announced with unfamiliar

satisfaction, "that our foes cannot move their ship. They have raised anchors and unfurled sails. They rush about, shouting. Their helmsman works his wheel to no purpose. They cannot move. They are fixed in place. Your iron has nailed them to the seabed. They will never return to their empire.

"And they dare not lower their longboats. From vantages which those cannon now cannot reach, Baron Plinth's men have begun to rain flaming arrows at the ship. Already sails burn, fire feeds on the midmast, and a structure that I take for the galley is alight. Should those brigands hazard their long-boats, they must first show some clear sign of surrender. Other-wise their boats will be set aflame.

"Glare Estobate's forces," he continued as though he under-stood the hampered trudge of my thoughts, "were at first reluc-tant to accept Baron Plinth's authority. But when they were informed of their Baron's death, they began to obey. We now have men enough to attempt rescues within Venture, to combat the fires, and still to assail Riddance Glave's ship."

With an effort that threatened to overwhelm me, I contrived to croak, "How—?"

Still Vail understood. "I ripped your hands from your blade and bore you overboard. Having lost blood myself, I lacked strength to swim away. But Slew saw us. He joined us in the sea. With this aid, you were brought ashore. Now he rides to speak with Her Majesty."

When I had assembled Vail's tidings into a sequence that I was able to comprehend, I found that this afterlife was tolerable despite the state of my hand and the unpleasantness of other discomforts. Thereafter I renewed my acquaintance with oblivion.

L ater I returned to consciousness with a mind somewhat clearer. Without undue difficulty, I observed that my porters even now bore me through the gates into the Domicile's bailey. And when I lifted my head to consider my surroundings, I found that Inimica Phlegathon deVry herself had come to my side.

She appeared as I had last seen her, altogether drenched by the rain now past. With her hair dripping from her head and her raiment a shambles, she was a bedraggled mess. Yet she remained magnificent, a queen of unmarred beauty in every line and glance.

At Her Majesty's arrival, my porters stopped so that she might address me. When I endeavored to rise from my litter, however, she halted me with her own hand. "Rest, Mayhew," she commanded. "You will be taken to the physicians. Hear me but a moment, and you will be tended.

"We are saved, Mayhew. We have a common foe. That evil ship's coming promises war. Thus it rescues us from rebellion and barbarism. At the cost of your hand, and of my daughter's, you have redeemed us from enslavement. The dooms foretold have been averted. Now at last I am freed to become the Queen that my realm requires.

"Know that your fidelity and courage—like my trust in you— will not be forgotten."

No doubt I should have made some seemly reply. Beyond question, I wished to do so. However, a greater need ruled me. Ere my Queen could hasten to Excrucia's litter, I begged, "A moment, Your Majesty."

She remained at my side despite her open impatience for her daughter. "Yes, Mayhew?"

As well as I was able, I framed my query. "You informed me that I have a gift which others lack. What gift do you find in me that I do not find in myself?"

She regarded me gravely, but she did not hesitate to answer.

"You know your fears, Mayhew. Therefore you are able to overcome them. Others know only that they are afraid. Therefore their fears rule them—as mine have ruled me."

Without another word, as though she believed that her reply sufficed, she turned to Excrucia.

Lifting myself higher, I watched Inimica Phlegathon deVry's reunion with her daughter.

Clearly Excrucia had emerged from stupor. She raised her arms to her mother, and at once my Queen caught her child in a fierce embrace. For a moment, no longer, I heard them weeping together. Then Her Majesty withdrew her head—though not her clasp—and said so that all in the courtyard heard her, "You are my beloved daughter. My pride in you is greater than my power to express it. Your courage humbles my extravagances. When the physicians have treated your wound, and you have rested, I will hear every word of your tale—every word since the day when you first formed an alliance with my Hieronomer.

Until that time, know that my realm will one day be yours. It will be yours *now*, if you wish it. I will defy the Articles of Coronation if I must. Indemnie can have no better monarch."

"Mother," Excrucia replied, still weeping, her voice wan and much abused. "I want only Mayhew."

Did my Queen then retort, A servant? A hieronomer? A man of impure lineage? She did not. Rather she replied without pause or doubt, "Then you will have him, if your wishes are his as well."

While I lowered myself to lie in my litter again, and my porters bore me away, I considered that life was altogether preferable to the oblivion of death.

Thereafter much transpired that I did not witness. I was grateful to be rendered numb while my hand was removed, and the stump of my wrist much treated to relieve infection, the result no doubt of a long acquaintance with the contents of bowels. But when I returned to myself, I found Excrucia seated at my bedside. Her hand had been likewise removed, yet she bore the loss with a composure that exceeded mine. Also she appeared to heal with greater alacrity. For the long days of our confinement among the physicians, she served as my nurse, tending me with a tenderness that belied her severe frown and arid manner.

During those days, however, tidings were brought to us with some regularity by none other than the Domicile's Majordomo.

Though her demeanor remained stern, she was neither shrill nor censorious, and she spoke as though her visits to our infirmary gave her pleasure.

Her first reports concerned Venture and the black ship. The fires in the town had been quenched, and though much had been destroyed, a considerable portion remained. Better still, an unlikely number of Venture's inhabitants had been reclaimed alive. As for Riddance Glave's men, fully a third had surrendered. By my Queen's command, they were treated gently while they were questioned on every conceivable topic concerning their empire, its origins, its extent, and its designs. The ship itself, however, burned with fearsome concussions and screams until the flames reached the water-line and were extinguished.

To that extent, Excrucia and I shared the Majordomo's pleasure.

Later, however, the woman informed us that Opalt Intrix and other adepts of iron had been sent to the transfixed remnant of the vessel to study its cannon so that Indemnie might one day possess similar devices. Thereafter she described at some length the alterations which our sovereign had imposed upon the rule of the isle.

In Glare Estobate's absence, his place as Baron was given to Vail Immordson—how had I failed to ascertain that Vail was Slew's brother?—while Slew himself was set in imprisoned Thrysus Indolent's seat. The brothers were instructed to preside over their new lands justly—a command worthy of a now loved monarch. Yet there was more. Vail and Slew were also urged to raise and train new armies, armies equipped and supplied to march at any moment to any threatened stretch of Indemnie's coast.

Apparently war occupied a substantial portion of Her Majesty's thoughts.

Other tidings occasioned less concern. Praylix Venery was much ignored, though my Queen named his eldest son—he had an abundance of sons with an inordinate number of mothers—to be his heir, on the condition that the youth would be dispatched at once to spend five years in the household of Jakob Plinth. There he might conceivably learn the merit of such qualities as rectitude and fidelity, and would certainly be taught the requirements of command.

As for Quirk Panderman, my Queen made no attempt to disturb his habitual carouse. However, she commanded the delivery of his archives to the Domicile. Also she asked the loan of several scribes to aid in the study and interpretation of the documents. Thus Indemnie—in the person of its monarch—at last acquired an interest in its singular history.

This alteration gratified Excrucia, though it discomfited me. Beyond question, I had gained much by my love's study of the isle's past. Nevertheless I had sensed a theme in the Majordomo's discourse, a preponderance of import that undermined my ease.

Subsequently our visitor's reports chiefly concerned the rebuilding of Venture and its harbor by teams of timber-men, carpenters, and alchemists drawn from every barony. Even there, however, I detected the same theme. The Majordomo did not

neglect to mention that the remade town would have fortifica-
tions unheard-of since the arrival of our people upon the island,
barricades and gates of stone strategically placed within Venture
itself as well as between the town and the harbor. Also Her Majesty had charged the isle's adepts of stone to raise obstacles from
the seabed of the harbor, obstructions hidden by the waters in
locations that would be known to our sailors, but that would
endanger or perhaps cripple any unwelcome vessel. Such a task
would demand years of effort, many alchemists, and much
chrism, but Inimica Phlegathon deVry deemed it a necessary
ward against subsequent intrusions, of which she appeared to
expect a great number.

Clearly war and defense were much on my Queen's mind.
Therefore they were much on mine. I had begun to understand
that she was born to give battle and protect her own.

In due course, I became well enough to quit my bed. When
my strength had returned to an extent that exceeded the bounds
of the infirmary, Excrucia slipped her truncated arm through
mine, and together we exercised our renewed health by explor-
ing the intricacies of the Domicile—passages, chambers, and
halls intimately known to her, largely unfamiliar to me. We
circled the bailey, revisited the ballroom, entered her apartment
when we desired rest, peeked briefly into the far larger and more
munificent private chambers of her mother, and engaged in long
circumnavigations of the high balconies. Elsewhere the vistas
were much as I remembered them, placid and pleasant, but to
the north we were able to observe the beehive of labor that was

Venture, the still smoldering wreck of the black ship, and the skiffs and rowboats of men who plied the waters of the harbor, apparently taking soundings to gauge the seabed's depth.

Everywhere we were greeted warmly by persons of every station, sometimes with applause, occasionally with effusive shouts. Nevertheless Excrucia frowned incessantly, a woman who wished to reclaim her reputation for plainness, and thereby to pass unnoticed. And I received both common greetings and extravagant commendations with an increasing chill. Wherever we gazed—at the courtyard increasingly crowded with men at training, at the much augmented number of guards within the house, at the stone walls among the wooden structures of Venture, at the tense alacrity with which commands were obeyed on all sides—I witnessed evidences of the theme that the Majordomo had disclosed.

The peace of Indemnie had been replaced by preparations for war. Its prosperity had been dedicated to the service of those preparations.

This was an alteration in which I had played no small part, and though I did not regret what I had done, I could not regard its outcome—apart from my place at Excrucia's side—with any satisfaction. Much that I had treasured had been lost ere I knew that I treasured it. Now I did not require entrails and blood to foresee that Indemnie's future—once a blank wall of doom— had become a succession of perils and culling.

Perhaps such an outcome had been inevitable from the first. Perhaps prosperity and peace were unnatural, and uncertainty and strife were the fate of all the world's folk. Nevertheless I had participated in delivering the world's fate to Indemnie. For that reason, I no longer regarded the use that I had made of my gifts with any clear sense of good purpose and worthy service.

When Excrucia and I were entirely recovered, I resolved to pursue a new ambition. I had once tasted *chrism*—and thereafter I had witnessed augury in an entirely changed manifestation, a chicken with its heart still beating after death. If *chrism* could work such an alteration in me, or in my impure blood, it could do as much or more for others of my gift-kin. For that reason, my goal became to form an academy for hieronomers, a place to discover and refine the effects of nature's catalyst upon our ability to scry.

Inimica Phlegathon deVry IV had become a woman altogether changed, no longer manipulative, willful, or cruel, but rather devoted to the freedom—indeed, the survival—of her people. Therefore she would require more precise and insightful auguries if she hoped to find her balance between the attractions of peace and the necessities of strife.

To serve that balance, hieronomy itself must become altogether changed. As I had.